"Strong characters, a clever story... all team up to make *Paranormalcy* the most refreshing paranormal debut of the year."

(((((LISA MCMANN)))))

New York Times bestselling
author of the Wake trilogy

"*Paranormalcy* seduced me. The two sexy paranormals who vie for Evie's affections each had their own victory; one won Evie's heart and the other won mine."

(((((APRILYNNE PIKE)))))

#1 *New York Times* bestselling
author of *Wings*

"A fast, flirty roller coaster of a ride. This story was everything I hoped for—sassy, light-hearted and downright scary. Oh, bleep! I'm in love!"

(((((BECCA FITZPATRICK)))))

New York Times bestselling
author of *Hush, Hush*

"Kiersten White creates the perfect blend of light and dark. Even as the stakes rose higher, *Paranormalcy*'s narrator, Evie, kept a smile on my face with her cunning wit. I can't wait for more!"

(((((CARRIE RYAN)))))

New York Times bestselling
author of *The Forest of Hands and Teeth*

PARANORMALCY

KIERSTEN WHITE

SCHOLASTIC INC.
New York Toronto London Auckland
Sydney Mexico City New Delhi Hong Kong

FOR
MOM AND DAD
AND FOR
NOAH, MY LOVE

PARANORMALCY

OH, BITE ME

Wait— did you— You just yawned!" The vampire's arms, raised over his head in the classic Dracula pose, dropped to his sides. He pulled his exaggerated white fangs back behind his lips. "What, imminent death isn't exciting enough for you?"

"Oh, stop pouting. But, really, the widow's peak? The pale skin? The black cape? Where did you even get that thing, a costume store?"

He raised himself to his full height and glared icily down at me. "I'm going to suck the life from your pretty white neck."

I sighed. I hate the vamp jobs. They think they're so suave. It's not enough for them to slaughter and eat you like a zombie would. No, they want it to be all sexy, too. And, trust me: vampires? Not. Sexy. I mean, sure, their glamours can be pretty hot, but the dry-as-bone corpse bodies shimmering underneath? Nothing attractive there. Not that anyone else can see them, though.

He hissed. Just as he reached for my neck, I tased him. I was there to bag and tag, not to kill. Besides, if I had to carry separate weapons for every paranormal I took out, I'd be dragging around a full luggage set. Tasers are a one-size-fits-all paranormal butt-kicking option. Mine's pink with rhinestones. Tasey and I have had a lot of good times together.

The vamp twitched on the ground, unconscious. He looked kind of pathetic now; I almost felt bad for him. Imagine your grandpa. Now imagine your grandpa minus fifty pounds plus two hundred years. That's who I'd just electrified.

Tasey's work done, I reholstered her and pulled out the vamp-specific ankle bracelet. I placed my index finger in the middle of the smooth black surface. After a few seconds it glowed green. Grabbing the vamp's ankle, I pulled his pants leg up to reveal the skin. I hated looking at these guys and seeing their pure white, smooth skin at the same time as their shriveled corpse bodies. I clamped the tracker on, and it adjusted to the circumference of his ankle. Two soft hisses sounded as the sensors activated and shot into his flesh. His eyes flew open.

"Ouch!" He grabbed at his ankle, and I backed up a few steps. "What is this?"

"You're under arrest under statute three point seven of the International Paranormal Containment Agreement, Vampire Protocol. You are required to report to the nearest processing facility in Bucharest. If you fail to report within the next twelve hours, you will be—"

He lunged for me. Sidestepping, I let him trip over a low gravestone. "I'll kill you!" he hissed, trying to pick himself up off the ground.

"Yeah, you really don't want to do that. That shiny new piece of jewelry I gave you? It's got two little sensors— think of them as needles—jammed into your ankle. And if your body temperature were to suddenly rise, say by the addition of human blood, the sensors would inject you with holy water."

His eyes widened in horror as he tried to pull the bracelet off, scraping against its sides.

"Don't do that, either. If the seal is broken, holy water, poof. Got it? And I activated the timer and beacon. So not only do they know exactly where you are, they also know your time limit to get to Bucharest. Miss it, and—do I really need to tell you?"

His shoulders slumped. "I could just snap your neck," he said, but I could tell it was halfhearted.

"You could try. And I could tase you again so hard you wouldn't wake up for six hours, giving you even less time to make it to Romania. So, can I keep reading you your rights?" He didn't say anything, and I picked up where I left off. "If you fail to report within the next twelve hours, you will be terminated. If you attack any humans, you will be terminated. If you attempt to remove the tracking device, you will be terminated. We look forward to working with you."

I always thought that last line was a nice touch.

The vamp looked dejected, sitting there on the ground and facing the end of his freedom. I held out a hand. "Need help up?" I asked. After a moment he reached out and took it. I pulled him up; vamps are surprisingly light. Having no internal fluids'll do that to you. "I'm Evie."

"Steve." Thank heavens he wasn't another Vlad. He looked uncomfortable. "Um, so, Bucharest? You wouldn't happen to have money for a train ticket?"

Paranormals, honestly. I reached into my bag and handed him a bunch of euros. Getting from Italy to Romania wouldn't be easy, and he needed to book it. "You'll want a map and directions," I called as he started to slink off through the graves. Poor guy. He was really embarrassed. I handed him the sheet of directions to the Bucharest Processing and Assignment building. "It's okay to use mind-control tricks to get through borders." I smiled encouragingly.

He nodded, still morose, and left.

Finding Steve hadn't taken as long as I had worried it would. Excellent. It was dark, I was freezing, and my vamp-luring outfit of a wide-necked white blouse wasn't exactly helping. Plus I stuck out like a sore thumb in Latin countries, with my platinum blond hair in a braid trailing halfway down my back. I wanted out of here. I punched in the number of the Center on my communicator. (Think cell phone, without a camera. And they only come in white. Lame.) "Done. I need a ride home."

"Processing your request," a monotone voice said on the other end. I waited, sitting on the nearest gravestone. The communicator flashed five minutes later. "Sending transport now."

The trunk of a large, gnarled tree about fifteen feet in front of me shimmered, and the outline of a door appeared. A tall, slender man walked out. Well, not man, really. His figure was distinctly male, although it seemed stretched—a little too narrow. With delicate features and almond-shaped eyes straight out of an anime cartoon, his face was, simply put, beautiful. It made your heart ache with the desire to do nothing but stare at him for the rest of your life. He smiled at me.

"Shut up," I said, shaking my head. Did they have to send Reth? Sure, the Faerie Paths were the fastest way from here to there, but that meant going from here to there with him. And unlike the happy fantasy of faeries as delicate, tiny winged things who love nature—yeah, not so much.

Faeries are a *lot* more complicated than that. Complicated and dangerous. Walking briskly up, I held out my hand and clenched my jaw.

"Evelyn," he purred. "It's been too long."

"I said shut up, didn't I? Let's go."

He laughed, a silvery sound like bells, and traced one long, slender finger along my wrist before taking my hand in his. I tried not to shiver. He laughed again and we stepped through the oaken doorway.

I closed my eyes; this part always freaked me out. I knew what I would see if I looked—nothing. Absolutely nothing. Nothing under my feet, nothing above me, nothing around me. I put one foot in front of the other and held onto Reth's hand as if my life depended on it. Since it did. No human could walk the Faerie Paths alone without being lost forever.

And then it was over. We stepped out into one of the cool, fluorescent-lit hallways of the Center. I yanked my hand away from Reth's; his special brand of warmth had already spread through my arm and was creeping even farther.

"Not even a thanks?" he called after me as I stalked down the hall toward my unit. I didn't look back. Suddenly he was right next to me. "We haven't danced in so long." His melodic voice was low and intimate. He reached for my hand again and I jumped back, pulling out Tasey.

"Back off," I hissed. "And if you come out without your

glamour on again, I'll report you." His glamour wasn't much less good-looking than his real face, but it was regulation for faeries.

"What is the use? I could never hide anything from your eyes." He moved closer.

I shoved down the feelings bursting through me. Not again. Not ever again. Luckily we were interrupted by a shrieking alarm. Something was loose. A hairy little gremlin, mouth open wide and acidic saliva dripping from sharp teeth, was booking it on all fours toward us.

I watched it as if in slow motion. The gremlin made straight for me, a rabid gleam in its eyes. It leaped into the air and I kicked out hard, sending it sailing down the hall, right into the arms of the containment worker chasing it. "Goal!" I shouted. Dang, I was good.

"Thanks," the worker said, voice muffled through the mask.

"You betcha." Reth's hand had found the small of my back. I wanted to lean into him, let his arms wrap around me, let him take me away. . . . Then I remembered the time. "Oh, crap!" I ran down the hall past the worker and still-snarling gremlin. After a couple of turns, I put my palm on my door pad, bouncing impatiently until the door slid open. Reth hadn't followed me. I was glad. Okay, maybe a little disappointed. And then mad at myself for being disappointed.

I dashed inside, grateful that my settings kept the unit

at eighty-five degrees, and flopped onto the purple couch. Turning on the flat-screen TV that took up nearly the entire pink wall, I sighed in relief. My favorite high school drama, *Easton Heights*, was just starting. Tonight's episode promised to be spectacular—a masquerade ball in which tiny masks somehow hid identities enough for everyone to make out with the wrong person. Where did they come up with this stuff?

A POPULATION
OF NIGHTMARES

The vid screen next to my couch buzzed again. It had been doing that off and on for the last thirty minutes. Finally, my show over, I hit the connect button. I was staring into a pair of green eyes, right in the middle of a green-tinged face. The image wavered, like always, since Alisha was underwater.

"Why haven't you checked in yet?" a monotone voice asked. I always wondered what her real voice was like. All we got was the computer program translating what she said into something we could hear.

"Got done early—my show was on."

Her eyes crinkled up into a smile. It was good that she had expressive eyes, since her mouth barely moved. "How was it?"

"You wouldn't believe it. It was a costume party. First Landon? He totally made out with Katrina. Who's dating Brett, right? But then Brett thought he was with Katrina, but really it was Cheyenne, her sister, who knew that he thought she was Katrina and tricked him into kissing her, then took off her mask and he was, like, what on earth? And *then* Halleryn filmed Landon kissing that tramp Carys."

Alisha blinked her transparent eyelids slowly.

"Man, high school must be awesome." I found myself wishing I could be part of normal drama for once. Paranormal drama didn't have nearly as much kissing.

"You need to check in with Raquel," Alisha prodded, her eyes still smiling.

"Fine, fine." I adored Lish. She was my best friend. Once you got past the weirdness of her robo-voice, she had a great sense of humor for a paranormal. Of course, unlike most of them, she was grateful to be here. Her lagoon had become so polluted it was killing her. Now not only was she safe, but she had something to do. Apparently being a mermaid is dead dull. I watched *The Little Mermaid* with her once a few years ago—she thought it was freaking hilarious. She couldn't stop laughing about the shell-bra thing, given that mermaids aren't mammals. Plus, as she put it, Prince Eric was far too hairy and "peach colored" for her taste. I always thought he was pretty hot, but then again, I *am* a mammal.

Leaving my unit, I walked down the cold, sterile halls to Raquel's office. We could have just done follow-up over the vid screens, but she always wants to see me in person after a job to make sure I'm okay. I kind of liked that.

I knocked once and the door slid open. The room was white—white walls, white floor, white furniture. Can you say boring? Raquel was a nice contrast. Her eyes were so brown they were nearly black, and her dark hair, pulled into a severe bun, was streaked with just enough gray to be distinguished without looking old. I sat, and she looked up from a stack of papers on her desk.

"You're late." Her voice had a slight Spanish accent that I loved.

"Actually, I'm early. I said I'd need four hours; it only took me two."

"Yes, but you got back almost an hour ago."

"I figured I'd take a little personal time as a reward for a job well done."

Raquel sighed. She was a professional sigher—the woman conveyed more emotions with a single exhalation than most people do with their entire faces. "You know how important follow-up is."

"Yeah, yeah, I know. Sorry. My show was on." One of her eyebrows rose ever so slightly. "You want a recap, too?" Most of the paranormals didn't care about my shows, but Raquel was human. She'd never admit it, but I was sure—

sure—that she liked television dramas as much as I did.

"No. I want you to debrief."

"Fine. Walked through the cemetery. Froze my butt off. Saw the vampire. Vampire tried to attack me. Tased the vampire. Tagged the vampire. Read the vampire his rights. Sent the vampire along. His name was Steve, by the way."

"Any trouble?"

"Nope. Oh, wait, yes. How many times have I asked to stop working with Reth? Do we need to go for an even hundred?"

"He was the only available faerie transport. And if we hadn't sent him, you would have missed your show." A small smile played at her lips.

"Fine, whatever." She had a point, after all. "Just, could you send one of the girls next time?"

She nodded. "Thank you for reporting. You may return to your room." She turned her attention back to the papers. I started to leave, then paused. She looked up. "Is there something else?"

I hesitated. But what did I have to lose? It'd been a couple of years. Might as well ask again. "I was wondering, you know, about maybe— I'd like to go to school. Normal school."

Raquel sighed again. This was more of a sympathetic, *I know what it's like to be a human wrapped up in all this nonsense, but if we didn't do it, who would?* kind of a sigh. "Evie, honey, you know you can't do that."

"Why? It wouldn't be too hard. You could just send for me whenever you need me. It's not like I have to be here 24/7." Truth was, here was kind of nowhere. The whole Center was underground. Not much of an issue when you have access to the Faerie Paths. It did, however, lend itself well to the occasional overwhelming bout of claustrophobia.

Raquel sat back in her chair. "It's not about that. Do you remember what it was like before you came here?"

This time I was the one who sighed. I remembered. I had been bounced through the foster care system my whole life, until that fateful day when I was eight. I'd gotten tired of waiting for my newest foster mom to take me to the library, so I decided to go by myself. I was cutting through a cemetery when a nice-looking man approached me. He asked if I needed help, and it was like he was two people at once—the nice-looking man and a withered corpse, both there in the same place, the same body. I screamed bloody murder. Lucky for me, APCA (the American Paranormal Containment Agency) had been tracking him and stepped in before he could do anything. When I started babbling about what he looked like, they took me in.

Turns out my ability to see through paranormals' glamours to what they are underneath is unique. As in, no other human on Earth can do what I do. That's where things got really complicated. When other countries got wind of what the APCA had, they freaked out. The UK especially—you wouldn't believe the level of paranormal activity they deal with there. They hammered out a new treaty, forming IPCA (the International Paranormal Containment Agency), the key items in the treaty being international paranormal control cooperation and, oh yeah, yours truly.

So I had to admit Raquel was probably right. My life of containment sometimes sucked, but at least I had a home. One where I was wanted.

I shrugged, pretending I didn't care about school anyway. "Yeah, cool, whatever. I'll talk to you later."

I felt her eyes on me as I walked out. It's not that I'm not grateful to IPCA. I am. They're the only family I have, and things are better here than they had been in the foster system. But I've been working full-time since I was eight, and sometimes I get tired. Sometimes I get bored. And sometimes all I want, more than anything else in the world, is to go on a freaking date.

I went back to my unit. I had a pretty nice setup. A small kitchen, bedroom, bathroom, and the main room with my awesome TV. The white walls in my bedroom had long since been covered. One was dedicated to posters of bands and movies I liked. Another was draped with an awesome hot pink and black leopard-spotted curtain. A third wall was my canvas. I wouldn't call myself an artist, but I had fun painting whatever came to mind—sometimes nothing more than just splashes of color—and changing it when I got bored. The paint was probably two inches thicker now than when I moved in.

I pulled on my favorite pair of pajamas and undid my thick braid. Somehow microwaving dinner and watching a movie won out over doing homework. I must have drifted off to sleep at some point, or maybe I was half asleep, I don't know. But I'm sure I was dreaming, because I kept hearing a strange voice, almost singing. "Eyes like streams of melting snow, cold with the things she does not know." Over and over again, that line, in the most haunting way. It was as if the voice was pulling me, calling to me. I wanted to answer. Just as I was ready to call out, another alarm jarred me awake.

I rubbed the sleep from my eyes and reached over to check my vid screen for an announcement of what was going on. I pulled the screen up, but all it showed was a flashing red WARNING. Lots of help there. I pulled on my robe, grabbed Tasey, and poked my head outside. I knew alarm procedure called for me to stay in, but I wanted to figure out what was going on, and now.

I ran down the empty hallways; strobe lights were going off to warn any paranormals that couldn't hear the alarm, although you could *feel* the dang thing it was so loud. Reaching Raquel's door, I palmed it. That's the nice thing about being me—all access, all the time. I ducked inside; she was at her desk, calmly rifling through some folders.

"Raquel," I panted. "What's up?"

"Oh, don't worry about it." She looked up at me and

smiled. Or rather, the thing wearing Raquel's face looked up at me and smiled. Raquel's face shimmered over— What? I couldn't describe it. It was somehow featureless, with eyes the color of water. If it hadn't been wearing Raquel's face, it would be like it wasn't there at all.

I forced a smile to mask my terror. "Woke me up from the freakiest dream."

"I'm sorry. I've got some work to do. Why don't you scoot along?" It went back to the files.

"Sure, as long as you don't need me." Turning toward the door, I casually walked closer to the desk. "Oh, Raquel?"

"Hmm?"

I flicked Tasey onto her highest level. "You dropped this." The thing wearing Raquel's face looked up as I lunged forward and jabbed it in the chest with the Taser. Its water eyes opened briefly in shock before it collapsed to the ground.

Horrified, I made my way around the desk. I had heard of things that could eat a person alive and wear her skin. The idea gave even me nightmares sometimes, and my life was populated by nightmares. "Please, not Raquel," I whispered, trying not to throw up. Raquel melted away, leaving the strangest thing I had ever seen. Which, given my job, is saying a lot.

NOT-ME AND I

My eyes couldn't seem to focus on the creature. They kept slipping down its sides, unable to find anything to hold on to. It wasn't invisible, exactly, but it was as close as a physical being can be. Imagine trying to walk up an eighty-degree incline covered in six inches of ice. That's what trying to look at this guy was like.

I was pretty sure it was a guy, at least. He kinda wasn't wearing any clothes, and I was grateful that he'd collapsed in such a way as to cover himself. I was at a loss for what to do next when the door slid open and the real Raquel rushed in, followed by two security guards.

"He didn't eat you!" I threw my arms around her, on the verge of tears.

The guards rushed by us, and Raquel patted me stiffly on the back. "No, she didn't eat me. She just punched me very hard in the face."

"It's a guy," I said.

"*What* is it?" she asked. We walked over to look at him. The guards stared down, perplexed. One scratched his head. Big guy, a hulking French werewolf named Jacques. Werewolves are a bit subtler to see than vampires. If the moon isn't full, the only thing that gives them away to me is their eyes. Whatever color they seem to be to other people, I can always see the yellow wolf eyes underneath. Most werewolves are pretty decent people. And, since they're extra strong all the time, we take a lot of them on as security. Of course, during full moons they're on complete lockdown.

Jacques shrugged. "I have never seen anything like it." He, too, was struggling to focus on the inert form.

The other guard, a normal human, shook his head.

"How did he get in?" I asked Raquel.

"She—he—it was wearing Denise."

"Denise from zombie duty?" Denise was a werewolf whose main job was zombie cleanup. I never went on zombie missions—no glamours, so anyone could do it. Plus they weren't ever hard to pinpoint, although agents had a heck of a time covering it up with the terrified locals. Just another service of IPCA: keeping the world blissfully unaware that most of the supernatural beings of myth are, in fact, real.

"Yes. It—it as Denise—called for a pickup. The zombie was a false alarm. I saw them as they came out of the faerie door. Denise turned and knocked Fehl, the faerie, back through. I pushed my panic button and went to confront her when she punched me and grabbed my communicator."

"How did he know where your office was?"

"She—he—ran into Jacques and pretended to be dizzy, asked for help getting here."

Jacques shuffled his feet, embarrassed. "How should we neuter it?"

He wasn't talking about *literally* neutering it. Yuck. "Neuter" is just our little term for rendering a paranormal harmless. Werewolves get tracking bracelets with massive amounts of sedatives set automatically for the full moons. Vamps get the holy water bracelets. Faeries are easy once you know their true names, since they have to obey whatever you tell them to do when you use it at the start of your command. Well, easyish, since they always seem to find little ways to work around their strict boundaries. Never underestimate faerie ingenuity for deliberately misinterpreting commands.

Raquel frowned. "I don't know. Just use the standard volt/sedative combo. When we know more about what it is, we'll find something with more finesse."

Jacques pulled out an ankle tracker. He looked hesitant

to touch the thing and shook his head. "I can barely see it. Where is the leg?"

Raquel and the two guards frowned as their vision slid around the figure on the floor. I sighed. "I can see his leg. I'll do it." I held out my hand and Jacques, relieved, gave me the tracker. Kneeling down, I paused, nervous. Would my hands go right through him, like plunging into cold water? But he had to be corporeal, otherwise Tasey wouldn't have worked. Suppressing a shudder, I put my hand on his ankle.

He was solid. His skin was warm and as smooth as glass—but no glass had ever been this soft. "Weird," I muttered, activating the ankle tracker with my finger, then fastening it. It took the self-adjust mechanism several tries before it sealed around his ankle. He twitched as the sensors jabbed in but didn't wake up.

I stood, still feeling his warmth on my hand. "Well, that's that. And I'm not carrying him to Containment, if that's what you were gonna ask next. You'll be able to feel him even if you can't see him. Besides, dude's naked—I'm not touching him again."

I held back a laugh at the looks on the guards' faces. They reached out like they would get burned, grabbed Water Boy, and carried him out of the room.

"I'd better find out what happened to Denise. And Fehl, too." Raquel gave her best *why is it always me that has to deal with these things* sigh (one I was well familiar with at this point), then patted me on the shoulder. "Good work,

Evie. I don't know what would have happened if you hadn't found it."

"Just—keep me in the loop on this one, okay? He's the weirdest thing I've ever seen. I want to know what's up."

She smiled, a tight, noncommittal smile that I knew meant *not a chance*, then picked her communicator up off the desk. I walked out, seriously bugged. IPCA had a tendency not to tell me much more than where they needed me to be and what I needed to do. Screw that. I skipped my room and headed straight for Containment. If she wasn't going to keep me informed, I'd just have to inform myself. I palmed the door and walked into the long, brilliantly lit cell-lined corridor.

My gremlin buddy from before was snarling and jumping at the electric field just inside the six inches of Plexiglas that lined its cell. Each time it hit the field, it yelped and flew backward, only to start the whole thing over again. Gremlins? Not smart.

Jacques wasn't too far down the hall. Wrapping my arms around myself, I hurried toward him. I was always cold in the Center, but Containment was downright frigid. Jacques stood there, a disturbed look on his face as he stared into a cell. I turned and my jaw dropped in surprise. There was Jacques again, leaning casually against the wall of his cell and staring out. When he saw me, his expression changed. Agitated, this Jacques moved as close to me as the electric field allowed.

Not Jacques. I walked right up to the glass as well, my eyes narrowed in concentration. There it was—behind Jacques's square face.

"It woke up right after I sealed the cell and has been doing that ever since," Jacques whispered, standing next to me.

"Please," Not-Jacques said, his voice identical. "That monster overpowered me and threw me in here! Let me out so I can help you!"

"Oh, sure," I said, pleasantly, "because I'm stupid."

The pleading look on Not-Jacques's face fell, replaced by an enigmatic smile. He shrugged, putting his hands in his pants pockets.

"How do you do the clothes?" I was genuinely curious. No other glamours I'd seen were anything more than a second skin. Only a few species (like faeries) could put them on and take them off at will, but none could change what the actual glamour looked like.

"How did you know?" His transparent eyes stared intensely at me behind the image of Jacques's.

Most of the paranormals have no idea what I can do. I like to keep it that way. "Raquel would never say 'scoot.'"

Not-Jacques shook his head. He leaned even closer; I examined his face, trying to find his real features. The only things I had an easy time focusing on were his eyes. He stood up straight, shocked. I'll give him this: He managed to make Jacques's face more expressive than Jacques ever did.

"You can see me," he whispered.

"Um, duh? You're right in front of me. Wearing Jacques. Looks better on you than Raquel did."

He smiled again. Then his skin rippled like water disturbed by the wind, and Jacques melted away. Now nearly imperceptible except for the ankle bracelet, he walked to the other side of the cell and, without warning, dropped flat to the ground.

I found his eyes staring right at me and realized too late that he was testing me, seeing if I could follow his movement when he was in invisimode. Color bloomed from his features and in a sudden shift of light I was looking at myself—myself exactly, right down to the bright pink fuzzy robe. "You can see *me*," my voice, tinged with wonder, said from his mouth.

"Evie!" Raquel was booking it toward us in her sensible (read: ugly) black pumps, a frown etching a deep line between her eyebrows. Busted. "You should not be here."

"Well, if it makes you feel any better, I'm there, too." I pointed at the cell. Raquel stopped short, surprise erasing her frown lines as she stared at Not-Me behind the glass.

"Remarkable," she whispered.

"Lame." Not-Me yawned and reached up to play with his—my—platinum hair.

"What are you?" Raquel was suddenly all business.

Not-Me gave her an impish grin. Watching myself do all this was really odd. I was getting angles of my face that

I had never seen before—way different from looking in a mirror. Not-Me glanced at me again, then shook my—err, his?—head. "I can't quite get your eye color." He stood and walked right up to the field, staring at my face. I couldn't help but check myself out. I was pretty. Too skinny, but I'd always been something of a beanpole. And, dang, really flat.

This was freaking me out. I frowned. "Take it off."

He just stared at me with my face. I was focused on his real eyes when I realized that he was sorting through colors. "Not quite right," he muttered. "Too silver. Now too dark. They're so pale."

It was true. My eyes were such a light gray they barely had any pigment at all.

"What color?" Not-Me mused. His eyes were flickering now, shifting colors like he was on fast-forward. "A cloud with the slightest hint of rain."

"Streams of melting snow," I answered without thinking.

He shot straight up and backed into the corner of his cell. I watched an expression of fear and mistrust spread across my features. "Yes, that's it," Not-Me whispered.

LEND ME YOUR EARS . . . AMONG OTHER THINGS

Where's Denise?" Raquel demanded, glaring at Water Boy in his cell.

I breathed a sigh of relief as my face melted from his, replaced by Denise's. "Right where I left her," Not-Denise said. He kept glancing over at me.

"And where was that?"

"In the cemetery. You should be able to find her."

"Find Denise or find her body?" Raquel's voice was hard.

Not-Denise rolled his eyes. "She'll have a headache. Honestly, it's like you think I'm some sort of a monster."

His mouth twisted in an ironic smile.

"What *are* you?"

"So rude. We haven't even been introduced."

She gave a *can I just start shocking him into submission now* sort of sigh. I jumped in before he got himself into more trouble. "My name's Evie. Raquel you already know—punched her and then stole her face, remember?—and Jacques over here is your new best friend, because he's in charge of the feeding schedule around here. Assuming you eat. And you are?"

"Lend."

"Lend?" Raquel asked.

"Yes, as in, lend me your self." He shimmered into Raquel again.

"Why not Borrow?" I asked. "Better yet, Steal?"

"I'll ask again," Raquel snapped. "What are you?" Given what this guy had done, I didn't blame her for being impatient.

"Good question. Maybe you could tell me?"

"Why are you here?"

"I love a nice dose of electric current in my body."

"What were you looking for?"

"Answers."

"Well." Raquel gave him a thin-lipped smile. "So am I." Her communicator buzzed. Relief flashed across her face as she read the message. Looking up, she nodded at her mirror image. "Tomorrow, then."

She turned and started down the hall with Jacques. I was still staring at Lend-as-Raquel, watching his real face beneath hers. I could almost pick out features now. He stuck his tongue out at me and, before I could stop myself, I giggled. It was too ridiculous coming from Raquel's face.

Raquel barked from down the hall. "Evie! Now!" Giving Lend-as-Raquel a final glare, I ran to catch up. "They found Denise, she's fine. And Fehl got back, too. I don't want you talking to that thing until we know what it is and why it's here."

No way, I thought. "Okay," I said.

"What do you see when you look at it?"

"I don't know. At first I couldn't really see anything, I could just tell there was someone under your face. But when he's not wearing anyone, it's like—I can't catch onto anything. I was getting better, though, staring at him in there. His eyes are the only things I can really focus on. Other than that it's like a silhouette or a clear shadow or . . . I don't know—a person made out of water and a hint of light."

"I'm going to call in some researchers. First we find out what he is, then we find out what he wants."

I shrugged, feigning nonchalance. "Cool, whatever."

"You should be in bed." Her voice was stern. You'd think the whole not-having-a-mother thing, or the whole being six-freaking-teen years old, would get me off the hook for bedtimes. But no. "And don't forget your class tomorrow."

"Fine. But if any more alarms go off, I'm going to ignore them instead of saving the day."

She heaved a *give me vampires and gremlins over pouty teenagers any day* sigh and waved as she turned off down another hall.

After heating up some milk for hot chocolate, I curled up with a blanket on my couch. My mind was racing too much to sleep. Today had been weird. And for something to be weird in *my* day, it's downright freaky. I popped in another movie and let my mind glaze over. The light from the screen flickered hypnotically. I didn't notice the light coming from behind me.

"Come and dance with me, my love." His voice was like the color gold—bright and sparkling with the promise of warmth. So much warmth. I smiled, closing my eyes and letting myself be pulled up off the couch and into an embrace. He rested his cheek against mine and the heat spread out, through my face and then down my neck, inching toward my heart. "*My* heart," he whispered. I nodded against his cheek. His heart.

My vid screen beeped, jarring me out of the trance. I jumped back and shoved Reth off me. The heat slowly drifted away from my heart. It had been close. Too close.

Reth looked disappointed. He held out his arms. I swore. "What is your freaking problem? Get out! Now!"

"Evelyn." His voice was a magnet with his warmth still in me. I leaned forward against my will.

"No!" Ripping myself away from the pull, I ran to the partition dividing the TV room from the kitchen and grabbed my communicator. "Get out." I glared, my hand over the panic button. His beautiful face fell. I wanted to comfort him. Closing my eyes, I lowered my finger. "Out. Now."

I could see the light of a door from behind my eyelids and waited until it faded to open them again. Reth was gone.

I went over to my vid screen and turned it on. "What good are freaking palm-coded locks when faeries can make their own doors any time they want to!" I shouted at Lish. Her green eyes widened in surprise and concern. I took a deep breath. It wasn't her fault. "Thanks for the interruption," I added.

"Reth?"

"Yeah. Can you file a report for me?"

"Yes, of course. We will try to make his instructions more explicit."

I shook my head. He always found a way around them. My guess was when they told him to go get me today he applied it as a blanket statement rather than a simple one-time retrieval command. "What did you need?"

She looked embarrassed. "I wanted to ask about the disturbance. I will talk to you tomorrow."

"Yeah, I'm kind of exhausted. I'll come visit and tell you everything, okay?"

"Do you want to spend the night here?" When I first came to the Center and had bad dreams, I would drag my blanket and pillow in and sleep on the floor next to Lish's aquarium. She'd tell me stories until I fell asleep. I was tempted, but felt too silly about not being able to spend the night alone because of a stupid faerie.

"I'll be okay." I forced a smile. "Thanks, though. Good night, Lish."

The mermaid's eyes smiled, and the vid screen went blank. I plopped back down on the couch. Reth had been so close. Again. And—worst of all—part of me wished that we hadn't been interrupted. But I had learned the hard way with faeries. It's all about possession and taking advantage, and, unlike human boys on all the TV shows, they aren't in it for sex. They couldn't care less about that. They want your heart, your soul. I was never giving mine back to Reth.

Deciding that hadn't stopped the ache of missing him, though.

I spent the rest of the night wide awake, wrapped in three blankets and freezing. When the clock read 4 A.M. I gave up. I got dressed in my warmest clothes and walked to Containment. Lend was curled up asleep on the floor. I sat against the wall and watched, fascinated, as his body flicked through identities the way I click through channels. After maybe an hour he went into his strange water-and-light state. I was so tired I could barely focus my eyes at all—and suddenly I could see him. It was like once I stopped trying so hard to *look*, he was just there. He actually had hair and normal features—cute even, if he had pigment. Even more surprising, he didn't look much older than me.

After a moment his eyes opened and met mine. Color flooded through him—he was wearing me again. The eyes were still flickering, trying to find the right shade.

"What are you?" I whispered.

"What are *you*?"

Offended, I frowned. "Human."

"Funny, me, too."

"No, you're not."

"Funny, neither are you."

I set my jaw and glared. What a jerk. "Why did you come here?"

My voice came from his mouth, disconcerting as always. "I could ask you the same thing. Are you going to kill me?"

HAVE A
BLEEP BLEEP DAY

I— no, that's not what IPCA does," I said. "They don't kill paranormals, they—"

Lend raised a hand to stop me and sat up, large eyes narrowing. "Are *you* going to kill me?"

"Why would I kill you?"

After a moment he let out a deep breath. "I don't think it's you."

"What's not me?"

Standing, he stretched. Did I mention how weird it was watching my body do this stuff? He even had the hair right—a little messy this morning, since I hadn't bothered to brush it yet.

"Can you please go back to normal?" I wanted to look at him more now that I could see him better.

He smiled, flashing my perfect teeth at me. I had to go through three years of braces for that smile; no fair that he could copy it in a second. "Normal? What's that?"

"How you really look."

"Can you take off all your clothes?"

Okay, weirdest thing ever—I just asked myself to take off all my clothes. It doesn't get much creepier. "Why on *earth* would I do that?"

"You asked me to be naked; I thought it was only fair."

"I just meant stop wearing me. Be yourself. But yourself with clothes."

"These are my clothes. But, if it bothers you." I melted off him and he grew a few inches. In my place was a teenage guy. Black hair, dark brown eyes, olive skin, and, oh yeah, absolutely gorgeous. Like, belonged on one of the shows I loved so much gorgeous. "Better?" His voice had changed, deepened, and I wished I was talking with an actual teenage guy.

"Definitely." I looked closer. Still Lend under there. Even the dark eyes didn't hide his water-colored ones; I could see him shimmering through.

"This seems to be a popular one."

"Yeah, I can imagine." Then I frowned, curious. "What does your real voice sound like?"

"What makes you think this isn't it?"

"I think it would sound different. Softer. Like water." I realized how stupid that sounded, but his smile dropped off and he gave me a considering look.

"If you didn't come here to kill me, why *are* you here, Evie?"

Awkward. Here I was, no makeup, ratty hair, in front of the hottest teenage guy I'd ever seen, fake or not. Why *was* I here? "It's my job."

His smile returned, this time with the usual ironic twist to his lips. "Oh. Your job. Quite the career for someone your age."

"You're not much older than me." Now that I'd seen him better, I was sure of it. Corrupted mortals like vampires show their real bodies' ages—old and nasty—underneath. True immortals, like faeries, have eternal youth, but there's something different in their faces. All those years don't add lines; they smooth, like a piece of glass turned around forever on the ocean floor. No mortal has that polish. His face was neither old nor ageless.

The shift in his expression confirmed it. "Ha!" I smiled smugly. "I'm guessing . . . fifteen." I went low on purpose.

He looked indignant. "Seventeen."

"See? You told the truth. That wasn't so bad, now, was it?"

Lend shook his head, then sighed. "Trouble."

"You bet I'm trouble," I countered with a smile. Sure,

maybe I was flirting, a little. Could you blame me? The only guys I ever met were too old, half monsters, living corpses, or immortal creeps. At least Lend was close to my age, whatever else he was.

"No, you're *in* trouble." He looked and I followed his eyes right to Raquel, who was not happy. At all. She finished crossing the hall and fixed a steely glare on me.

I was about to apologize, but then I rolled my eyes. "What are you going to do, ground me?" Maybe I shouldn't have been so flip about it, but really. After the night I had, the last thing I wanted was a lecture.

"Out. Now."

I walked past her, turning my head to glance back at Lend. He winked at me and I couldn't help but smile.

Instead of going to my room, I made my way to Central Processing. It was still early but that's another great thing about Lish: she doesn't sleep. I loved Central Processing. Unlike the rest of the Center, it didn't look sterile. The entire room was a circle, with desks placed against the wall and everything based around Lish's gorgeous aquarium. About fifty feet in diameter, it was fifteen feet high and a perfect circle. They even managed to transplant a living coral reef, complete with tropical fish in the crystal blue water. Way better than my unit.

Lish was staring at the series of screens that lined the front of the tank. She was like the ultimate personal assistant. No sick days, no vacations, no sleep, and she wanted to be there. A lot of the paranormals couldn't be trusted with too much. Even though they're neutered, most of them harbor a bit of resentment toward IPCA because of the loss of freedom. But Lish loved her job. She was in charge of scheduling, monitoring, transports, you name it. Girl knew everything.

Apparently not today, though. Her green eyes widened with interest when I walked up to the tank. I smiled. "What's up, Lish?"

"How are you feeling? Are you okay after last night?"

Lish knew me better than anyone else at the Center. Raquel was in charge of me, but she was hard to talk to about feelings. After all, when the main way you communicate is through sighs, it makes it hard to relate to teens. Lish understood how bad a new run-in with Reth would mess me up. I could (and did) talk with her about everything.

"Been better. Didn't sleep."

Lish tried to swear—which is always funny, because the computer won't translate it. It went something like this: "Bleep stupid bleep bleep faeries and their bleep bleep bleep obsessions. He had better stop bleep bleep bleep the bleep bleep rules or I will bleep bleep bleep the little bleeeeeeeeeeep." All in a completely robotic monotone. Awesome. Lish could really get going sometimes. I loved her for it; she was like the big sister I never had. The big sister who happened to be shiny green and covered in scales, with a long, finned tail and webbed hands. But she was beautiful in her way.

I laughed. The robot voice tirades always cheered me up. "Okay, you bleep bleep do that." She shook her head, still mad about Reth. Something on one of her screens took her attention and she waved her webbed hands in front of it for a few minutes. I wasn't sure how all the tech worked in there, but it always looked cool.

Once she was done, she looked back at me. "So, tell me about what happened yesterday with the break-in."

"What don't you know?" Lish was usually the font of all information. Granted, most of that information was classified, but we were best friends. We told secrets, and kept them, too. Like the time when I was twelve and the Center was processing a load of pixies. Lish knew how badly I wanted to see them and slipped me the when and where information—even though Raquel had grounded me for wandering off on a bag-and-tag mission. Too bad pixies turned out to be dirty, ugly little things, even their wings coated with mucous. Yet another cartoon dream shattered.

"They are not releasing much intel. What is it?" She looked worried.

"Don't know. I've never seen anything like him. Neither has Raquel."

"Why was he here?"

"Don't know again. I caught him in Raquel's office, but he hasn't said why."

"And he can take the appearance of anyone?"

"Yup. Pretty freaky when you're standing there talking to yourself."

A small, wheezing laugh sounded. I looked over and noticed one of the office vamps standing close by, listening. "Something funny, Dalv?" I glared at him.

He glared back. "It's Vlad and you know it."

"You and half the other vamps out there." Vlad—or Dalv, as I liked to call him just to piss him off—was one of my least favorite parts of the Center. After neutering, IPCA always set the paranormals up with some mandatory job. Werewolves had the most job flexibility, depending on what they were before. Vamps usually worked in the satellite buildings or did cover-up for sightings using their persuasion skills. Vlad was pretty useless though. I guess I can't blame him for feeling bitter. Going from being the terror of Bulgarian nights to a janitor would kinda suck. And, since I was the one who had done the bag-and-tag, he especially hated me.

He shrugged as he swept the already spotless floor. His glamour was less flashy than most; he looked like a forty-year-old man, not handsome, not ugly, just thin and slightly balding. Underneath all vamps looked the same. Ugh. "He could be a doppelgänger," he said, a sneer of a smile creeping onto his face.

"What's a doppelgänger?" I immediately regretted asking as his smile spread.

"Good news for the rest of us, if he took your form." Giving another wheezy laugh, he walked out.

I turned to Lish; she was already looking it up on one of her screens. Her eyes narrowed. "What?" The look on her face was making me nervous. "What's a doppelgänger?"

"Doppelgängers appear to people as harbingers of—" she paused "—death. The tale was that if you saw yourself, it meant you were going to die. They were also bad spirits who would take your form and destroy your life, again leading to your death."

I frowned. Not cool. "Wait, spirits?" She nodded. "Nope, dude's corporeal." I had dealt with a few ghosts and poltergeists in my time. The great thing about them is they can't touch you. Their only power is fear. And there's a whole lot you can do with fear—make people see, hear, and even feel things that aren't there—but if you know that going in, it's a lot easier to see past it. "Besides, if I'm going to die, Raquel, Denise, and Jacques are all going with me."

She blinked thoughtfully. "And why would a doppelgänger want to look through Raquel's files?"

"Exactly. Plus, he's only seventeen."

Lish tilted her head. "He is not an immortal?"

"Nope. Oh, whoops, probably should have told Raquel that." I frowned. I'd tell her when she decided to include me. "Listen, don't say anything, okay? I want in on this one, and info's the only leverage I have."

Lish closed one of her transparent eyelids at me in her

best imitation of a wink. "They are not giving me research clearance anyway. I have no reason to tell."

"You're the best, my fine fishy friend."

Lish's eyes smiled at me. Different as we were, we were both exactly what the other needed—a friend. As was my custom, started when I first met Lish as a ten-year-old, I smashed my face against the glass and blew my cheeks out at her.

DEAD MEAT IN ANY LANGUAGE

I had finally fallen asleep later that morning when the alarm went off. I jumped out of bed, confused, thinking there was yet another break-in or emergency. Then I realized it wasn't the Center's alarms, it was my personal alarm. The alarm that meant my tutor, Charlotte, would be here in exactly ten minutes.

"Oh, bleep." I hadn't done any of my homework.

The last few years I'd tried to convince Raquel that I really didn't need to study math, English, science, world history, and four—yes, *four*—foreign languages. It wasn't like I was going to go to college or anything. Sure, I wanted to attend real high school, but that had more to do with being around actual teenagers than learning stuff. Besides, I doubted IPCA cared whether or not I had my GED. As long as I could keep seeing through glamours, I had a job for life. But every time I brought it up, Raquel looked at me with those almost-black eyes and heaved her patented *I know you think it's not important to know these things but one day you'll appreciate that I've made you into a well-rounded adult* sigh.

I pulled out my Spanish book, pretty sure that's what I had this morning. Hastily filling in my irregular verb chart for *morir*, I wrote out example sentences. *Tú eres muerta carne*. Scratched that—adjective after the noun. *Tú eres carne muerta*. Oh, who was I kidding, I wasn't even using morir in the verb form anyway. *Yo soy carne muerta*. Translation: I am dead meat.

Right on time my unit door beeped and I let Charlotte in. She was a pretty woman, looked to be in her late twenties. A couple inches shorter than me with shiny brown hair that was pulled back into a ponytail and these adorable rectangular glasses over her blue eyes, which were over her bright yellow wolf eyes.

Charlotte always smiled so sweetly. Teaching had been her life's passion until she was infected. After she realized what she was and what she had done—attacked a family member—she tried to kill herself. Fortunately we found her before she could figure out the few things that can bring down a werewolf. I could never tell if it was my lack of motivation as a student or her pain and regret about the past that made her look sad even when she was smiling.

We sat down on the couch and pulled up a table. She glanced over my worksheet and suppressed a smile. "You are dead meat?"

I gave my best *don't get mad, aren't I cute?* grin and shrugged.

"That's an American expression—the meaning doesn't translate. And you didn't finish your verb charts or the short story you were assigned." She looked up at me with those sad, sad eyes. Those eyes killed me.

"I'm sorry." I hung my head. "Yesterday was crazy. First I had a vamp job, and then there was the break-in, and then Reth paid me a late-night visit, and then I couldn't sleep."

"It sounds like you had a rough day. But you've had this assignment for a week. Perhaps next time if you didn't leave it to the night before?"

"Hey, now, let's not start talking crazy, Char." That, at least, got me a less-sad smile.

We spent the rest of the morning conjugating (a word that sounds dirty but is, in fact, boring) and conversing in good old *español.* She stayed and ate lunch with me, and then it was time for my afternoon training session.

Bud, my self-defense and combat skills teacher, was still trying to get me to learn knife fighting. "Silver knives! Painful and sometimes deadly to nearly all paranormals!"

"Tasey!" I countered. "Hot pink and sparkly!"

"You can't always count on technology." Bud was human, but you'd think he'd grown up in the Middle Ages. In case you were wondering if he was cute, well, maybe thirty years ago. Now, not so much. "And, since we've had this argument before, I made you something."

I perked up. "A present?"

He nodded, an annoyed look on his face. Pulling out a cloth-wrapped bundle, he revealed a slender dagger with a bright pink, pearlescent handle. "No way!" I yelled, taking it from him.

"I can't believe I made a pink knife."

"It's so cute! I love it. Finally, a companion worthy of Tasey." I gave him a quick hug. Hugs always freaked poor Bud out, but he was relieved I'd finally agreed to take a knife. "Oh, gosh, what should I name her?"

"Whatever it is, please don't tell me. Just keep it sheathed and on your belt."

I took the sheath—which was black. "Can you make me one in brown, too? And pink?" You'd think Bud was a werewolf by the way he growled as he shooed me out of the training room.

The rest of my afternoon free, I banked on the hope that Raquel would be in meetings. She was pretty high up in IPCA. I used to think she was only assigned to me, but it turned out she ran the entire Center and was in charge of all bag-and-tag missions. I guess I was just her favorite. That, or the most useful.

I had been thinking about Lend on and off all day. He was the most interesting person/thing in here right now, so I went to Containment. I stopped in front of Lend's cell, then did a double take. He wasn't there. And not in an almost-invisible way, in an actually-not-in-the-cell-anymore way. Not cool.

Jacques was at the very end of the long corridor. "Jacques!"

He walked down. "You are not supposed to be here, Evie."

"Yeah, yeah. Where's Lend?" What if they had let him go? Not likely, once I thought about it. He'd broken into the Center. I couldn't remember that happening—ever. But what if he was in more trouble than I thought, and they were hurting him? That idea bothered me. Then the rational part of me wondered if maybe he was dangerous and they'd taken him to a higher-risk placement area.

Jacques shrugged. "Raquel wanted him moved."

"Why?"

"We are not equipped for long-term holding here. No beds, no bathrooms."

"Oh." Made sense. "Where is he?"

The werewolf shook his head. "Sorry. You are not cleared to know." Today his normally cute French accent was seriously bugging me.

"Not cleared?"

"No. Raquel told me not to tell you."

My face melted into a pout. This was so not fair. I turned on my heel and stalked to Raquel's office. I had just put my palm up to enter when the door opened.

"Oh, good," Raquel said.

"What's the deal with—"

"I've got a job for you. You need to leave right now. A transport's waiting."

I frowned. "What is it?"

"Vampire activity in Istanbul. We've got a location, but you have to hurry."

"I— Okay." We ran to my room and I grabbed my bag with the ankle trackers. I always had Tasey on me, and now she was joined by my dagger. "I'm not really dressed for vamping." I was wearing skinny jeans and a long-sleeved V-necked tee, my hair back in a ponytail.

"You look fine," she said dismissively. "Your neck is showing—that's all that matters."

We were almost to Transport when I remembered. "Hey, why can't I know where Lend is?"

Raquel rolled her eyes and heaved an *is this really the time* sigh. "You don't need to know." The Transport room door opened in front of us to reveal the waiting faerie. I hadn't seen her in years, and my stomach immediately clenched with guilt and nerves. All the human employees were required to memorize two faerie names, the faeries assigned at random so no faerie had too many people attached. This faerie was one of mine, and I couldn't remember her name for the life of me.

Hers had been the first one they'd told me; I was ten. They also told me to never, ever use it unless I absolutely had to, then explained all the ways in which I could be killed if I screwed up. It was a little traumatic; can you blame me for forgetting? I knew I should ask again but was too embarrassed that I'd forgotten in the first place. Raquel would flip.

The faerie didn't even look at me. "Do you have the location?" Raquel asked her. She nodded. Her skin was creamy white and her ruby hair contrasted sharply with it. Like all faeries, she was beautiful in a way no person could ever be. She held out her hand and blurred as her glamour went into place. The faeries were all required to tone down their looks during transports in case someone caught a glimpse of them. You don't forget a faerie face. The faerie's hair softened to auburn and her face took on more normal proportions, the eyes shrinking and moving closer together. She was still beautiful, but normal now. Unless you were me and could see right through it.

I walked forward and took her outstretched hand. It was warm, but not in the same way Reth's was. The usual outline of brilliant light formed on the blank wall in front of us and we walked together into the black. I put all my attention on the feeling of her hand in mine and just moved forward. It surprised me when she spoke—faeries don't usually deign to speak to mortals. Unless they're trying to kidnap you, of course.

"Oh, you are Reth's," she said in recognition, her voice discordant but oddly lovely, like glass raining onto concrete.

I missed a step, almost tripping. Her grasp never wavered. "No, I'm *not*." As if the Faerie Paths weren't creepy enough already. Where did that come from?

She just laughed—more glass, falling faster. Then I felt cool night air on my face and opened my eyes. We were in a filthy alleyway between two old stone buildings. I let go of her hand and wiped my palm on my pants. She smiled at me, her faerie eyes glowing underneath the glamour. There was a cruel cast to her smile that made me shiver. She pointed toward the alley opening. "You should find the creature in this market."

"Thanks a lot," I muttered, turning and walking out of the alleyway. I hoped they'd send a different faerie for the return trip. Heck, I hoped they'd send a jet. I was sick of traveling by faerie. They were getting more and more intrusive.

The market was one of those sprawling open-air types, totally packed. The air beckoned with alluring spices, none of which I'd get to taste. Still, *Easton Heights* wasn't on tonight, so I was in no hurry. Lucky for me it seemed to be a big tourist spot and I didn't stand out too much.

I wandered around, pretending to look at the stalls but really scanning people. I liked this kind of job much better than the cemetery runs. There's no real reason for vamps to hang out in cemeteries. They just do it because so many of them have bought into the whole pop culture concept of how they *should* act. Besides that, cemeteries are boring and lonely. Nights like this I could wander around and people-watch. People—normal people—fascinated me. Tourists and locals clashed in a wonderful mix of jeans and silk, baseball caps and black hair.

It was also nice to get out on my own. I used to always have one other person (usually a werewolf) go with me, but the last couple of years they'd sent me solo for the basic runs. Vamps weren't a threat now that I knew what I was doing. If it was something more dangerous I'd always have backup.

A guy called out to me in broken English from a jewelry stall. He was Turkish, kinda cute in a stretched out, throes-of-puberty sort of way. I was about to stop and pretend like I really was a shopper when I caught a glimpse of something walking by. Something not human. Smiling my regrets at stall boy, I turned and hurried after the person. All it took was one good look to confirm—through the cover of the man's thick, dark hair I could see the last stringy remains of actual hair clinging to his shriveled and spotted head.

It didn't look like he was stalking anyone; he moved purposefully through the market. I almost had to jog to keep up until he entered a derelict building near the very end of the market. Waiting about thirty seconds, I went in after him. A small hallway led to a single door. I pulled out

Tasey, walked forward, and kicked it open, striding into the room.

The vamp I was following turned and looked at me; so did the twenty other vampires in there.

"Oh, bleep," I whispered.

THERE'S NO PLACE
LIKE HOME

One vamp I could handle. Heck, I could probably even handle five at a time—shriveled corpse muscles and all. But twenty vampires? I was not liking my odds. What was going on? Vamps were solitary by nature. This was weird. And very, very bad.

I gave my best embarrassed smile. They wouldn't know I knew what they were. "Whoops. I'm looking for the theater. Wrong building."

Maybe if I made it back through the door fast enough, and then—click. Another four vamps had come in behind me and locked the door. I reached to my belt and hit the panic button on my communicator. Then I pulled out Tasey.

Taking a deep breath, I put on my best stern face. "You're all under arrest under statute three point seven of the International Paranormal Containment Agreement, Vampire Protocol. You are required to report to the nearest processing—"

"You're IPCA?" one of the vamps asked. The others were shifting nervously in place.

"Yes. I'm going to have to ask you to line up for tagging." I waited for them to start laughing.

"You aren't going to kill us?" the speaker asked, giving me a suspicious look.

"Why does everyone keep asking me that?" Seriously, did I look like some sort of psycho assassin? Maybe it was the pink sneakers. Or the heart earrings?

The vampires turned toward one another, holding a whispered conversation. I inched closer to the door, Tasey at my side, as I pushed the panic button over and over again. Lish would see it. She'd send help. She'd never failed me before, but if they didn't answer my distress call soon, I would have to do something I *really* didn't want to.

Freedom was a foot away when they turned back to me. The one who kept speaking, a tall vamp with a handsome curly-haired glamour, shook his head. "Sorry." He bared his fangs in an apologetic grin. "We're glad you aren't what's hunting us, but we're no friends of IPCA.

And we're all very, very thirsty."

"What, no flirting?" I asked, trying to buy time. "Aren't you going to at least try to be sexy? Think of all those vampire fans out there—they'd be so disappointed." I pulled out my silver knife. Probably should have paid more attention during my knife training. "Tell you what. Let me go and I promise not to tell anyone that you aren't suave."

"Sorry, kid."

"Okay." I held up the knife in one hand and Tasey in the other. "Guess I am here to kill you then." If I could get through enough of them—I just needed to get out of the room—I could outrun them.

Three jumped me and I flailed wildly. I hit two of them with jolts and they collapsed. The third tried to catch my arm, but I slashed at him with the knife and he drew back, howling in pain. I ran for the door but couldn't get it open. I turned and put my back against it.

"Everyone at once," the leader shouted, and then it was a mass of hands—nice, normal flesh over the decay underneath—all grabbing at me. I struggled, but even vamps are strong enough when they outnumber you twenty to one. It only took a few seconds for them to have me pinned against the wall; I managed to hold on to Tasey and the knife but couldn't move to use them. The leader stood right in front of my face. I tried to look at his glamour, just his glamour, but the pure white eyes staring at me from sunken sockets were all I could focus on. He smiled. I wanted to cry.

My rescue would come too late.

"Aren't you going to scream?" he whispered, leaning in and tracing my neck with his lips. His dead, dead lips. I felt his mouth open and closed my eyes. All the horror from my first childhood run-in with a vampire flooded back in. No one would save me. I was out of options. A single tear traced down my cheek.

"Lorethan!" I shouted. The vamp hesitated; clearly it wasn't what he was expecting. "I need you! NOW!"

The pause was enough to save my neck. White light exploded into the room and the vamps jumped back instinctively. A pair of arms wrapped themselves around my waist from behind and pulled me into the darkness.

"You called," Reth murmured in my ear as he held me in the nothingness. "I knew you would." I could hear the smile in his voice, the triumph. I had sworn I'd never use his real name again, never call on him. Instead I'd just negated all the commands to stay away from me. And my wording—why had I said I needed him? He could twist that any way he wanted. But the memory of the vampire's lips on my neck made me shudder. It didn't matter tonight.

"Just take me home, okay?"

He tightened his arms around my waist, his torso pressed against my back. I could feel his heart through my shirt, its beat strong but far too slow. "Home then." He laughed his silver laugh.

That should have warned me.

I kept my eyes closed, trying to ignore his body against mine. Faeries couldn't care less about sex and physicality, but they did care about manipulation, and Reth knew how much I craved contact—any kind of contact. Growing up the way I had, there was never enough affection, never enough attention. More than Raquel, more than Lish, more than anyone, he knew how deeply lonely I was. I hated him for it.

I expected him to take my hand and walk; instead all I felt was a slight breeze, then it was bright and warm. I opened my eyes to a room. Not mine. The light was soft, emanating from an unidentifiable source. Elegant furniture was placed at random, and the walls appeared to be solid, pale rock. The fabrics were all silks and velvets; deep reds and royal purples with gold accents. There was no door.

"I said home."

He laughed again. "You didn't say whose." Furious and too tired to deal with any more faerie crap, I opened my mouth to tell him exactly where to take me and where he could go after that. I wasn't sure a faerie could obey a command to go to hell, but I was going to find out. Before I could say a word he lifted his slender hand and stroked my throat.

"Shhh," he whispered.

My voice was gone. Not scratchy-throat-rasping gone. Completely gone. I couldn't scream. I couldn't even whisper. I wanted to find the genius who thought we could control faeries and kick him where it hurt. Twisting away from Reth's arms, I rushed over to put one of the antique-looking couches between us. "Fix it," I mouthed.

He smiled at me. His eyes were golden like ripe wheat and his hair shone nearly the same shade. Everything about him was gold, except his laugh. That had always been silver. I couldn't look at his face anymore without risking never wanting to look away, but I didn't want to take my eyes off him and let down my guard. I was so dead.

"Evelyn." My name in his mouth was like a caress. "Why are you fighting me? You want to be with me. And I want no one else forever."

I had goose bumps. Reth had probably taken countless mortal girls into the Faerie Realms. He knew we didn't last forever. Either he was manipulating me again, which was likely, or was up to something seriously frightening. "Why?" I mouthed. I knew he was telling the truth—he wanted me. And that made everything even harder; not many people in my life ever wanted me. My own parents had abandoned me when I was a toddler.

He sat gracefully. A small claw-footed table next to his chair held a crystal bottle and two goblets. He poured a clear liquid into both of them, then held one up to me. "Drink?"

I shook my head. I wasn't born yesterday. You never, ever accept food or drink from a faerie anywhere, especially on their turf. You'll never get out again.

Nonplussed, he drank it himself. I racked my brain for

what to do without my voice. Then, idiot that I was, I realized I still had Tasey and the knife. I was clutching them both so hard my hands ached. Glad my actions were hidden by the couch, I put Tasey away—not any good for more than a few seconds with faeries. With a hand free, I pushed the panic button again. I had no idea where we were, but really, really hoped it was somewhere Lish could send a retrieval.

"Aren't you tired of being cold?" he asked, trying to draw me in. "Cold and alone. You don't have to be. Our time grows short." His eyes were pools of amber, deep and eternal. Pools you could drown in. "Dance with me again."

I squeezed my eyes shut. He was right. I was tired. I had been alone my whole life. The foster homes, the Center— what was the difference? Why was I resisting him? I felt his hand on mine; he was so warm. The heat started to spread up my arm, slow and insistent. Why not give him my heart, my soul? No one else wanted them.

He could feel my surrender and pulled me close. "There is no one else for you, my love. Let me fill you." There was no one else for me. I opened my eyes and looked into Reth's golden ones—and the image of other eyes, eyes as clear as water, flooded into my memory. Why I thought of Lend right then I have no idea, but it was enough to pull me back. I lifted the silver knife and held it between us like a talisman.

Reth looked surprised, then angry. "What are you

doing, child?" He hadn't let go of my other hand, but I resisted the warmth. It was barely past my shoulder, now slowing. "Don't you know what I'm trying to give to you?"

I shoved the flat of the blade against his chest and he let go of my hand, backing up a step. Iron is the best against faeries, but they aren't fans of silver, either. "Enough," I mouthed, pointing to my neck. Glaring, he flicked his hand and my throat tingled.

"Why are you fighting this?"

"Because you're a lunatic! I don't want this! I don't belong to you! I never will!"

A half smile twisted his perfect face. "You're wrong."

"Well, I've got a silver knife that begs to differ. Now—"

"Take you home?"

I nodded.

His smile spread. "That wasn't a command, and you've got to sleep sometime." Before I could command him to take me home he disappeared, his silvery laugh lingering in the absence.

I was starting to miss the vampires.

FAERLY STUPID

$\mathcal{I}$ screamed for him to come back, then sat heavily on one of the couches. He was right. I was exhausted from not sleeping last night plus a very full day and rather stressful evening. And if I fell asleep, I couldn't hang on to the knife. And if I couldn't hang on to the knife . . .

It was a problem. I didn't know what he was trying to do to me, and I didn't want to find out.

Not surprisingly, there was no signal on my communicator. I didn't even know if I was technically on the planet anymore. The Faerie Realms coexist with ours, but cross time and space and all sorts of other boring and weird physics things that I never cared about before now. I added Faerie Realms and knife fighting on my list of things to pay more attention to.

I could call for him using his real name again, and he'd have to come. But that worked out *so* well before. The phrasing I used still killed me. I *need* you? The way I figured it, he took that as the command and would now fill what he thought my need for him was. If I called him back and negated my command before he took my voice again, there was no telling how he would interpret it. If you give a faerie conflicting commands, they can't fill them and therefore come up with something completely different (and always bad). I was so screwed.

Faeries are the slipperiest things in the world. IPCA (before it was IPCA and back when it was APCA and all sorts of individual country acronyms) worked for decades to find a faerie, any faerie, and learn his true name. Their plan involved using pretty young girls as kidnap bait. Dozens of pretty young girls, none of whom were ever seen again. Except one girl, who discovered a great secret.

Faeries are unaffected by alcohol, but much to her surprise—and the faeries' undoing—they get very, *very* drunk on carbonation. Using copious amounts of Coke, she was able to discover a single faerie's true name. With that she was able to force that faerie to do her will and reveal several other faeries' names—who were forced to reveal other faeries' names, as well. Thus followed the great Faerie Catalog and Control Operation of '95.

It sounds more impressive than it was. A whole bunch of workers on the project ended up dead or missing, and faeries guard their names closely even from one another, so IPCA only got a fraction of them. Here's what IPCA should have learned, still hasn't quite learned, and probably never will learn: you cannot control fairies. Can. Not. They aren't logical or rational. They don't obey the same laws (physical, social, emotional, traffic—you name it) that we do. They always have their own agendas and are just plain smarter than us. Plus, in finding and using their names, we were messing with paranormal magic deeper and more powerful than any of us understood.

I say us. I mean arrogant IPCA.

I pondered all this as I sat on Reth's couch, trapped in the Faerie Realms and wondering how long I could hold out before I had to sleep, eat, or drink. Or pee for that matter, because I wasn't seeing a toilet. Stupid immortals. Was faerie magic really worth all the mess and risk we incurred by working with them?

There had to be another option. I couldn't—wouldn't—call Reth back. I knew he would never let me out, and there was no way to escape other than the Faerie Paths.

Another faerie! It was perfect. The faerie names I had been assigned were to be used only in dire straits. These were dire enough for me. I opened my mouth and stopped.

I still couldn't remember. The names were so strange,

and I had been so scared I'd blocked it out. Lying back on the couch, I stared at the ceiling; it shimmered with crystals. I watched it and racked my brains for the ruby-haired faerie's name.

The crystals reflected an unidentifiable source of light. It seemed like there was some sort of meaning, a pattern. And now I was detecting faint colors, too. They were telling me something. If only I stared long enough, hard enough, didn't think about anything else . . . and if I closed my eyes and didn't think, it would be even better and it would all work out. . . .

"No!" I sat up, blinking to keep my eyes open. No more ceiling.

What was her name? I knew that I knew it. And then I remembered—she was the faerie Lend had hitched a ride with. Fehl! Fehl was her nickname. And her full name was . . .

"Denfehlath!" I shouted, triumphant. After a few seconds the outline of a door formed on the wall and she walked through, still looking bored.

"Oh." She frowned.

I jumped up, giddy with relief, but stopped myself before I said anything stupid. This time I would be careful. Specific. "Please take me back to the IPCA Center where I live."

She held out her hand and I took it.

"Stop!" Reth commanded from behind us. I didn't let go of Fehl's hand as I turned to look at him. "She's mine."

Fehl gave him a sharp smile. "It's a named command. I

have no choice."

Reth's golden eyes brimmed with rage. That's another thing about faeries. Nasty tempers. I had seen him lose control once before—it was what finally shocked me into giving him up.

"Let's go, now." I pulled on her hand. The ambient light in the room had shifted; now everything seemed to glow with a red, menacing hue.

We darted through the door and into the Faerie Paths. More frightened of what was behind me than around me, I kept my eyes open for once. Fehl squeezed my hand so hard it hurt; the look on her face was pure fury, tinged with a hint of smugness. I wondered if there was something going on. Those two had a weird dynamic. Whatever. I didn't care as long as I got home.

But then I had a brilliant idea. "Can you open a door to Lend's room?"

She gave me a glare so cutting I was surprised I didn't bleed. A few more steps and the white lines opened in front of us. She shoved me out and disappeared into the black.

The room was the same boring color scheme as the rest of the Center. A door to a small bathroom was open; other than that the room was a simple square with a gray bed against the wall. Lend, wearing me of all things, was sitting on it. He glanced over, surprise flitting across his/my features. Then he looked away, and I realized Raquel was talking.

I backed up against the wall. She must have been standing in the hallway, because I couldn't see her and was pretty sure from the lack of reaction that she hadn't seen me. Not busted. Yet. And now I knew where Lend was. Sometimes faeries came in handy, after all.

". . . would all be much easier if you'd just give us some simple information. I'll let you think about it." Raquel finished and I heard her pumps tapping away down the hall.

Lend-as-me looked over and raised one eyebrow quizzically.

"Hey, no fair!" I whispered. I'd never been able to raise just one eyebrow at a time. And not for lack of trying, either. He looked confused, so I gestured to my own eyebrows and shook my head. He grinned in response and I melted away, replaced by the dark-haired dark-eyed hottie.

"What are you doing here?"

I shrugged, sliding down the wall and sitting against it. "Just thought I'd drop by for a visit."

"Really."

"Yeah. I was bored."

"Me, too." There was a long, awkward silence. "Are you planning on staying for a while?"

"Not sure. I think I'm missing."

"Raquel did seem very on edge."

I sighed. "Yeah, I should probably let her know I'm not dead." I didn't get up.

"You look tired." He briefly shifted back to wearing me, showing me my heavy eyelids and the dark circles under my eyes.

"Gee, thanks. I love hearing that. Why not just tell me I look like crap?"

He laughed and switched back to the cute guy. "I still can't get your eyes."

"I'm an original," I said cheerfully.

"More than you know, I think."

"What's that supposed to mean?"

He shrugged. "Just that I've never met a human I couldn't replicate exactly."

I stood, scowling. "Look, Water Boy, the only paranormal in this room is you."

"If you say so."

I was too tired for Lend's nonsense. The doorway was wider than a normal door and totally open. "What's the security on this room?"

He lifted the foot with the ankle tracker. "If I cross the threshold of the room, an alarm goes off and my ankle thing goes zap."

No problems for me then. "Excellent. I'll see you later." I walked out without another word.

I didn't spend much time in the security sections of the Center. By the time paranormals got here, my work was done. Guessing, I turned left and followed the hall to a familiar area. I was pretty close to Central Processing, so I went in and found Raquel talking frantically with Lish. "That's not acceptable! The werewolves have to be able to find *something*!"

Lish looked up, saw me over Raquel's shoulder, and

promptly burst into tears. At least, I think that's what she was doing. I'd never seen her cry, and there weren't tears since she was already in water, but the facial contortions and shoulder movements were enough to clue me in.

Raquel turned around and yelped, then threw her arms around me. "They didn't eat you!"

"No, they didn't eat me." I had to laugh at the odd symmetry, pushing back my own tears of relief. I was so glad to be back here, with Raquel and Lish. For a while there I'd honestly thought I might not ever see them again.

Regaining her composure, Raquel pushed me out to arm's length, holding onto my shoulders. "What on earth happened? Where have you been? And why did you kill all those vampires?"

"I— Wait, what? Kill the vamps?"

She nodded, looking severe. Killing paranormals is *not* okay for employees of IPCA. All paranormals are classified as endangered; that's why even the icky ones just get neutered instead of, well, dead.

"I didn't kill them! They were one bite away from killing me! I tased a few and slashed around with my silver knife, but I'm sure I didn't pierce any hearts."

"How did you get away?"

I looked down at the ground. "I called for Reth."

She let out a *this is going to be an even bigger mess than I thought* sigh. "Then who left twenty-five vampires dead?"

DUMBBELLS, BOYS, AND OTHER DENSE THINGS

Raquel's vampire explanation came first. "When the panic team got there, they found all the vampires dead."

"Were they staked?" I asked.

"We have no idea what killed them. There were no marks of any kind, no indication that any of the ways to kill vampires were used. What were they all doing there in the first place?"

"Not a clue. I followed my vamp and burst into the room to find them all waiting. A few more followed me and locked me in." Frowning, I thought back. "They *did* seem to think I was there to kill them, though."

"Are you sure you didn't do anything?" Raquel asked, the line between her eyebrows deepening.

"Besides almost get sucked dry? Yeah, I'm sure."

She sighed. Pretty much the same *why me* sigh as before. "Well, where have you been?"

I rubbed a weary hand across my eyes. "I messed up. Big time. No one was coming and I was gonna die, so I called for Reth."

"That's fine, that's why you were assigned names."

I shook my head. "It wasn't calling for him that was the problem. Everything was happening so fast, and I could feel the vamp's teeth on my neck and I— When I called for Reth I yelled out, 'I need you.'"

Raquel's face went from understanding to seriously pissed. When IPCA gives you faerie names, they also make you take a yearly two-week—*two-week*—course on appropriate named commands and how to use them. "I need you" was about as open-ended and stupid as they get.

"'I need you'? That's what you said? That was your named command?"

"Don't get mad." I was on the verge of tears. "I already paid for it, trust me. I told him to take me home and he took me to *his* home, tried to take my heart again."

"Evie, honey, I know you have a history with Reth, but he can't just take your heart. It doesn't work like that."

This was too much. On top of everything else, she was going to tell me—again—that what happened was all in my head and wasn't some sort of faerie freakiness. She had never felt the warmth, felt it sneak in and surround her heart, felt it consume her. She didn't know. She couldn't. And I was sick of her acting like I was some sort of stupid little girl, still mad over an ex. "Whatever," I snapped. "I'm going to bed."

I turned and stalked out of the room without saying good-bye to Lish. She would sympathize, I knew, but she still just didn't understand.

No one understood. Well, that wasn't true—Reth understood. Everything. And he was right, too. I was completely alone and it sucked. When I got to my unit, I went straight to my bedroom and dug around under my bed until I found the three-pound dumbbells I had stolen from one of Bud's training sessions. They were iron, the best protection against faeries. Or at least, I was pretty sure they were iron. Okay, I really, really hoped they were iron, because my only other option was to sleep with my knife on my chest. Images of impaling myself during a nightmare flew through my head. Dumbbells it was.

Putting the weights on either side of me, I closed my eyes and was instantly asleep.

I woke up late the next morning; half-formed memories of a woman's voice calling to me tickled the edge of my thoughts. Both dumbbells were still in place, tangled up in the covers, and my heart was still mine. The night appeared to be a successful one.

I took my time getting ready for the day, pretty sure it was Saturday. Sometimes it was hard to tell the days apart in the Center, but since none of my daily tutors had shown up wondering why my homework wasn't done yet again, Saturday seemed a good guess.

After eating breakfast I went to talk to Lish. I felt bad about running out yesterday. When I walked in her eyes lit up. "Evie," the monotone voice said, but I could tell that she was saying it with an exclamation point. "I am so glad you are okay. I was so worried about you."

I gave her the best smile I could manage. "It was a bad day."

"I am sorry."

I wasn't sure what else to say. "Any leads on the vamps?"

"None."

Weird. Also, not my problem. I wasn't especially heart-broken about it, either, so I shrugged. "How about Lend? Do they have any more ideas on who or what he is, or why he broke in?"

She shook her head. Then her eyes crinkled in a smile and she leaned toward the glass conspiratorially. "I did hear that he requested paper and pencils. Raquel thought he was going to write down information, but all he did was draw."

I smiled. Whatever else he was, Lend was a professional at annoying Raquel. Usually that was my job, but I kinda liked sharing the duty. "Speaking of Raquel, do you know

where she is? I want to talk to her." Whether or not she
believed me about Reth, she had to help me figure out how
to negate my named command.

"She is in meetings all day today." If anyone at the Center worked harder than Lish, it was Raquel. She lived here,
too, and pretty much worked every waking hour of every
day. I'd never known her to take a vacation. In a way it was
nice. It would feel lonelier without her here.

I frowned, frustrated. But then it clicked: if Raquel was
in meetings all day, that meant I was free to do whatever—
and see whomever—I wanted. I smiled at Lish. "That's
okay. I'll talk to her later. Thanks!"

I ran back to my room. After checking myself in the
mirror, I gathered up all my magazines, my mini-video
player, and a couple of books. Then I tucked Tasey and the
knife into my belt and headed for Lend's room.

I turned the corner just in time to see Jacques walking
away. Perfect. I ran down the hall and ducked in. Lend was
sitting on the bed eating lunch, wearing an attractive black
guy. "Don't you look nice today," I said. He looked up,
surprised, then smiled.

"What're you doing here?"

I dumped my armful onto the floor. "I'm bored, you're
bored. Thought we could hang out."

He narrowed his eyes. "This isn't some bizarre good
cop, bad cop thing?"

I laughed. "I don't care what you tell or don't tell Raquel.

But you're the only semi-human person here that's my age, and I thought it would be fun to, you know, just hang out." I was hit by a horrible thought: What if he didn't *want* to hang out?

I mean, sure, there were worse things. Like if he was actually a psycho paranormal assassin and had been waiting for the perfect moment to kill me. But I didn't think so. And somehow that would hurt my feelings less than if a teenage guy didn't think I was cool enough to spend time with. Especially a teenage guy who could be cute in so many different ways.

To my relief he smiled again. "Sounds good." He got off the bed and walked over, glancing through the magazines. "You like reading this stuff?" He raised an eyebrow at all the girly teen and star-stalking content.

"Hey, don't judge. I happen to like popular culture. There's a reason it's popular, you know."

He shook his head but looked amused. Picking up the mini-video player, he sat down on the floor with his back against the bed and started it up. "Do you have anything besides *Easton Heights* on here?"

"*Easton Heights* is the best show on television right now, bar none. But if it's not good enough for you"—I sniffed haughtily—"then find the movie folder." He laughed and the black guy melted off to be replaced by none other than Landon, the freaking hottest guy in the world and conniving lothario of Easton High. "Shut up!" I practically yelled. "That's awesome!"

He laughed at my reaction, then went back to looking up movies. Part of me was giddy that I was sitting in a room with Landon. And the other part was still looking at Lend underneath, and actually liking his face a little bit better.

"Is there anyone you can't do?" I asked, curious.

He shrugged. "I can't do some paranormals. I also can't go up or down in height more than a few inches, so I can't be a little kid. Bulk's about the same as height when it comes to stretching, so I couldn't weigh three hundred pounds. And I can't do your eyes."

"So you keep saying," I muttered. I lay down on my stomach, propped up on my elbows as I paged through one of the magazines. Lend settled on something and we spent the next hour in companionable silence. It was slightly dull and utterly normal. It rocked.

After a while I looked up and noticed a bunch of papers under his bed. "Oh, are those your drawings?" I grabbed them.

"Oh, I—don't—" he said, but I had already started looking at them. He was amazing. He had drawn a portrait of Jacques that was so exact it could have been a photo. Apparently he could copy people on his own body and on paper. I flipped through to the next page and stopped. It was me.

"Holy crap, Lend, these are amazing. You're really, really good." He looked embarrassed, shrugging. "I mean, with a subject as cute as me, of course it's going to turn out well, but still," I teased. He smiled. Gosh, was I getting good at flirting, or what? You'd never know I only practiced during daydreams. I went back to the papers. Now it was my turn to be mildly embarrassed since the majority of the drawings were of me. Mildly embarrassed and really flattered. One of the last ones was a close-up of my face, focused on my eyes, which he had left unfinished.

Turning to the last drawing, I was surprised. He had been trying to draw himself—his real self—with much less success than all his other portraits. "You've got a stronger jawline, and your hair has a bit of wave to it."

"You really can see me that well." He sounded awed.

"It's what I do."

"Yeah, I've been meaning to ask you. What *do* you do? Why are you working here?"

"I help identify and bring in paranormals."

"Do you have any other powers? Super strength or anything?"

I laughed. "Oh, yeah. Absolutely. That's why I nearly got killed by a room full of vamps yesterday. Because I'm such an awesome fighter." He looked confused. I rolled my eyes. "No, I don't have any powers. I'm normal, I can just see a little better than your average person." I didn't explain that I could see through all glamours, since that was classified information.

"How did they find you?"

"Long story. Or not so long. Just boring. I've been here

since I was eight. There's this whole international treaty that I'm pretty much the star of."

"So they own you."

"No! They don't own me."

"So you can leave any time you want?"

I gave him a funny look. "Why would I want to leave?"

"I don't know—it just seems like you aren't very . . . happy."

"I'm plenty happy!" I said, frowning. "Besides, I do a lot of good. I've neutered—" He looked horrified, and I quickly corrected. "Neutralized! Like, made hundreds of vampires harmless over the last few years, identified werewolves before they could hurt themselves or others, helped track down a troll colony, and done countless other things to make the world a safer and more organized place." Had I just said I made the world a more organized place? Wow. Lame.

"Could you leave if you wanted to?"

I shrugged, uncomfortable with the topic. I had been pretty happy here for a long time, but ever since Reth, I'd been wondering more and more what my options were—and kind of worrying that I didn't have any. It was easier not to think about it. No one else ever brought it up, and hearing it so bluntly from Lend made my stomach clench. "I don't know. It's safer for me here."

"Safer for you, or safer for them?"

"Just drop it, would you? This is my job, my life. I'm fine with it."

He held up his hands. "Sorry. It just seems to me like you're more of a possession than an employee."

"They can't hold humans," I snapped. "Under international regulations they're only allowed to detain or monitor paranormals."

He gave me that look again, the one he was so good at. I watched his water eyes; they were sad. "Evie, you aren't exactly normal."

Standing up in a huff, I gathered my magazines and pulled my mini-video player from his hands. "At least I know what I look like." I stormed out of his room, furious.

Halfway down the hall I slumped against the wall, barely able to breathe. He was exactly right.

THERAPY BILLS

Stupid, stupid, stupid," I muttered as I stomped down the halls. I wasn't sure what exactly was stupid, but it seemed like a lot of things were lately. Lend, for one, with his dumb questions, making me think about stuff I'd rather not. I stopped in front of Raquel's office. She needed to believe me about Reth, do something about the command I'd given him. She still thought that faeries didn't care about humans at all. Sure, she knew the histories, how they kidnapped mortals to take to their realm and dance (yeah, it's as weird as it sounds), but since IPCA gave their faeries a named command not to, they figured it was a non-issue now.

I knocked and the door slid open. Raquel was standing at her desk, gathering papers and looking tired and stressed out. "What is it, Evie? I'm due back in five minutes."

I walked in and sat down, scowling at her desk. I was all set to tell her about Reth, using as evidence the creepy comments Fehl had made about me being his, but when I opened my mouth the first thing that came out was, "What if I want to leave?"

She looked surprised. "What do you mean?"

"I mean, what if I quit? What if I'm tired of doing this? What if I'm sick of stupid vampires and clueless werewolves and poltergeists and trolls and the Center? What if I'm done dealing with psychotic faeries? What if I want to go to college?"

She sat down. "Honey, where is this coming from?"

"I don't know, I'm just— You didn't answer the question. What if I left?"

"You don't want to leave." She looked at me with understanding, a motherly smile on her face. It pissed me off. She wasn't my mother.

"Maybe I do. What are you going to do—slap an ankle tracker on me?" I waited for her *don't be ridiculous, Evie* sigh. It didn't come. In fact, not only did she not sigh, she looked anxious. My eyes widened in horror. "Holy crap. You would, wouldn't you?"

She shook her head. "Don't be silly. You know I care about you, and I want the best for you. I—"

I stood. Her pause had been enough to confirm it; no amount of pretending to be my surrogate family would erase this. I really couldn't leave. Without a word I walked out, heading straight to Central Processing.

Lish was surprised to see me again. "What is up, Evie?"

"What's my classification?"

She frowned. "What do you mean?"

"I mean, what's my classification, Lish. Look it up. Now."

"They only classify paranormals. You know that."

"Well then, I shouldn't be in there, so it won't matter if you try to look me up."

"I suppose not." She shrugged and waved her hands in front of her screens. Then her eyes narrowed. "Oh."

"What?" My stomach felt like a brick, heavy and sharp in my abdomen.

"I—you—there is a classification." She looked up at me, concern shadowing her face.

"What does it say?" I whispered.

"Evie, it does not change anything. It does not change you."

"What does it say?" My voice was hard. After a few seconds, Lish looked back at the screen.

"It says you are a 'Level Seven Paranormal, unknown origin, mortal form.' Your status listings are 'protected, in use,' and 'under observation.'"

I shook my head in disbelief. Paranormals were categorized

according to several factors: level of power, how common they were, how dangerous they were, and how much was known about them. Vamps were a two. Lish was a four. Faeries—*faeries*—were a six. I had never met a seven.

I felt like my mind had short-circuited. I always knew I was weird. But I figured I was a normal human who could do something paranormal. Not a paranormal who could do some things human.

"Evie," Lish said, waiting until I met her eyes. "You have always known you were different. Do not let this change the way you see yourself. IPCA is—" She paused, then moved closer to the glass. "IPCA is not always right about everything. You are not paranormal." She smiled at me, sadness behind her wide, green eyes. "You are special. There is a difference."

I couldn't cry, not yet, and being with Lish right now hurt. I knew she understood, but I wasn't ready to face this, so I just nodded and walked slowly out. I wandered, numb, through the Center. When I was nearly back to my room, the white outline of a door showed up on the wall ahead of me. I paused, waiting to see who would come out. I might even have welcomed Reth at that point.

It turned out to be a different faerie. She had done a few transports for me but I didn't know her name. She walked out with a werewolf, then turned to go back through.

"Wait!" I called. The Faerie turned to me, her large, violet eyes disinterested. "I need a transport."

"I don't have transport orders for you."

"Just came in; you know I have clearance." I tried to look impatient. "This has priority."

Nodding impassively, she held out a hand. I took it and we walked into the dark. "Where?"

I bit my lip. I hadn't actually thought about it. "Umm—" Then I remembered one of my bag-and-tags a couple months back. It had been in Florida, near a mall. What was the mall's name? "The Everglades Shopping Center, in Miami." I hoped that was enough. Usually their instructions came from Lish—I didn't know how specific the directions had to be. The way Lish explained it to me once was that all names are powerful for faeries. If you could name where you wanted them to go, they could find it.

Weird, but it came in handy today; after a few more steps a door opened in front of us. I stepped out. "Thanks," I said, but the faerie was already gone.

Nearly all my trips out were at night. Lifting my head, I enjoyed the feeling of the sun on my face, the tickle of humidity. It was March but the weather was perfect here. The entrance to the mall was just ahead of me. Nearby, surrounded by palm trees and hibiscus with brilliant red blossoms, were a couple of benches. I sat down, soaking the heat in through my T-shirt. I was still a little cold—I was always a little cold—but this was a world of improvement from the Center.

After a few minutes I went in, wandering through the

crowds and annoyed at the excessive AC. Watching normal people usually cheered me up whenever I got a chance to do it. Today it made me feel even worse. What if I really didn't belong here? I had always felt almost smug toward the paranormals, because at the end of the day, no matter what, I was still human. I didn't have to be monitored or neutered. I wasn't stuck in a glass tank. They made my life look a lot better. Now I wasn't so sure.

Depressed and worried, I found a bathroom and stared at myself in the mirror. Maybe I had been missing something. If Lend didn't know what he really looked like, maybe I had never looked at myself closely enough. I searched for anything underneath, lingering on my pale eyes, looking for any clue that I, too, was more than what I seemed.

Nothing.

There was nothing there. No shimmering hint of something, no glowing eyes, no body underneath my body. It was just me, just like every other human I'd ever looked at.

Except not just like them, because I could see things no one else could.

I left the bathroom dejected. I had nothing. No wallet, no purse, no identity. There was nothing for me in the real—in the normal—world. Whether or not I was paranormal, I didn't belong here. I sat down on another bench and watched. Couples that couldn't seem to get their hands out of each other's back pockets. Girls with their arms linked as they gossiped about who liked who and who said what and OMG, are you kidding me. All of them going about their wonderful, normal lives. They didn't know anything. I envied them.

I was still sitting there when someone sat next to me. "Evie." Raquel took my hand. "Hon, what are you doing?"

I shook my head. "I don't know."

"I should have told you about your classification a long time ago. I'm sorry."

I sniffled. If I started crying in the mall I would never forgive myself. "Why didn't you?"

"I didn't think it mattered. All it really means is that you can do something no one else can and we don't know how or why. It doesn't mean you aren't human, or that you're somehow the same as the vampires or faeries or unicorns."

"Wait—seriously? There are unicorns? You're lying." I narrowed my eyes.

She laughed. "Maybe if you're really good and start doing your homework I can take you to see them."

"Shouldn't being a Level Seven get me out of homework?"

"Not on your life." She brushed some stray hair away from my face, smiling. "I let you get away with quitting piano lessons when you were ten because that troll teacher scared you, and I've never forgiven myself. No slack on homework. Now, since we're here, we might as well do a little shopping, don't you think?"

I sighed. Mine was nowhere near as impressive as one

of Raquel's sighs, but maybe if I worked at it someday I wouldn't need to talk at all. "I'm not really in the mood."

She looked worried. "You're kidding, right?"

"Yeah. Come on." I loved shopping but did all mine online. Raquel used to buy my clothes for me, but I put a stop to that years ago. A girl can take only so many navy blue skirts and starched white shirts. But being here, actually being able to try things on, feel them, and see the color in real life was way better than pointing and clicking. By the time we were finished Raquel and I were both loaded down with bags.

She shook her head. "I don't know how I'll fill this out on my expense reports."

"Just list it as therapy bills," I suggested. She laughed and we headed for the door. A small store caught my eye. "Oh, just a sec!" She gave a *you've got to be kidding me* sigh, but followed me into the art supply store. I picked out a nice sketchbook and some charcoal pencils. Then, for good measure, I threw in colored pencils and pastels.

"Taking up a new hobby?" Raquel asked as she paid for all of it.

"I figured my wall could use a break, right?" She had patiently ignored my decorating, but I knew it bothered her.

We walked out and into a delivery alley. When she was sure no one was watching, she called for a pickup and a door appeared. I guess that was a perk to being Raquel—

my pickups always took a few minutes. The same faerie who had dropped me off stepped out and took our hands. You'd think she'd be mad after I lied to her, but faeries only care about the things they care about, if that makes any sense. She didn't so much as give me a second glance.

When we walked back into the Center, Raquel helped me carry the stuff to my unit. We set the bags down and she put her hand on my shoulder, searching my face. "You're okay?"

I smiled. "Yeah, I'm fine." She seemed satisfied and left. My smile dropped off. Things weren't fine, and I had no idea if they ever would be again.

I CAN SEE RIGHT
THROUGH YOU

The next morning I was still feeling down. My marathon of *Easton Heights* last night hadn't done anything to cheer me up. If anything, it kinda made me feel worse. I knew it wasn't like real life, but it still reminded me of all the things I wouldn't have: proms, catfights, best friends who actually had legs and breathed air, boyfriends. Boyfriends especially.

I pulled Lish up on my vid screen. "Raquel available today?"

She shook her head. "She is not in the Center. More meetings. Do you want me to call her?"

"Oh, no, no big deal. Just wanted to ask her something; there's no rush." I smiled and waved to Lish, then shut off the screen. Going through my bags of new stuff, I pulled on a zebra-print wrap dress and fitted hot pink stiletto boots. My style was a little over-the-top, but if you lived in a place where everything was white you'd want to liven it up a bit, too. The boots didn't make me as happy as I thought they would. Still, I looked good.

I grabbed the bag of art supplies and was about to walk out the door when I had a better idea. A few years ago Raquel had given me a pair of Rollerblades for Christmas. I wreaked such havoc zooming through the hallways and smashing into everyone and everything that she took them away. I did, however, have a rolling chair at the desk in my room. If riding that through the halls didn't make me at least a little happier, I didn't know what would.

I hooked the bag around the back of the chair and pushed it into the hall. Backing up a few feet, I got a running start and jumped on. It shot down the hall, veering to the left until I slammed into the wall. I took the long way, with very odd stares (and a few swear words if they had to dive away) from the people that I passed. In Lend's hall I leaned so that the chair would roll into his room and made it half-way to the bed before tipping over. I looked up at his very surprised face. "Hey." I giggled.

"Hey?" He raised one eyebrow. Dang that one eyebrow! Today he was wearing the dark-haired, dark-eyed hottie again. I liked that one.

"So." I jumped up, straightening my dress. "You were right."

"I was right?"

"Yup. IPCA has me right up there with faeries. All this time I thought I was part of the family; turns out I'm under observation. Awesome."

"I'm sorry." He sounded like he meant it.

"Yeah, well, I think they're wrong. Because when I look at myself, all I see is me. Nothing else." I had been thinking about it pretty obsessively and it made sense. If I were a paranormal, I'd see something.

"So you can see through other things? Not just me?"

I wasn't supposed to talk about it, but I didn't care. "Sorry, you're not that special." I grinned at him. "If it's a paranormal, I can see what it is, no matter what's on the top."

"Wow. Nice trick."

"Comes in handy. So, I brought you a present." I handed him the bag. He looked inside and a smile spread across his face.

"Thanks! This is great."

"I thought you could teach me a little bit. I'm not really great at figures."

"What are you talking about? You've got a great figure."

He was flirting with me! I laughed, blushing. "Dork." He laughed back and sat on the edge of his bed, patting the space beside him. He spent the next hour explaining proportions and how to depict them. By the end of the hour I was still terrible but getting better. And having fun, too, which was nice.

"So, can you see through anything?" he asked, sketching me again.

I watched his hands, fascinated by the interplay between the hands he was showing me and his real hands underneath. "No. I can't see through clothes or anything. Just glamour skin. Except I can see through all of you, since your clothes aren't real." I stopped, horrified. "I mean, I don't look— It's hard to see you, and I like looking at your real face, but I don't try to see anything, because— Oh gosh, this sounds terrible."

He had a funny look on his face, like he wasn't sure what to think. "Huh. That's never been an issue before. Maybe next time you could bring me some shorts."

I nodded, still mortified. Desperate to change the subject, I said, "So what about you? Are you just, like, projecting things, or can you actually make your hair longer and stuff?"

He shimmered, a long-sleeved shirt replacing his short-sleeved one. He held out his arm and I hesitantly touched the fabric. It was tangible, but felt too smooth to be real. "Hair's the same way."

"That is so freaky." I took the fake material between my fingers. "Can you feel this? Is it like part of you or something?"

He shook his head. "Not really. I have no idea how I do it or how it works."

"Is that why you broke in? To find out what you are?"

He laughed. "No. I don't care what I am according to IPCA."

I frowned. "Yeah, me neither. Why *did* you sneak in?"

After a pause, he shook his head. "I'll tell you later, okay?"

Much as I wanted to know, I realized it didn't really matter. Neither of us were going anywhere. "Sure."

"How can you stand traveling that way here, though? When I took that woman's hand, I had no idea what was going on. It was all I could do not to freak out."

"Oh, yeah, the Faerie Paths. They suck. You didn't know she was a faerie?"

"I don't know much about faeries, really."

"Lucky. You don't want to."

"Why? Seems pretty useful, being able to open doors to anywhere."

"Oh, sure. Super useful. But then you have to deal with the faeries." I got started talking and somehow ended up telling him all about faerie history. I wasn't sure how many faeries IPCA controlled, but the ones we did have hated us for it. I'd also heard that there were different types of faeries, but as far as I could tell there was just the one—beautiful, powerful, and psychotic. I explained as much as I could about how they manipulated the natural world to some extent and traveled pathways between Earth and the Faerie Realms, but that was one area Raquel wouldn't talk much about. She always acted like faeries were around just for transportation, but I suspected there was more to it. I finished by telling him about all the operatives that had been lost over the years by screwing up a command.

"Why does IPCA use them if they're evil?" he asked, confused.

"They aren't *evil*. They aren't even really immoral, per se. They're amoral. They don't operate on the same level that we do. For a faerie, the only thing that matters is what they want. That's their good. Anything else is superfluous. So like how they kidnap people, not a big deal—they want the person, they take him. Or killing someone. If you live forever, how much does one mortal life matter in the scheme of things? When you exist outside time, cutting off the forty years a person has left is a non-issue. They don't even notice."

"So you like faeries?"

"Oh, heavens no. I think working with them is the dumbest thing IPCA could possibly do."

"Why do they keep using them, then?"

"The first named command every faerie gets is to serve IPCA. They think they can control the faeries—I *know* they can't," I muttered darkly. I looked down at his sketch. "Man, you are so good at that."

"Nice subject. And I like your outfit." I couldn't tell

from his smile whether he was serious or poking fun at me.

"I can bring you some boots like this along with the shorts, if you want."

He laughed. "Just because I can look like a girl doesn't mean I want to dress like one."

"You're right. You probably don't have the calves for them, anyway." Standing, I stretched. "I'd probably better go. Technically I don't even know where they're keeping you." I winked at him.

"You should take these, then. You can practice." He handed me the sketchbook and pencils. "You'll come back, right?"

"Sure. You're the coolest person here." He started to smile, so I shook my head, putting on a mock-serious face. "Don't be flattered—most of your competition is undead."

I sat down on my chair and rolled backward out of his room. He watched me, laughing silently, and I gave him a jaunty salute. Back in my unit, I pulled out the sketchbook and looked at his drawings. Mine were pathetic in comparison, but I was much, much happier than I had been before I went to see him. Pulling out the pencils, I started practicing.

The whole next week I didn't get a chance to sneak into Lend's room. Between my usual classes and Raquel being extra attentive (read: annoying) I didn't have any free time. Every day that I didn't see him got more frustrating. Finally, the weekend came again. I was hoping against hope that Raquel would be busy.

The buzz at my door as I finished getting ready Saturday morning made me think otherwise. Raquel walked in, smiling. "Don't you look nice," she commented.

Of course I looked nice—I wanted to go see Lend that day. I forced a smile. "What's up?"

"I don't know, I thought maybe we could go somewhere today. Anywhere you like—the beach, the mall again, a movie."

"Really?" This was new. Usually field trips were carefully scheduled and coordinated. For the most part we visited museums that had to do with my current curriculum. I used to like that when I was younger. We'd walked around and I'd pretended Raquel was my mom and we were a normal mother and daughter. Of course, taking the Faerie Paths back always ruined the illusion.

"Things have been pretty hectic; we could both use a break."

"Okay, sounds good!" I meant it. Much as I wanted to see Lend again, I hadn't been out of the Center all week.

Her communicator beeped. She looked down at it and a deep, worried frown crossed her face. And then, just when I was expecting a sigh, Raquel swore. She *swore*. That had never happened before, not as long as I could remember. Whatever the news was, it had to be really, really bad.

"I'm sorry," she said, already racing for the door. "It's an emergency."

"Don't worry about it." I watched her go. I wanted to know what was up, but I knew that unless it involved me she wouldn't say anything. Never one to waste an opportunity, I grabbed my art supplies and the shorts I had ordered online, then headed for Lend's room, surprisingly fluttery at the thought of seeing him again.

POETRY AND
HOLDING HANDS

Lend was lying on his bed with his back to the door when I got there. It must have been dead dull for him, trapped in here. I thought about letting him nap but figured he probably wouldn't want to. I tossed the pair of basketball shorts at his head. It would be nice to look at him without having to worry about seeing through his projected clothes.

He sat up, startled. Then, seeing me, he grinned. He was wearing the cute black guy again today. I liked this one's smile, but underneath Lend's smile was just as nice. "Hey," he said. "Took you long enough."

I sighed, feigning nonchalance. "Some of us have a life, you know."

"Yeah, I remember what that was like." He pulled the shorts on underneath the covers. "Weird to have real clothes again."

"Aren't you freezing?"

He gave me a funny look. "It's not cold in here."

"You're crazy."

Pulling off the covers, he stood up. I laughed; the shorts were hanging over a pair of khaki pants. The pants dissolved, leaving a great set of legs.

"So, have you been practicing?"

I sat on his bed. "Yeah, but I'm still not that good." I handed him the sketchbook. He flipped through it, nodding.

"No, these are a lot better. And you're really good with color."

I beamed. He passed the sketchbook back to me and our hands brushed. I smiled and shook my head. "So weird."

"What?"

"I just—I don't know, I always expect you to feel like water or something. The first time I touched you to put on the ankle tracker, I was worried my hand would go right through you."

He laughed. "Nope."

"I thought it would be like putting my hand in cold water. But you're really warm."

He put his hand on top of mine. My heart did a happy jump inside my chest. "Your hands are freezing."

"See? Cold in here. Told you." I couldn't help but frown a little when he moved his hand away.

"How was your week?" he asked.

"Pretty boring. Probably not as boring as yours, though."

"Probably not."

"What are they even doing with you? Are they going to just keep you in here forever?"

"Hopefully not. I've got some things I need to be doing. They've run tests on me, but I'm afraid I wasn't very cooperative. And Raquel's been to talk to me, trying to figure out where I came from and why I was going through her stuff."

"I'm a little curious about that as well."

He smiled. "I'll bet. Of course, it's your fault I'm stuck in this room in the first place."

I had to admit he was right. Actually, I didn't have to. "No, it's your own fault your plan was so crappy a helpless teenage girl caught you."

"Helpless? Hardly. I seem to recall being electrocuted."

"Oh, yeah, there was that."

"You're not wearing your Taser today. You didn't last time, either." He looked at me thoughtfully.

"Planning something?" I wasn't nervous. Well, maybe a little, now that he said that.

"Nope, not at all. I'm glad you trust me."

"Once again, how much threat can a guy be whose grand plan for breaking into the Center included punching people and running?"

He put a hand on his chest. "Ouch. You're right, though, I didn't have any idea what I was doing. It was pretty desperate."

"That's all right. We all do stupid things. Last week I was following a vamp and burst into a room that I hadn't checked out first. Turns out there were a whole bunch more. I nearly got killed."

"How did you get out?"

"Reth." I frowned.

"Who's Reth?"

"It's a long story."

Lend leaned back. "I've got nothing but time."

My shoulders sagged under the weight of memory as I thought of how wonderful Reth had made my life—for a while, at least. "When I started here, I thought faeries were angels. They were so beautiful and mysterious. Then Reth came when I was about fourteen. At first he was like all the others—cold and distant. But when he found out what I could do, he started talking to me, taking an interest. Not only was he one of the only guys—well, I guess males— around, but he was the most gorgeous thing I had ever seen. Pretty soon he was coming by my unit, telling me stories, listening to me. When we talked he held my hand and it was like he was warming me from the outside in. I lived for the times I got to see him, and he told me about how he was going to take me away to his dreamland. What lonely girl doesn't want to hear that?"

Lend frowned, looking bothered. "So, were you guys, like, dating?"

I sighed, heartsick remembering how much I had loved Reth, depended on him. Life had been easier then. "Not like *dating* dating. I mean, we didn't kiss or anything normal. Anyway, every time he held my hand I got warmer, faster. He'd come and take me in the middle of the night, dance with me until I swear we both glowed. I thought he was perfect. Sometimes when he held me, my heart would be so warm it felt like I would burst.

"Then one day I went on a simple retrieval, just a werewolf. Those are pretty easy—the people are so freaked out they're relieved to have someone explain things. I guess this guy had been a werewolf for a couple of years and he actually liked it. So when I found him and told him he was under arrest, he got really angry and hit me. Before I knew what was happening Reth was there. His face—it was pure fury. There was nothing human there. He put his hand out and the werewolf flew back into a tree. Then Reth was muttering and the tree started shaking and cracking, growing out and—the werewolf was— It crushed him alive," I finished hurriedly, trying to get the image and the screams out of my head. "As much as I still loved Reth, it scared me so bad that I wouldn't talk to him or see him for a month.

The heat faded, and I could finally see things clearly. I don't know what he was doing—Raquel thinks it wasn't even real." I scowled. "So now every time he sees me, he tries to touch me and I can feel the heat spreading again, trying to get to my heart."

Lend was quiet for a while. "Why don't they just send him away?"

"IPCA is too dependent on faerie magic. They think because they know a faerie's name they can control him, so they don't care. They don't know how stupid they're being."

"IPCA doesn't know a lot of things."

"Yeah." I frowned, trying to get the memory of Reth's warmth out of my head. "So, your turn. What did you do out there? Do you have a family? Did you go to school? Where do you live? Have you always been like this?" All the questions I had been saving up for him spilled out. Except if he had a girlfriend. I managed to keep that one inside.

He just laughed. "I think, considering Raquel has decided to join us, we'll have to talk about those things another time."

I looked up. Raquel stood in the doorway, hands on her hips and looking like she could spit fire. "Oh, bleep," I muttered. Then, smiling, I waved. "Hey, Raquel. What's up? Did you change your mind about the movie?"

"What are you doing here?"

"You know, just hanging out. Lend's been teaching me how to draw."

"Get up and move away from him, now."

"Oh, relax." I waved my hand dismissively. "If he wanted to kill me, he already would have. I brought him all these sharp pencils, ideal for stabbing, and he's been a perfect gentleman."

"Evie." Her voice was dangerous now. She meant business. I went to stand, but Lend took my hand.

"You want answers?" he said to Raquel. "Let her hang out with me and I'll tell you why I came."

Raquel looked from me to him. She had this strange expression on her face, calculating but almost sad. I could tell she was desperate for answers, but there was something more. I didn't know what. Finally, shaking her head, she sighed. It was a sigh I rarely heard from her—the sigh of defeat. I couldn't believe it.

"Fine," she said.

Lend let go of my hand. "How many dead paranormals did you find this week?"

Raquel looked surprised, then suspicious. "Paranormals don't die very often. What makes you think we found any?"

He rolled his eyes. "How many?"

She paused, then said, "Thirty."

"Wait, what? Seriously?" I couldn't believe it. Thirty dead paranormals? That just didn't happen. We'd lose five, maybe ten a year. And most of those were vamps that activated their ankle trackers' holy water function.

"You're missing a lot then," Lend said. "I'd guess it was probably closer to fifty, if the numbers are holding steady."

"Where are you getting this information?"

"Do you really think IPCA is the only group that keeps track?"

Raquel looked triumphant, sure she was finally going to figure Lend out. "What is your group?"

Lend shook his head. "I'm not stupid. We're not interested in being tagged. We're also not interested in being slaughtered."

"Where are you getting your information?" she repeated.

"A banshee. She said—"

"You know a banshee? Where?" Her eyes were practically bugging out of her head now.

"Please stop interrupting. She told me that the answer was with IPCA, and then spouted off a strange poem."

Raquel waited expectantly. "Well?"

Lend turned and looked at me. "Evie, you wanna start it?"

"What?" I was completely confused.

"'Eyes like streams of melting snow,'" he said softly.

That's what I'd said to him when he was first trying to figure out my eye color. No wonder I had terrified him. I had forgotten about it until now—but how did he know what I'd heard in a dream? "What are you talking about? I—I don't even know what that means."

"What was the rest of it?" Raquel asked, impatient.

He turned to her. "I'll tell you when you let me go."

"We're not letting you go. For all I know, your group is behind the attacks. Maybe you broke in to find our tracking records for more victims."

"I'd say whatever this thing is, it's doing just fine on its own."

"Why did you break in, then?"

"I already told you. The banshee said the answer was here. I thought maybe you had info on it, had figured out a pattern or something. That's what I was looking for. Obviously I was on the wrong track, since it seems you know even less than we do."

Raquel was seriously pissed. I'd never seen anyone who could push her buttons as well as Lend. "When you're ready to give me anything *useful*, let me know. Evie, let's go."

"I think I'll stay here for a while." Oh, baby, that was the wrong answer.

Her mouth barely moved as she snapped one word: "Now."

"I guess I'll see you later, Lend." Leaving the drawing stuff with him, I followed Raquel out, turning to give him a sheepish grin.

"I can't— Why you were— You could have—" Raquel stopped, taking a deep breath. "I'm very disappointed in you."

I rolled my eyes, walking next to her down the hall.

"Yeah, well, maybe if I actually had a life or some friends I wouldn't have to hang out with the prisoners. But as it is, he's very nice, and I think if you were nice to him, you might have learned something by now."

"You don't understand how this works."

"No, I don't, because you don't tell me anything! What's up with all the dead paranormals?"

Raquel rubbed her forehead wearily. "I don't know. The vampires last week, and there have been several more the last few days. Either we haven't been picking up on it, or it's getting worse."

"What are you gonna do?"

"We've got research and analysis working on it, but we haven't been very lucky coming up with answers lately. Like your friend in there—we have no idea what he is or where he came from."

"Kinda like me?"

She gave me a sharp look that softened quickly. "You're a very different case."

"Yeah. Okay." I wanted to add a whatever, but knew it would push her over the edge. "Oh, did you figure out a new command for Reth? I'm tired of sleeping with weights on my bed."

"You're sleeping with weights on your bed?"

"Gotta stay safe somehow."

She heaved an *I can't deal with this right now* sigh. "You know that the faeries can't take you. They're all strictly prohibited from kidnapping."

"Someone should tell Reth. Besides, it's not the kidnapping, it's what he does to—"

"Enough, Evie. Maybe hanging out with Lend isn't such a bad thing if it will get you off this obsession you have with the faerie."

I stopped in my tracks. She kept walking for a few steps before she noticed. "My obsession with *him*? Why won't you believe me about this? I thought you cared about me!" Angry tears stung my eyes, and I closed them before I could say anything else. Taking a deep breath, I shook my head. "Whatever. I'm going back to my room."

"Just be sure and tell me before you go and see Lend again."

"Sure, because we're big on trust here, right?" Before she could answer I turned and walked off.

LIGHT MY FIRE

The next day (after sending a rather snippy message to Raquel informing her that I was going to see Lend) I went into his room, laptop in hand. He was Chinese and utterly adorable this morning. "What do you have planned for today?"

I gave him a stern look. "I'm going to make you realize that *Easton Heights*, while popular with viewers, is severely underrated by critics."

He looked up at the ceiling and sighed. "So Raquel's resorted to torture."

I hit him in the shoulder and continued. "I've picked

out three episodes that not only showcase superb acting but also have unparalleled writing. And you *are* going to love them."

"Is that an order?"

"No, it's a threat."

He put his pillow against the wall as a cushion and sat all the way back on his bed. I sat next to him, not minding that we had to be touching so we could both see the screen. That's when it hit me—right then, when our arms were touching—that I was totally crushing on him. It should have been obvious since I thought about him pretty much all the time, but at that moment I knew. I liked him. *Like* liked him. A lot. Not in just a fun-to-finally-have-someone-to-flirt-with way, but in an I-wanted-to-hold-his-hand-and-kiss-him way.

And suddenly even *Easton Heights* couldn't make me feel better. I was overwhelmed with insecurity. What if he was nice to me because I was the only person here who was nice to him? What if he had a girlfriend in the normal world? The way he could change his looks, he could have fifty girl-friends and they'd never know! And what would happen if IPCA let him go? I'd never see him again. The thought was crushing. But what would happen if they didn't? He'd get bitter and angry and blame me, since it really was my fault that he got caught.

Lend nudged me. "It wasn't that bad," he said, smiling, and I realized the first episode was already over.

I managed a weak smile. "Wasn't that bad? It was awesome."

He narrowed his eyes. "Are you okay?"

"Yeah, sure. Why wouldn't I be?"

He reached out and put his hand on top of mine. My heart skipped a beat—he liked me, too!

"You're worried about what's killing the paranormals, aren't you?"

Crap. He didn't like me. "What does it have to do with me?" I asked before I thought about it. "I mean, it's bad, yeah, but not really my problem. IPCA will figure it out."

He moved his hand. "You don't get it, do you? Evie, it has everything to do with you. You're a paranormal, whether you like it or not."

Okay, I *so* didn't like that. I was about to say so, but he just kept going.

"They're our kind, and whatever's killing them is not only a threat to the few special things that are left, it's a threat to us, too."

"I'm sorry that paranormals are dying, but honestly, not too sad that the vampires who were trying to kill me ended up dead."

"It's not just vampires; there are whole species out there you have no idea exist. And if this goes on much longer, they won't. The world will be a much colder, emptier place for it."

"Isn't it already?" Bitterness saturated my voice. I

couldn't be one or the other—by being both normal and paranormal I didn't belong anywhere. I was sick of not belonging.

"Trust me when I say it's not. And I want to show that world to you. But we've got to make sure it's still there to see."

I sighed. "What can I do?"

"Where did you hear that line? About the eyes?"

I put down the laptop and turned sideways so I could see him. "I don't know, really. It was just in my head. I think I was dreaming about it the day you came. 'Eyes like streams of melting snow . . .'" I paused, trying to remember. "'Cold with the things she does not know'?"

His breath caught and he nodded. "Do you know the rest of it?" I shook my head. "Maybe you can help me figure it out. I'll—" We both looked up as extra light filled the room from a doorway appearing on the wall. "Are you expecting anyone?"

"No." I scooted closer to him. We both watched as a figure came out of the door. Reth. "Oh, bleep," I whispered. I didn't have my knife. I didn't have anything.

"Here you are," he said, smiling pleasantly.

Raquel hadn't done anything to stop him. "Lo—" I didn't even get to the second syllable of his name before he waved his hand and whispered a word, disappearing my voice again.

"There's no need for that." His smile didn't change.

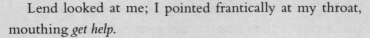

Lend looked at me; I pointed frantically at my throat, mouthing *get help*.

"Stay away from her," Lend said, standing and moving in front of me.

"Evelyn is mine. You are irrelevant." Waving his hand dismissively, he sent Lend flying across the room and into the wall. Lend slid down into a heap at the bottom. I screamed, but nothing came out.

Reth glided across the room and settled down on the bed next to me. I tried to hit him, but he grabbed my arm, laughing. I struggled as he took his free hand and traced a finger down my spine, paralyzing me. It was like one of those nightmares where you have to watch everything happen and you can't do anything.

Lend was completely still. Tears filled my eyes.

Reth kept his hand on my forearm, encircling my wrist with his long fingers. "I'm sorry for the haste, but circumstances have changed and we can't afford the same leisurely pace." His heat crept up my arm. Closing my eyes, I willed it to stop. It slowed, and then stilled. It felt like I was damming the flow by sheer force of will. I couldn't last long.

"Don't be difficult. Once I finish, everything will be better—you'll see." He smiled at me tenderly, stroking a finger down my cheek and leaving a trail of heat. "We've got things to do—what fun we'll have." I didn't stop concentrating. "Evelyn." He sounded annoyed. "I'm giving you a gift; moving you forward. It was only a matter of time. You belong with me, and this is the best way." He squeezed my wrist. The warmth burned hotter and hotter. Now instead of pleasant, it was painful. It was like his hand was searing itself to my arm; in my mind the flesh was sealing, his hand permanently attached to me. I couldn't hold this back anymore. It was too hot, there was too much. The fire devoured my arm, moving faster and higher, ever closer to my heart. I screamed again, but no sound escaped my lips.

And then sound was everywhere. I opened my eyes. Lend was on the floor in the hall, his body convulsing from the electric shocks shooting through it. "Lend," I mouthed. He had triggered the alarm—thrown himself out there, knowing what would happen.

Reth sighed impatiently, squeezing my arm harder. "I hate it when people meddle." The fire was in my shoulder; the first tendrils of it touched my heart, nestling in like a small animal.

"Lorethan!" a voice called out, sharp and brilliant in my pain.

Reth turned his head, murder on his face.

Raquel spoke slowly and clearly over the sound of the alarm. "You will not touch Evelyn."

A fraction of a second, then his hand shot off my arm as though he were the one being burned. The rest of the fire split—half drained back down my arm to where his hand had been; the other half found its way into my heart. I still couldn't move or talk. He stood, regarding Raquel with the same cold fury I had seen when he'd killed the werewolf.

"Leave us now," Raquel said.

Reth was absolutely still, looking like an avenging god in the middle of the white room. I wondered if he would kill us all. After the longest silence of my life, he waved his hand toward me. I collapsed onto the bed, finally able to move again. Without another word Reth walked to the wall and through a faerie door.

Raquel pushed a button on her communicator, turning off the alarms, and rushed to my side. "Evie, hon, are you all right?"

The memory of the pain hurt as much as if it were still happening. I sobbed and clutched my burned arm to my chest.

"Let me see it," she said, pulling it out. "Oh, Evie, I'm so sorry." I looked up; her eyes brimmed with tears. "I should have listened to you."

On my wrist in brilliant scarlet was the imprint of Reth's hand. But Raquel could see only the burn. She couldn't see what my eyes could see.

Beneath the handprint, I was still on fire.

BURN, BABY, BURN

I stared at my arm. Underneath the red handprint golden tendrils swirled, warm and living. "What did he do?" I whispered, crying. What had Reth put inside me?

Raquel, thinking I was talking about Lend, stroked my hair. "He tried to run away."

I looked up, shaking my head. "No, he didn't. When Reth— Lend couldn't— He threw himself over the threshold to trigger the alarm. It was the only way he could help."

"Oh," Raquel said, her voice soft. She looked into the hall at Lend's unconscious form, or at least what she could see of it. He was wearing the shorts I'd given him; to

Raquel's eyes it probably looked like a pair of shorts and an ankle tracker floating in the hall.

Raquel called on her communicator and a couple of guards came, bringing Lend in from the hall. I moved to the end of the bed, clutching my arm. After they set Lend down, I put my uninjured hand on his chest, surprised as always that it was firm and warm. "He's breathing." I was so relieved I started bawling.

"It's okay." Raquel put an arm around my shoulders. "How did this happen?"

"How did it happen? Are you kidding me? How long have I been telling you that Reth was crazy, that he was doing this to me? How many times have I told you that you guys don't understand faeries, that you can't control them?"

"I'm sorry. I should have listened. But it must have been the 'I need you' named command you gave him—somehow he twisted it."

I rolled my eyes. "You think? That's what they *do*."

"Still, he can't touch you now, so that's taken care of."

She really thought it was that simple. She had no idea.

"Let's take you to the infirmary so the doctor can look at that burn."

I looked down at my arm; the gold glow hadn't faded. I couldn't believe she didn't see it—it was like I was lit up from the inside. "What about Lend?" I put my hand on his cheek.

"He'll be fine once he wakes up. It wasn't a lethal amount."

I let her take my good hand and walk me to the infir-mary. The doctor was a pleasant werewolf in her midforties. I hadn't been in here since I sprained my ankle two years ago. And, no, it wasn't in some exciting way, being chased through a graveyard by a vamp or anything. I sprained it while rocking out to my iPod alone in my room. Apparently hip-hop is not my calling. Remembering how embarrassed I was then was a stark contrast to the terror I felt now.

Raquel explained what happened and had me hold out my wrist for the doctor to see. She frowned; for a moment I was overwhelmed with panic, thinking she, too, could see what seethed under the skin. If IPCA was already watching me and considered me a paranormal, there was no telling what they would do if they thought I was changing.

"That's odd," she said. "It's a burn, but it doesn't look like it happened five minutes ago. It looks older, mostly healed now." My skin felt so hot to me I expected it to burn her as she ran her finger over it, but she just shook her head. "Still feels quite warm." She put her hand to my forehead and looked up. "You're freezing." If she gave me that con-cerned frown one more time I'd freak out. I didn't feel any colder than normal. In fact, I felt warmer. Especially inside my heart.

"Can I talk to you in the hall?" Raquel asked and the doctor followed her out. Trembling, I got off the table and walked over to a mirror hanging above the sink. I took a deep breath and unbuttoned the top three buttons of my shirt, pulling it wide. I sighed, relieved. My reflection was completely normal; just my pale skin, barely-there cleavage, and pink bra.

Then, buttoning my shirt, I looked down. "Oh, no," I whispered. Right where I could feel my heart racing in my chest the same liquid gold burned. It pulsed with life in time to my heartbeats.

I jumped as the door opened, yanking my shirt closed. The doctor smiled at me. "Everything okay?"

"I, yeah, everything's fine."

"I'm going to put some aloe on your burn and then wrap it up. Since it seems mostly healed, I don't think you need to keep it covered for more than a day. Now, I was talking with Raquel, and I'll admit I don't know much about faerie magic or wounds. Are you experiencing any other strange symptoms?"

"No." Besides the fact that I was glowing and for the first time could see myself like I saw paranormals. I knew I should mention it—tell Raquel that it was more than just a burn, that Reth had done something, changed me somehow—but I couldn't. I wasn't looking for an ankle tracker or to be some sort of freaky test study. Visions of being dissected ran through my head. I didn't think they actually did that, but I wasn't going to risk telling IPCA anything.

I looked down at the wrap the doctor put on my wrist, relieved that I couldn't see the flames anymore.

"I'm going to take your temperature; you feel very cool, and I'm worried it might be a side effect." She put a thermometer in my ear. After a few seconds it beeped. She pulled it out, and there was that surprised frown. Again. It was almost as bad as Raquel's sighs. "This is way too low. The thermometer must be broken. Do you feel okay?"

I jumped off the table, terrified that they would figure out something was seriously abnormal—paranormal— here. Aside from a complete physical when I first arrived and the ankle thing, I'd never been in here, never been sick that I could remember. I chalked it up to that whole living in near-seclusion thing. I didn't want her to start poking around and figure out I was even weirder than they thought. "Yeah, I'm fine, really. I'm always a little bit cold; the thermometer must be broken, no big deal."

"Okay. If that wrist bothers you, or you have any strange symptoms—anything at all—let me know."

"Will do." I walked out with Raquel following me.

"Why don't you go get some rest?" she asked, hurrying to keep up with my fast pace.

"I want to be there when Lend wakes up."

"I don't think—"

"Raquel," I said, giving her a flat look. "He saved me. He freaking electrocuted himself to save me. I'm gonna be there when he wakes up so I can tell him thanks."

After a small *I give up* sigh, she nodded. "Just be careful, okay? We still don't know anything about him." They didn't know anything about me, either. "And if he tells you where he's from or what he's doing, tell me immediately."

Yeah, right, I thought. "Yup," I said. She walked me to his room and stood in the doorway as I walked straight in.

"Okay—I'll check on you later then." She hovered for a moment, then left.

Lend was still out cold. I sat on the edge of the bed next to him, wondering how long it would take him to wake up. I felt horrible. It was my fault—yet again—that he had been zapped.

I stared, glad he had the shorts so I didn't have to feel guilty. He was amazing. He had the faintest luminescence about him, centered in his chest. I studied his face. When he was wearing other people I could see hints of his features underneath, but now that it was just him it was a little easier. I leaned closer and closer, trying to memorize the way he looked. It was kinda weird having a crush on a guy who was different every time I saw him, and I wanted to have this face, Lend's real face, in my mind. He was the most strangely beautiful guy I had ever seen—even more than the faeries, because his face was human.

I leaned in so far I almost fell on top of him. Rather than risk that again, I got off the bed and knelt, propping my elbows on the side of the bed and resting my head on my hands. Still curious, I reached out a hand and ran my fingers through his hair. It was the softest, smoothest texture imaginable. I was so busy trying to see his hair and playing with it that I didn't notice him wake up until the hair I was playing with turned black.

"Oh!" I said, moving back so fast I fell on my butt. "You're awake!" He was wearing the standard dark-haired, dark-eyed hottie and regarded me with a puzzled expression. Before he could ask what I was doing playing with his hair, I started babbling. "Are you okay? How do you feel? Can I get anything for you?"

He moved to sit up, then stopped and put a hand on his forehead. "Man, I hurt."

"I'm so sorry! This is all my fault."

He looked at me, frowning. "How is this your fault?"

"I got you electrocuted again."

"I think we can safely blame the crazy faerie."

I shook my head. "If you hadn't— I don't— Thanks." I smiled and took his free hand in mine. "Really, really thank you. I'm pretty sure you saved my life. Or at least my soul."

He sat up, not letting go of my hand. I liked that. A lot. "What was he doing to you?"

I sat on the bed next to him and stared at the floor. "I don't know. It was kind of like what he used to do—with the heat. But it was different this time—stronger. It was like he was burning me up on the inside, forcing it into me. And it didn't—" I stopped. I couldn't tell Raquel about what I saw in myself now. Could I trust Lend with it?

"It didn't what?"

I took a deep breath. "It didn't go away this time."

Taking my hand from his, I pulled off the wrapping and stared at the red handprint and liquid flames underneath. Lend drew his breath in sharply and I looked up at him, shocked. "You can see it?"

"Of course I can see it!"

HAGTASTIC

Lend could see the flames under my skin. I couldn't believe it. Maybe they weren't paranormal, after all. "Really? How can you see them?" I asked.

"It's bright red! How could I not see? He must have burned you really bad." Lend took my hand tenderly, looking at the burn. "Hand's still freezing, though."

My shoulders slumped in disappointment. "You can't see it, then."

He looked up, confused. "Is there something else?"

I bit my lip, then shook my head, avoiding his eyes. "No, nothing."

"Evie. What did he do to you?"

"I don't know." That part was the truth, at least. I had no idea what he'd done to me, or what would have happened if he hadn't been stopped.

"You can see something there, can't you?"

I shook my head again, then closed my eyes and nodded.

"What is it?"

"I don't know. It's like—it's like the fire I felt from him, it's still there, right under where the handprint is. Just swirling around, all golden and creepy. I've never been able to see anything under myself before."

"Not even when he was doing this to you earlier?"

"I don't know. It was different." I tried to remember; I knew it made me feel warmer, but it always faded after he left. "I never bothered looking because it wasn't permanent. The feeling always went away. Back then it was as if he was letting me borrow the warmth. This time it was like he was forcing it into me, making me take it."

"Maybe this will fade, too?"

"I don't know," I said, trying not to cry. "It's not just on my arm."

"Where else?"

My voice came out a whisper. "My heart."

Lend was quiet for a long time. "What did Raquel say?"

"I didn't tell her. They've already got me classified as a paranormal. I don't want to give them anything else that would make them—make me, I don't know, weirder?"

"I can understand that. I've hidden from them my whole life. But where else are you going to get any answers?"

"They don't know a bleep thing about faeries."

Lend laughed.

"What?" I asked.

"What's with the bleep? Didn't they teach you any actual swearwords here?"

I blushed, then laughed. "It's kind of an inside joke. Lish—Alisha, my best friend—she's a mermaid, and the computer talks for her. It won't translate swearing, so it all comes out as 'bleep.' I kinda picked it up."

"I guess that makes sense in a weird way." He was still holding my hand and looking at the burn. I really, really, *really* liked the feeling of my hand in his. It was amazing that even with everything that happened today such a little thing could still make me feel giddy. Granted, it would have been better if he wasn't staring at the wound that had gotten him electrocuted and possibly meant I was even more of a freak than before, but I'd take what I could get.

"Isn't there anyone you can ask about this? I'm kind of worried about it."

I laughed. "I'm the one who's freaking on fire on the inside. Lish would keep it a secret, but she doesn't know anything that IPCA doesn't. And I could always ask Reth what the bleep he did to me, but I kinda don't want to see him again. Ever. And I'm sure no other faerie would help. They don't really do helpful."

Lend had a weird look on his face. "Did you say you're on fire on the inside?"

"That's what it looks like on my arm and chest—kind of all swirly and golden, like liquid fire."

"Liquid fire." His tone was flat, disbelieving.

Feeling defensive, I shrugged. "Yeah."

He sighed. "'Eyes like streams of melting snow, cold with the things she does not know. Heaven above and Hell beneath, liquid flames to hide her grief. Death, death, death with no release. Death, death, death with no release.'"

What. The. Crap. That was what I thought. And what I said was, "*What the crap?*"

Lend let go of my hand and rubbed his hands over his face. "I don't know. It's what the banshee gave us, some sort of prophecy poem. I have no idea what it means. And a lot of it seems like it means you. Your eyes, and you're always talking about how cold you are. And now the liquid fire inside you."

"Umm, yeah, but you're forgetting that whole 'death death death' part! And I am *not* a killer!" I stood, insulted. I couldn't believe Lend would think that.

He laughed drily, shaking his head. "Trust me, I really don't think you're the killer. You're not exactly the slaughter-hundreds-of-paranormals type."

"Oh." Feeling stupid, I sat back down. "What do you think it means, then?"

"I don't know. I used to think it was describing whoever was doing this, but now I have no idea."

I thought about it. The whole thing was weird and creepy. "Hey, the part about heaven and hell—do you know any faerie mythology?" He shook his head. "Well, the traditional stories about them say that they were too bad for heaven and too good for hell, so they got stuck in the middle—Earth and the Faerie Realms. And they've been trapped here ever since, immortal, unchanging, trying to find a way back to heaven. Or hell. Or somewhere else entirely, I'm not sure. Trying to find a way out, I guess. Maybe it's about the faeries!" If it was about the faeries, then it wasn't about me. I *needed* it to be about the faeries.

He nodded thoughtfully. "Could be."

"And! And! Reth was the one who came and got me from the vamps, and then he left pretty soon after taking me to his home— He totally could have gone back and killed them all!"

"But why? And it says 'she,' not 'he.'"

I frowned. He had a point. "Still—there are lots of girl faeries. And he's the one who put the fire stuff in me. I think it's Reth."

"You could be right. Honestly, I'm in so far over my head. I should never have come here. Not only did I not figure anything out, I can't help anyone."

I nudged him with my shoulder. "You helped me."

He nudged me back. "That's something, at least."

I smiled, happy. Then I frowned. Lend didn't belong here. As much as I never wanted him to leave, the whole thing was stupid. "I'm gonna talk to Raquel, see if we can get you out."

He laughed, but it didn't have any humor. "They won't let me leave. And even if they do, it'd be with this ankle tracker, which would mean I could never go home." He turned toward me, his face serious. "You should leave, though. You could get out, get away."

I shook my head, sad. "I can't. I don't have anyone or anything outside IPCA. I'd have no money, no family, nowhere to go." Ever since I found out the agency that took care of me considered me one of the things they protected the world from, it was a lot harder to forget I was totally alone. Reth's words came back to haunt me. Stupid, stupid faerie. I sighed heavily. "Gosh, now I don't even feel like watching another episode of *Easton Heights*."

Lend put his arm around me and patted my shoulder. "At least there's one good thing to come of all this, then."

I elbowed him in the stomach, laughing. "Whatever."

"You don't have wireless on that thing, by any chance?" He had dropped his arm back to his side and was eyeing the laptop we used to watch the show earlier.

"Nope, sorry."

"Evie!" Raquel was standing at the door. "Why don't you have your communicator on you?"

"Forgot it. What's up?"

"You've got a job."

"A real one? Today?" Surely what I had just been through was enough to get me a sick day.

"Yes, today, right now. Hurry up."

Sighing, I stood, leaving the laptop. Poor guy needed something for entertainment. "See you later, Lend. And thanks again for that whole electrocuting-yourself-to-save-me thing."

"Anytime."

I followed Raquel out. "Not that I'm nervous or anything, considering the last job almost got me killed and Reth burned a hole in my arm today, but what exactly is this job?"

"Ireland. Possible hag."

"A hag? Oh, ick. Can't someone else go?" I'd only met one hag before, but it was horrible.

"No, it's unconfirmed. We'll need your go-ahead for the bag-and-tag. Remember what happened with Alex?"

I had to laugh. Alex was this awesomely shy, bumbling kind of guy who worked in our section of IPCA for a while. He was six foot four and about 150 pounds. Knew everything there was to know about any type of paranormal but was useless in the field. He came back once, triumphantly dragging a "hag" along. Yeah, turns out she was just a really old, ugly woman. That was a mess. Alex was never sent out again—permanent paperwork duty.

"I hate hags." They were creepy. Beyond creepy. Way worse than vamps.

"I'm sending Jacques with you. I don't want you going

out by yourself for a while."

"Fine by me." Jacques, besides the natural werewolf enhancements, was huge. Definitely the kind of guy you wanted with you when you were feeling a little nervous. I stopped at my room to grab my bag of ankle trackers, my communicator, Tasey, and my knife.

We met up with Jacques outside Transport. A faerie was already waiting for us. Fehl. Of course, it had to be one of the few who ever paid attention to me. I was all faeried out for the day, but I had a job and there was nothing to be done. Fehl didn't say anything, standing with her usual bored and annoyed expression. I had never noticed before, but her eyes were the same ruby color as her hair. Like her voice, it was creepy and beautiful at the same time.

"Be careful, okay?" Raquel cautioned.

"Yeah, yeah." Completely exhausted, I just wanted to get this over with.

Jacques and I stood on either side of Fehl. She held her hands out and we took them as a door appeared in front of us. Without thinking I had given her my hand with the burned wrist. She looked down and the briefest smile flickered across her face. "He didn't finish," she murmured in her breaking-glass voice. Sure that Raquel hadn't heard, I clenched my jaw and closed my eyes, walking through the Faerie Paths toward my date with a hag.

LOST SOULS

We stumbled out of the Faerie Paths into the dim sunlight of a hazy, cold field, surrounded by nothing but tall brown grass. Fehl quickly backed up through the door in a dead tree behind us. Good riddance. I pulled my arms around myself. "Shoulda worn a coat."

Jacques shrugged. "It is not so bad."

I could see the pond, a murky, lonely thing ahead in the distance, surrounded by a thin copse of trees. Why couldn't these creatures ever hang out on tropical islands? I wouldn't have minded a trip to Hawaii.

I frowned. "You should probably hide when we get

close, let me stand there alone. She's more likely to show, if she's even there."

"Are you certain you will be all right?"

"If I'm not, trust me, you'll know."

He smiled and we crossed the field in silence. When we were a few yards away from the edge of the pond, Jacques broke away and hid in a scraggly stand of trees. Putting one hand on Tasey, I walked to the edge of the water, picked up a rock, and threw it in. There was no reaction. I did it again. Nothing.

Granted, I hoped nothing would happen. Hags live in ponds and creeks and look like old, gnarled women. Not even a very cute glamour, but what's underneath is awful. They're sickly green, with big, round fish eyes—pure white. Their hair is like clumps of rotting weeds, and they top it all off with three rows of needle-like, blackened teeth. Did I mention they eat kids? Yeah. *Kids.* They ask for help and then pull them under the water until they stop struggling. Then the hag eats them whole.

Hag protocol was pretty simple. You couldn't get them in the water—too strong. But if you lured them out, it was easy enough to tase them, attach an ankle tracker, and call for transport. Unlike vamps, hags couldn't be neutered. They were kept in a special unit somewhere in Siberia. "Humane Detainment," IPCA called it—a little odd, considering there was nothing humane or human about hags.

After ten minutes of walking around and tossing rocks

into the pond I got bored. Maybe I was too old to attract a hag these days. I looked around the pond, trying to see any hints I wasn't wasting my time. Most of the vegetation was still dead; spring had yet to visit this part of Ireland. The trees were thicker than I'd noticed, though. Then I saw something to my right. About two dozen feet away was an odd little mound, mottled green and gray, that seemed out of place. Pulling Tasey out, I made my way cautiously over. As I got closer, the scent of mildew was nearly overpowering—that was the hag smell, all right. Holding my breath, I tiptoed around to her other side. I couldn't believe it.

She was dead.

I didn't even know how to kill a hag. They were just one of those things that always were, kind of like mermaids. But she was definitely dead. Underneath the glamour, her milky white hag eyes were opened wide, her horrible face frozen in confusion. How had this happened?

I glanced around for clues, but didn't see anything. Looking down at the hag again, I narrowed my eyes. There was something under the glamour, just where her heap of rags covered her chest. Finding a stick, I pulled down the cloth. There was the faintest trace of a handprint there—a handprint in pale gold, getting dimmer even as I watched, until it disappeared entirely.

Then I realized something else: the hag was steaming slightly in the cool air. Which meant her body was still warm. Which meant she hadn't been dead for long. "Oh, bleep," I whispered. I stood up straight, holding Tasey out in front of me and spinning around. The whole area felt sinister now, as though every clump of brown bushes or stand of trees held my imminent death.

"Jacques?" I called softly, backing away from the pond. I pushed the panic button on my communicator, hoping that Fehl wasn't far from the transport point. "Jacques?" I didn't want to yell. Of course, I'd been standing out in the open so long that whatever this thing was had probably already seen me. Far to my left I heard a twig snap. Dropping my bag of ankle trackers, I pulled out my knife.

"Jacques? Jacques, is that you?" My voice was shaking almost as badly as my hands. "Jacques?"

A scream ripped through the air, like a soul was being ripped from its body. Jacques's soul. Jacques's body. And, hating myself even as I was doing it, I turned and ran as hard as I could for the tree. If this thing could take a hag and Jacques, I didn't stand a chance. My breath tore at my chest as I pushed myself faster than I thought possible. I was running from death and expected it to catch me at any moment.

The tree got closer and closer—and nothing was there. Fehl hadn't answered the call yet. I sobbed as I ran. If she didn't come soon, I was going to die. I made it to the tree and still there was nothing. Shaking so hard I thought I would fall apart, I turned around, wanting to meet my end face-to-face. The field was empty. I sobbed harder. I didn't know whether I should wait for Fehl to come or risk using her name. Just when I was about to shout it, light burst from behind me and I grabbed Fehl's outstretched hand. "Go, now!"

From the edge of the trees I saw a flash of fire shaped like a person, and then the door closed.

SELFISH IS
AS SELFISH DOES

Raquel was sitting in a chair near my kitchen, talking quietly on her communicator when I woke up on the couch. She had stayed the whole night. I didn't want to be alone.

Her eyebrows were knit as she rubbed her forehead with her free hand. I sat up. She looked over and gave me a strained smile, then continued her conversation for a few minutes. When she had finished, I sat on my hands so they wouldn't shake. "Did they find it?"

She shook her head and heaved a new sigh. This one was laced with more stress and tension than any I had ever heard before—even more than her *Evie, Evie, Evie* sigh that showed up whenever I messed up big time, like when I was fourteen and stole her communicator in an attempt to reprogram mine to play music. I screwed up the entire system and locked everyone in their rooms for a few hours. It didn't go over well. I was on Containment cleanup duty for a month.

If only things were that easy this time.

I didn't want to ask, I didn't want to know, but I had to. "Jacques?"

She shook her head sadly. "He was dead."

I looked at the floor, tears welling in my eyes. I hadn't done a thing to help him—I hadn't even tried. Raquel sat next to me and put her arm around my shoulders. "There was nothing you could have done. If you had tried to help him, you'd both be dead now. And I know Jacques would be glad he died helping you escape."

Actually, I was sure Jacques would be glad to be alive right now. Still, he had been armed and had supernatural werewolf strength. If he could be taken out that easily, I really wouldn't have been able to do anything.

Telling myself that didn't erase his scream from my mind.

"I've got to go to a meeting with all the department heads. We'll figure it out and stop whatever's doing this."

I remembered my theory and sat up straight. "It's Reth!"

"What's Reth?"

"Reth, the killer! I think Reth's doing it!"

"Why would you say that?"

"The handprint! On the hag's chest—she had a hand-print that was glowing gold! Just like—" I stopped dead. I hadn't told Raquel about the glowing in me and I wasn't going to. "He left a handprint on me, I think it's him!"

Raquel shook her head. "I know you're mad at Reth, and with good reason, but it isn't him."

"How do you know? You don't know anything about faeries!"

She gave me a level stare. "I have been working with faeries far longer than you. And I know Reth didn't do this. While you were out there, he was in a disciplinary hear-ing."

"A—what?"

"His actions with you were under review. There were seven people on the council; they can all vouch that he was there the whole time."

A disciplinary hearing? Who were they kidding? Faer-ies didn't care in the slightest about us or our rules. Like I told Lend, they were only here because of the named com-mand they had been given in the very beginning—to serve IPCA. "So, what, are they punishing him?"

"His actions were deemed inappropriate and he was firmly admonished." The way Raquel said it, I knew she realized how lame it sounded.

"Ah, admonished. That'll teach him! I feel totally safe now!"

"You don't need to worry about him anymore. I gave

him a named command not to touch you. He can't, ever again. So please, stop letting it bother you so much."

I looked down at my wrist. It was mostly covered by my sleeve, but I could see the swirling glow where the skin stuck out a little. Yeah, nothing to worry about at all. "I still think he had something to do with this—or maybe another faerie. One IPCA doesn't know about."

"Well, I'll suggest your theory during the meeting, but we have no reason to suspect the faeries. You and I both know faeries don't do anything without motivation."

"Yeah, and we both *should* know that we really don't get their motivation."

Raquel heaved an *I'm done talking about this with you* sigh and stood up. "Lish wanted you to go see her as soon as you felt up to it. I would feel better if you spent the day with her. I don't want you alone. And, please, this time, take your communicator."

Raquel patted me on the head like I was five, then left. I was freezing, so I took a shower that was too long and too hot. I tried not to, but I couldn't avoid looking down. My chest still had its spot of liquid gold fire, undimmed.

When I got out, I stared hard at myself in the mirror, but I could see my freaky liquid flames only if I looked directly at them. It felt like my face should look different, but it was the same old Evie—cute but not gorgeous, button nose, pretty mouth. And my pale, pale gray eyes.

But then something hit me—something horrible. If I

could see what was paranormal about myself only by looking directly at it, I had no idea if there was something my
face was hiding. I could never look into my own eyes without a mirror and, for all I knew, I'd been glowing my entire
life. Maybe that's what was so weird about my eyes that
Lend couldn't imitate. Suddenly my face felt like a mask,
hiding whatever I really was underneath.

It was a terrible thought. A terrible thought that I had
no way to either confirm or deny. That was the great thing
about being one of a kind. No answers. Ever.

Upset, I dried off and pulled on my biggest, softest
sweater. It was a pretty pale blue and the sleeves came down
past my hands. That was a bonus, since I didn't have to see
my wrist. I braided my hair and grabbed my communicator. When I walked into Central Processing, Lish practically slammed herself into the glass in her urgency to talk
to me.

"Evie, are you okay? I have been so worried."

I smiled weakly. "Yeah, it's been kind of a sucky couple
of weeks."

"Please, sit down. You have not visited me much lately.
I missed you."

I dragged over one of the rolling chairs, sitting down
and pulling up my legs.

Lish made me recount everything that had happened
with Reth and then the hag. Being with her now made me
realize how much I had missed my best friend. Between all

the extra attention Raquel was giving me, the increasingly botched and dangerous jobs, and Lend, I had been busy. Lish, being a very clever amphibious immortal, narrowed her eyes in a sly smile.

"And this Lend—who saved you from Reth—is he very . . . cute?"

I laughed. "He can do a perfect Landon."

"Landon from *Easton Heights*? Oh, then you really must be in love with him."

I shook my head. "No, his real face is nicer. And he's funny, and nice. Don't tell Raquel, but I do kinda like him. . . ."

Lish nodded, still smiling. "Is he a raging bundle of human hormones like Landon?"

I laughed at the absurdity of her question. "Umm, I'm thinking no. I'm kind of glad, too."

"Ah yes. Too much—" Lish paused and winked one clear eyelid at me exaggeratedly "—baggage, right?"

"You know me—I like to pack light."

Lish blew bubbles laughing. "See how good I am getting at metaphors?"

"You're a pro!" We practiced metaphors and clichés a lot; it was important to her to be able to relate to me in spite of our differences.

"The most vital question, though, is does he like you?"

"Umm, probably not. I'm the girl who keeps getting him fried, remember? And he's stuck here because of me, too. He shouldn't be. It's stupid that they're keeping him."

"What else can they do?"

"I don't know—listen to him, help him! Wherever he's from, they know what's going on, too. If IPCA wasn't so concerned with bagging and tagging and tracking and all that other nonsense, if they'd treat him like an equal or an ally, they could probably work with Lend and figure this thing out before any other paranormals end up dead!"

Lish looked proud of me. Maybe she wasn't as pro-IPCA as I'd always assumed.

"Have you talked to Raquel about this?"

"Not really, no." I had been too nervous. I used to be secure in my place at IPCA, but knowing I was a Level Seven made me worry that everything I did would be suspect. Paranormals weren't equal around here—they were always, always *other*. Pushing for Lend's freedom was about as suspect as anything I could do right now.

But then I realized I was sitting there, worried about whether or not Lend liked me as more than a friend (if he even liked me as a friend), worried about my status with the normal humans at IPCA, worried about myself. Always about myself. Just like when I ran sobbing for my life and left Jacques alone. Paranormals were dying. It was easy to forget about hags and vamps being killed, but Jacques didn't deserve that. It had to stop.

"I'm going to talk to Raquel about it. Whatever they're doing isn't working."

Lish smiled with her eyes. "Good girl."

I smiled back, wondering if maybe Lish had been trying to help me realize this stuff for a long time. I'd never had a problem with her. I even liked some of the other paranormals, especially the werewolves. After all, it wasn't like it was their fault they were how they were.

Of course, once I thought about that, it really wasn't any of the paranormals' faults. It's not like hags woke up one morning and thought, hey, wouldn't it be fun to eat children? They were like vultures. Sure, they were disgusting and horrible, but that's just what they were.

But did that make it okay? Did that mean they should be allowed to continue hanging out in ponds and swamps, hoping for a nice snack? The whole train of thought was giving me a headache. I needed a break from thinking.

"So, umm, would you feel really bad if I left to go see Lend?"

"Bleep no. Go see your weird boyfriend."

I laughed, smashed my face against her glass as a good-bye, then made my way to Lend's cell.

He was still wearing his standard, the dark-haired, dark-eyed hottie, and drawing in the sketchbook I'd given him. When he looked up, relief flooded his face. "You're back."

I nodded, trying to smile. Then, to my immense embarrassment, I burst into tears. He jumped up and pulled me into a hug. "What's wrong? What happened?"

"It was there. It killed the hag and then it killed Jacques. I just ran."

He didn't let go of me. "Did you see it?"

"Sort of." I described what little I could to him. "Oh! And it left a handprint! On the hag, on her chest. A shimmering, pale gold handprint that faded and disappeared while I watched."

"On her body?"

"I think it was under her glamour. I doubt anyone else would have been able to see it. It kind of looked like what's under my skin now. But Reth has an alibi."

He frowned thoughtfully. "Are you okay?"

"I don't know. It was— I've never been so scared. I really thought I was going to die. And Jacques— I heard him die." I started crying again. Lend led me to the bed and sat next to me, his arm around my shoulders. "Sorry," I said, wiping my eyes.

"Don't apologize. I'm just glad you got away. And you're the first person to see anything. It helps a lot, actually."

"Or it would if you weren't locked up in here. But I'm going to talk to Raquel, try and make her realize that we need to work with you, not hold you like some criminal. This thing has to be stopped."

He nodded, and I think he looked a little proud of me, too. Leaning over, he kissed me lightly on top of my head. How could I feel so terrible and wonderful at the same time?

DON'T CALL ME

Determined to be as good as my word, I pulled out my communicator and sent a message to Raquel right then, asking her when we could talk. After a few minutes it beeped. "Oh. She's going to be gone for three or four days." I turned to Lend. "But as soon as she gets back, I'll talk with her. IPCA has it all wrong. They're so busy being scared and trying to control things that they can't see the paranormals who can help. Like you. I'm gonna convince her to let you go without a tracker."

"I hope you can."

"Me, too." I sighed. Everything had gotten so complicated,

so serious. "Tell me something about yourself—something fun, something easy." I scooted back and leaned against the wall. He did the same, staying next to me.

"What do you want to know?"

"What's your life like out there? I mean, you don't have to tell me any secrets," I added hastily. "But, like, do you go to school?"

"I'm a senior. Just got all my college acceptance letters." He smiled. "Of course, I don't know how I'll make up the work I'm missing."

"You're going to college? That's so cool! Wait, so normal high school? Wow. What's it like? Did you go to the prom? Do you go to a lot of parties? Do you have lockers?"

He laughed. "Lockers?"

"They just seem cool."

"Oh, yeah, they're the best. High school's actually kind of boring. It's a little bit like living in the Center. Everyone thinks they know everything about everyone else, but really there's a lot more under the surface. But you already know that, don't you?" He nudged me. "And as far as prom, no, I don't really date."

"Why? Look at you, you're hot!" I blushed. "I mean, you can look like whatever you want, I'll bet the girls love you."

"Yeah, they always like this face."

"Whose face is it really?"

He smiled enigmatically. "Mine. Kind of. But it's just

weird with other people—like I'm pretending, playing a part. And they only like the part. They don't really know me."

"I get that." I didn't add that I was really, really happy he wasn't dating anyone. Best news I'd had all week. If Lend were like one of the characters on my shows, he would have hooked up with every single girl, on- and offscreen. For once I was glad real life wasn't one of my television dramas.

Then I thought of something I really wanted to know. "Do you have a family?" My voice caught. More than high school or prom or dating—or even lockers—family filled me with the most regret and sadness about my life. Aside from Raquel and Lish, I didn't have anyone. I never had.

"That would fall into the category of things I can't tell you about." My face fell and he added, "Yet. What about you? How did you end up here?"

"They kind of found me." I told him the vamp-in-the-cemetery story.

"So you never had a family?"

"Nope, just the foster system. Some of the families were okay, but it wasn't a really happy or stable way to spend a childhood."

"I'm sorry."

"Yeah, me, too." I didn't like to think about it; it hurt too bad knowing that whoever my parents were, they didn't want me. Giving me away I could understand, but they had just abandoned me. I couldn't remember them, or any-thing before the foster homes and the series of families that took me in and then passed me along. "It's okay, though. Raquel's actually a way nice person—she nags me so much I can almost pretend she's my mother. She took me on my first bag-and-tags just to make sure I was comfortable, and she tries to make my life here as normal as possible. And Lish is an awesome best friend, even if she's the worst hide-and-go-seek player ever."

Of course, he hadn't met Lish, so we talked about her and then everything else under the sun for a few more hours. I made him describe his typical day to me in excru-ciating detail, where he wanted to go to college, what he would study there. I thought he should study art, but he laughed and said he wanted to do something more practi-cal. Then he asked about what life was like growing up in the Center. We traded stories, and I was grateful for the distraction.

Finally I was too tired to form a coherent sentence. "I need to go to bed. But I'll come hang out tomorrow, okay?"

He smiled. "Good. Oh, here." He opened the sketch-book and pulled out a page. He had written out the poem for me. "Just in case it helps you think of anything."

"Yeah, thanks. I won't show it to anyone."

"I know." Then he pulled out another page and handed it to me, grinning. It was the drawing of me in my zebra dress and pink boots.

Oh, heavens, I liked that boy. When I got back to my unit, I stared at the drawing. He really captured me, which made me hope he spent a lot of time thinking about me. I sure spent enough time thinking about him, after all. I cleared off my bed and lay down with the drawing next to me.

Reading over the poem a few more times, I didn't have any new brilliant ideas. The whole thing was too weird and vague. I could come up with a lot of explanations that kind of fit, but nothing was perfect. Plus I kept coming back to the fear that it had something to do with me, which made it hard to concentrate. I tucked the poem under the drawing, turned off the lights, and fell asleep.

I opened my eyes to the dark room. There was a pale light near me and someone hummed a soft, haunting melody. It made me ache inside. Reaching out in a panic, I almost knocked my lamp over as I switched it on. Reth was sitting on the end of my bed.

"Hello," he said, his voice and smile pleasant.

"You can't touch me!" I sat up and pulled the covers over myself.

"Yes, about that. You need to negate the command."

"Excuse me?"

He looked at me patiently, like he was explaining something to a stubborn child. "You need to break that command."

"And why on earth would I ever want to do that?" I glared at him. Lunatic.

"Because I wasn't finished."

"Oh, no, I really think you were." I held up my wrist. It still bore the scarlet mark of his hand and, to my eyes at least, was bright against the light of the lamp. Then, since I was holding up my hand anyway, I flipped him off.

"You're going to need more."

"Well, that's easy." I held up my other hand and flipped him off with that one, too.

His golden eyes shimmered softly in the dim light. "It didn't work; you're still cold."

"I'm just fine, thank you very much."

"'Eyes like streams of melting snow, cold with the things she does not know.'"

I glanced down at the poem; it hadn't been moved, still hidden underneath the drawing. "Yeah, I know that one. Ends with lots and lots of death."

He shook his head. "No, that's not yours. That's hers. Yours has a different ending. You'll understand everything if you let me fill you."

"What are you talking about?" I shouted. He was really starting to frustrate me. If he had to be obnoxious, the least he could do was be clear. The whole obnoxious and mysterious thing wasn't working for me.

"We need to finish. I cannot explain it to you now— court secrets and whatnot. Simply let me finish and then you'll be able to see."

"Tell me what you did to me or get out." He had answers, but I knew he wasn't going to give me any. I was too tired to deal with faerie nonsense tonight.

"There are many who would rather she be the one. If I don't finish, you might not survive. I'd like you to survive." He smiled affectionately at me.

"Who is this 'she'? One of your faerie friends?"

"Bless me, no."

Could he *be* less helpful? "Are you doing this? Killing the paranormals?"

He cocked his head to the side. "Why would I do that?"

"You tell me."

"I have no reason to kill those creatures."

I took a deep breath, trying again. "What did you do to me?" Every nerve was strained as I waited for his answer.

"I'm going to fill you, to create you. I tried to be gentle but you never held on to it. Then you wouldn't accept any more, so you left me no choice. It won't hurt if you behave and stop denying that you want it. Shall we finish?"

"Fill me with what?!"

"Please break the command, Evelyn."

"I won't! Not ever; you're never touching me again."

His large, ageless eyes narrowed and he smiled again. It had a touch of cruelty. "I will enjoy it when you beg me to touch you again."

"Get out of my room."

He raised his eyebrows. "Until you call for me then, my love." The light went out and I swore, not wanting to be alone in the dark with him. By the time I found the switch and turned the light back on, he was gone.

HEARTS AGLOW

What do you think he meant by that?" Lend asked, frowning. Today he surprised me by wearing a pudgy, acne-plagued blond boy. It made me laugh; usually he stuck with the whole hot thing. Still, I could see him underneath, so it didn't really matter what he put on the outside.

"I don't know—he's Reth. What does he ever mean by anything?" I had just finished telling him what Reth had said about the poem and needing to finish me.

"Well, as much as I hate the guy, he's probably got resources we don't. What were his exact words about the poem?"

"He said that ending wasn't mine, it was hers. Whoever that is. But that's good, at least, right? I mean, I'd rather not be bringing 'death, death, death, death, death' and so on and so forth."

Lend laughed. "Yeah, probably not. Death in sparkly platform sandals. It's a nice image, at least."

I smacked him on the shoulder. "Hey, I'm scary. You thought I was going to kill you, remember?"

"Oh, I remember. Man, that was a stressful day."

"No kidding. I wonder if things have always been this weird and I just never knew, or if they're getting worse."

"They're getting worse."

"Okay, so poetic prophecies and creepy faerie stalkers aside, I've got an important question."

"What?"

"Do you have a driver's license?"

He laughed. "That's important?"

"Oh yeah! I'd kill for a driver's license! Hey, maybe that's what the poem means! I'm going to go berserk and start attacking people because they won't let me drive. . . ."

"Could be, you never know. But, yes, I have a driver's license."

I leaned back against the wall, sighing. "Man, that must be so cool."

"It ranks right up there with lockers. In fact, sometimes I put my license inside my locker, and it's so cool I worry that the whole thing might explode with the sheer coolness of it all."

I smacked him on the shoulder. Again. I was doing that a lot. "Shut up. You try living your whole life here and then tell me what you think is cool." He gave me a funny look; he'd been watching me closely this whole time.

"You really don't care about this face, do you?"

"What face?" I asked, confused.

He smiled, showing off braces I hadn't noticed. "This one."

I laughed. "Why would I care? You wear a lot of different things."

"Yeah, but this one isn't very cute."

"Not really, but it's not you." He got that funny look again. I smiled. "The only thing that bugs me is that your voice is always different. I wish I knew what it really sounded like. Oh, and also I think it's a little creepy when you're a girl, but you haven't done that in a while."

He shook his head. "You're weird."

"Says the invisible shape-shifting boy."

He laughed a little, then leaned back against the wall like me. "We aren't figuring this out."

"I know. Sorry." I had racked my brains but didn't know how to begin to put together all Reth's random tidbits and the stupid poem with what I had seen. And even more bothersome, I couldn't stop wondering what the ending to my poem was, if there even was one. Have I mentioned how much I don't like faeries?

"Evie?" His voice was tentative. "Is there any way you could email someone for me? If I could get this information out, maybe my—my group could help."

My heart fell. Was Lend just using me? But then I remembered the whole trying-not-to-be-self-centered thing. So what if he was? He should be. IPCA wasn't solving this, and they were stopping him from doing anything. Still, I hoped he liked *me* and wasn't just trying to manipulate me.

"I don't know. I've got a computer, but the only thing I do online is shop and I know IPCA monitors every single thing I click on because they cancel about ninety percent of my purchases. I could try to set up a new email address or use yours or something, but I'm pretty sure they'd catch it immediately. Maybe it would already be sent by then, though." I bit my lip, nervous.

"What would happen if they caught it?"

I smiled, feigning nonchalance. "Umm, I'd be imprisoned indefinitely for treason. Probably. But you never know—they really like what I can do. And I think Raquel would stick up for me. Maybe I could get out of it." I'd never been sent to a disciplinary hearing; the idea terrified me.

Lend shook his head. "No, I'm sorry. It's not worth the risk."

"It really is, if you think any of the information we have will help your group figure it out and stop this thing." Gosh, was I being brave or what?

"It won't do any good to get us both locked up. I've got another goal besides finding and stopping the killer."

I frowned. As much as I liked him, if he was asking me to help him take down IPCA I'd have to say no. It wasn't a perfect organization by any means, but they were doing a lot of good. I, for one, thought the world was a much safer place without free-ranging vamps and hags and all the rest of the nasty creepy-crawly blood-sucky flesh-eating things of legend. "What's your other goal?"

"I want to get you out of here."

"Don't you mean you want me to get *you* out of here?"

He took my hand—yeah, my hand again. I was liking this. A lot. "No, I mean I want to get you out. This shouldn't be your life. You deserve a lot more. Like a locker."

"And a driver's license?"

"Let's not get carried away."

I smiled. As much as I wanted to get out and live a real life (whatever that was; I didn't pretend like I knew anymore), I didn't think it would ever happen. If I was classified as a paranormal, IPCA had complete jurisdiction over me. Which meant I couldn't exactly turn in my two weeks' notice.

My communicator beeped. I pulled it out with my free hand. I wasn't letting go of Lend's till he let go of mine. His skin was the coolest thing ever. Warm, but perfectly smooth and soft. Not to mention the happy tingles it gave me that had nothing to do with anything paranormal.

I glanced at the screen. It was Lish. "What's up?"

"Come to Central Processing. There is trouble. Raquel

is coming back and the Supervisors are following. You should not be caught alone with Lend."

"I'm leaving right now. Thanks, Lish." I hooked the communicator back on my belt. Lish always looked out for me. "I don't know what's happening, but Raquel and a bunch of bigwigs are headed to the Center, so I probably shouldn't be here."

He gave my hand a quick squeeze (which made my heart do all sorts of happy dances in my chest) before letting go. "I'll see you later, then."

I hurried to Central Processing. Lish looked downright panicked. "What's going on?" I could tell by her expression that something big was up, and it scared me.

"The Birmingham Tracking and Placement Center in England was hit today."

"Wait, hit? What do you mean hit?"

"Every paranormal there is dead." That phrase said in the robot voice was so startling and horrible I didn't know how to react.

"It—was it the same thing?"

"Yes. Just dead, no traces of weapons or anything that should have been able to kill them."

"Did anyone see anything?"

"No. It is a small facility. None of the humans saw any-thing."

That was something, at least. Apparently this thing didn't go after humans. I was relieved until I remembered that I might not be quite human. Not very comforting. "Anything else?"

"I do not have any more details right now. We will probably go on lockdown."

"What's that?"

It took her a minute to respond; I watched as her eyes darted around all the various screens she was managing. I swear she did the work of twenty people. "Lockdown procedure calls for all our assets in the field and satellite buildings to be brought to the Center. When everyone is secure, we go into complete lockdown—no one in, no one out."

"Oh, wow." That was a big deal. "How long until that happens?"

"We should be secure in two hours." Gotta hand it to IPCA—for a government-type agency, they were efficient.

"And how long is the lockdown in effect?"

"Until they are certain that the risk has passed."

"So, a long time."

"No way to tell. The information is coming in; I need to get back to it." She looked away, focusing on one of her many screens. I wished that Lish wasn't stuck behind the glass. She was my best friend, but sometimes she seemed so inaccessible.

I turned to the side as the brilliant outline of a door formed on the blank wall. Raquel walked out with a faerie. I wondered when the Supervisors would get here. I had seen a few of them before, back when IPCA was officially forming. I didn't remember too much, just a lot of head patting. I hated that.

Raquel looked like she had aged about ten years in the past few days. "Initiate lockdown protocol," she said, not even bothering to acknowledge Lish with a nod, a hello, or a how's the water this morning.

"Lockdown protocol initiated." Lish darted her hands around, the movements quick and precise.

"Call the other faeries," Raquel said to the faerie who had brought her here. Looking annoyed, the faerie opened another door and disappeared through it.

Raquel finally noticed me. "Oh, Evie. You're here. Good. We need to talk."

"Yeah, we do." Before I could launch into the speech I'd been mulling over since I decided to stick up for Lend, a brilliant light traced a line through the wall and a whole section opened up into the black. Faeries stepped out— more faeries than I had ever seen before. More than I even knew IPCA had. There were at least a hundred of them.

It was overwhelming. One faerie alone is distractingly beautiful. This many at once and it was like a tidal wave for your eyes—stunning and inescapable. I had a hard time focusing on what Raquel was saying to them. Besides the faerie sensory overload, I noticed something, something I had never seen before.

Faerie clothing is similar to ours, but it always seems

older, more refined, and simple at the same time. Many of the male faeries had their shirts unbuttoned and chests bare. (How's this for freaky: no nipples or belly buttons.) Faeries always have a hint of a glow, but now they seemed to have a bright spot—right where I assumed their hearts were. It wasn't dramatic, but there was definitely something extra there. I hoped it didn't have anything to do with my now-glowing heart.

Then I looked at their faces. A lot of them were just bored and annoyed. Standard faerie. But there were some— and these seemed to be grouped together—that had sly twinkles in their eyes, like something about all this was terribly amusing. That look bothered me; anything that amused a faerie couldn't be a good thing. Then my eyes met Reth's. He wasn't with that group, but his smile was the biggest of all.

I wanted to get out of that room. All those faeries—I felt almost dizzy. I did my best to ignore Reth's stare, waiting until Raquel finished issuing instructions and the faeries started leaving to pick up their assigned groups. "Raquel, we need to talk."

She turned to me, an intense look on her face. "Yes. I need you to tell me everything you know about Lend."

"Why?"

"Because the Supervisors are coming, and he's one of our only links to what's happening."

"That's stupid! That makes it sound like he's connected

to it. He's not a link, he's a resource."

"I'm afraid we see it differently. What has he told you?"

I folded my arms, glaring at her. "What makes you think he's told me anything? And, even if he has, why would I tell you?"

Her voice was flat and a little dangerous. "You'll tell me because it's your job."

"My job? I'm sixteen! I didn't ask for any of this! Besides, why is it that I can prance around here without an ankle tracker, but you won't even let him out of his cell? Maybe if you'd stop being so scared of him and let him go, we could work with him and his group and actually have a chance at figuring this all out!"

"You know we can't do that. It's against the charter to release a paranormal untagged."

"What the crap am I, then? Huh? You can't stand here telling me that Lend is automatically an enemy because he's an unknown paranormal when I'm a freaking Level Seven!"

Her expression softened. "Please, don't do this. Not now. I've worked long and hard to make certain that the Supervisors see you not as a paranormal but as a girl who can do something unusual. We can't help Lend, honey, not right now."

Angry tears pricked my eyes. "Don't call me honey. I'm not your daughter. I'm your *employee*."

Her dark eyes went wide with hurt, then her face quickly hardened. "If you won't help us with Lend, you'll be confined to quarters."

I let out a harsh laugh. "Great, now you're grounding me." I couldn't believe how stupid I had been, pretending and wishing that Raquel was really my mom. Whatever else she might be, she was always professional. She was not my family.

The room around us had grown noisy, filling up as faeries dropped off more and more paranormals. Werewolf security guards milled around the edges and tried to direct the traffic into an orderly line in front of Lish's tank.

Raquel sighed. "I think it would be best if you went to your room. You're in no state to be around the Supervisors and they'll be here any minute."

I was about to come up with a snotty retort when shouting distracted both of us.

"I won't!" a vampire screamed, yanking his arm away from one of the guards. "Not here, not this! The tracker is bad enough, I won't be a rat in your lab!" I realized with a shock that it was Steve. It felt like a lifetime since that night in the cemetery.

"Is there a problem?" Raquel asked, stepping forward. "If you'll just be patient, we'll get everyone processed and settled in."

Steve looked at her, a desperate, manic gleam in his eyes. "I'd rather die," he whispered. Before anyone could react, he leaped forward, lunging for Raquel's throat.

I screamed as he bit down on her neck. No one else

moved. "Do something!" I shouted, fumbling for my Taser. But it wasn't necessary. He jerked away from her neck, a look of—peace?—on his face as his ankle tracker was activated. The glamour faded and in a matter of seconds he was nothing but a corpse crumbling to the floor, unnatural life gone.

We all stared, shocked, at dead undead Steve. Raquel put her hand over her neck to stop the flow of blood. She looked pale and scared.

"Raquel!" I rushed forward, putting my hands on her arms. What if he had killed her? What if those mean things were the last words I ever said to her? "Are you okay? I thought— I was so scared that—"

Another light flashed and five of the Supervisors walked into the room. Raquel straightened and brushed my hands off her arms, her face an emotionless mask as she turned to the group of people. I dropped my hands to my sides, shattered by her rejection. She walked forward to greet the Supervisors, leaving me surrounded by paranormals.

I guess I knew my place.

OH, BLEEP

Two days later and I was going crazy. Everyone was on edge with the Center packed to capacity. The timing with the lunar cycle couldn't have been worse. Since werewolves make up the bulk of IPCA security forces, we always operated on minimum capacity during the full moon. So now most of our security would be unconscious tomorrow night with every single member of IPCA locked in the Center. This included a whole bunch of things you wouldn't want to meet at night in a dark alley (unless you were me and that was your job—and, let's face it, even I didn't usually want to meet them).

Frustrated and scared, I got dressed in a dark gray wrap dress and my pink boots. I hadn't been able to get to Lend with things so crazy, and I was determined today would be different. I bundled up some cookies and headed out. Usually I could walk anywhere I wanted and run into only one or two people, if that. Today everywhere I went there were werewolves, people carrying things in cages, personal assistants bustling about, and vamps. I went out of my way to avoid them after the Steve incident. They didn't exactly like me to begin with, and everyone was so tense. I didn't want my blood to be someone else's suicide.

I tried to visit Lish, but Central Processing was very literally like a zoo. Looking in, I realized just how few paranormals I usually came into contact with. I didn't know what most of the things in there were. I gave up trying to work my way through and went to the detention block. Although this area was quieter, more of the cells were taken. I couldn't help but peek through the open doorways at what was in them. It was depressing. All the paranormals I saw were sitting listlessly on their beds, totally broken.

The hall was clear by the time I made it to Lend's room, and I ducked in as fast as I could.

"What's going on?" he asked, jumping up.

"It's crazy—total lockdown. This thing took out our Birmingham Center—everything. They called everyone in. No one can come or go until they figure this all out."

"Well, at least that'll protect the paranormals IPCA knows about. That's something."

"I guess."

"Had some visitors last night," he said. I just now noticed he was wearing the handsome black guy again. I was so focused on his real self that what was on the outside barely registered.

"Oh, the Supervisors?"

"Mm-hm. Man, if I were in charge of some massive, covert international organization, I'd choose a better title than Supervisor."

I laughed. "No kidding. Are you okay?"

"Sure. They asked me a bunch of questions, I didn't answer any. It was productive."

I nodded glumly. "Raquel and I had a . . . fight . . . about you. She hasn't seen me since, or let me talk to the Supervisors, either." I held out the cookies. "Figured you might like a treat. It's kind of the least I can do."

"Thanks." He took them from me, setting them on the bed. We stood there awkwardly.

"I'd probably better go. I don't want to get us in trouble right now."

He looked disappointed. "Yeah."

On impulse, I leaned in and kissed his cheek. When I pulled back, he was smiling. "I'll see you soon," I said, beaming back and blushing as I walked out, practically floating.

• • •

I finally saw Lish the next morning. Everyone in Central Processing was super stressed, gossiping and spreading rumors in the hallways as they rushed to and fro. Lish, however, was in her element, flicking through screens and giving orders to people and paranormals standing in front of her.

"Hey, what's up?" I leaned against the glass, ignoring the queue in front of her.

"Quite a bit. I am rearranging duties since all the were-wolves will be out of commission tonight. Plus there is the issue of finding more permanent quarters for everyone."

"Why don't you use the gym for the werewolves to zonk in? That frees up space for tonight at least." The gym was a massive room where they could let the more energetic (read: rabid) paranormals run around.

Lish looked up at me and smiled with her eyes. "That is a great idea. Thank you." She went back to her screens.

Near the front of the line was a vamp I didn't know; his glamour was a teenage guy, devastatingly handsome with dark hair and crystal blue eyes. He gave me his best come-hither smile. "Hey," he said.

He was already trying to work his mind mojo on me. Vamps have slight mind control powers. They can influence you, push you in a direction as long as you're already leaning that way. So if you're kind of scared, they can make you terrified. Kind of attracted, they can make you down-right lustylicious. Unfortunately for this particular vamp, I could see straight through him to the corpse underneath. Oh yeah, baby, hot stuff.

I busted up laughing. "Not a chance."

He scowled, offended. "What are you talking about?"

"I prefer my guys with a pulse. Lish, let me know if you need anything. I'll see you later." She glanced up and waved. I missed her. It would be nice to get to spend some time together again when this mess was over.

I was surprised when my communicator beeped with a page from Raquel. I thought about ignoring it but had nothing better to do, so I went to her office. She looked up at me from her desk with a tight smile. Dark circles ringed her eyes and her hair was falling out of its bun. That was a first. "Evelyn, thanks for coming."

I shrugged. I thought about making some remark about how I didn't have a choice, but the bandage on her neck made me think twice. Thank goodness one bite wasn't enough to turn her.

"I know things have been stressful lately and you've been struggling. When all this is over, I'm taking you on a vacation."

Didn't see that one coming. "Wait, a real vacation? Like, we actually spend the night somewhere else and just walk around or sleep or hang out during the day?"

She smiled. "Yes, a real vacation. Anywhere you'd like."

Oh, the possibilities . . . I couldn't help but smile back. Things weren't all right between us, not by a long shot, but this was huge coming from her. I had never known her to take even a day off. "That sounds okay with me." It sounded more than okay. The two of us, in some gorgeous, warm place. Almost like a family.

"Good. Now I've got a lot of paperwork to go over and some interviews to do."

"Oh, yeah. Sure." I don't know what else I expected, but I was disappointed as I left. We hadn't talked about anything important, anything that needed to be addressed. I wanted to help out around the Center. She probably wanted me far, far away from the Supervisors after my outburst. And I was sure she didn't want to talk about Lend again.

Lonely, I tried to sneak over and see Lend, but the hall was packed with werewolves making sure everything was secure before sedation. I figured I could make it back later; it didn't ease my disappointment at having to wait.

Lucky for me *Easton Heights* was on that night, even if it was a rerun. I changed into some black leggings and a tank top (I bumped up the heat in my unit from 85 to 90—why wait for a tropical vacation?), then snuggled up on the couch, just barely warm enough. When the show began I was startled by my buzzing vid screen. Lish.

"What's up?" I asked, trying not to panic. Surely something else hadn't gone wrong already.

"*Easton Heights* is on tonight, right?" the monotone voice asked.

"Yeah, I just didn't think you'd have time."

"All the werewolves are down; the rest of the Center is

finally secure and settled. I am looking forward to seeing who Landon kisses this week."

I laughed. "Me, too." I turned my vid screen toward the television. It wasn't as good as actually hanging out in the same room, but it was pretty close. I pretended Lend was on the couch next to me, holding my hand. I had been going over all the times we'd held hands, trying to decide if they counted as *really* holding hands. I wanted them to, but it had always been in the context of comforting each other. Not, hey, I like you and I want to sit here and hold your hand because touching you makes me happy.

About halfway through the episode Lish spoke up. "What the bleep?"

"What?" I asked, turning her screen toward me.

"I just had five new ankle trackers pop up on the grid. This does not make sense."

"Wait, like five new tags?"

She nodded, frowning. Then, vid screen still on, she called Raquel. "Raquel, I have five new ankle trackers."

"What?" Raquel asked.

"Five new ankle trackers were just activated."

"How? Who?"

"I do not know. The activation was incomplete, so there is no data. They are all in the same area, a suburb of Paris. Do you want me to send someone to investigate?"

"No, we can't risk it. Actually, yes—send a faerie. Just have him pop in and look at what's happening, then come right back."

"Any other instructions?"

"No—unless it's an operative who didn't get back in time, then bring him in."

"Okay, I will call the faerie on duty."

Lish looked up, realizing I was still on the vid screen. "Sorry, Evie. I have to go."

"Sure, yeah." I closed the connection, half paying attention to the show as I thought about what I had overheard. That was weird. I mean, who would be out there on a bag-and-tag right now? Everyone had been called in. Maybe someone somehow missed it and was using this as a way to contact us. How anyone could have been missed in the lockdown I didn't understand. Like I said, IPCA was efficient.

And then I remembered something. On the hag trip, I had dropped my bag with ankle trackers in it.

Five ankle trackers.

NOT OKAY

I tried to connect back to Lish on the vid screen, but the channel was busy. Punching Raquel's number on my communicator as I pulled on one of my boots, I swore. It was busy, too. I yanked on my other boot, nearly falling over in my haste, then grabbed Tasey and my knife. I sprinted down the hall, praying my hunch was wrong, that it was just a weird coincidence. No alarms had gone off yet; surely that meant everything was okay. Everything had to be okay.

As I turned the corner to Central Processing I slipped, flying backward and hitting my shoulder hard against the wall. The floor was covered with water and my leggings were now soaked. I couldn't breathe. Everything was not okay. Pushing myself up, I ran the last few feet, nearly slipping again, and palmed open the sliding doors.

"No," I whispered, so shocked it felt like everything around me had slowed, disappeared, stopped. I knew I had to move forward, but my body wasn't working anymore. All I could do was stare at the jagged hole smashed into Lish's aquarium. About a foot of water remained in the bottom and lying there, near the hole, was Lish.

She couldn't be dead. She couldn't. Lish was forever. She was my friend, my best friend. There couldn't be a reality in which Lish wasn't. She was probably just hurt—I needed to get her more water, right away.

I ran forward. "Lish! It's okay. I'm here, I'm going to help!" I ducked through the hole and sloshed over to her. Her eyes, her beautiful, beautiful eyes, were wide, the clear eyelids half shut. She wasn't moving. And on her chest was a handprint of golden flame, slowly fading. "Lish?" I dropped to my knees next to her, picking her up and cradling her in my arms. She wasn't gone, she couldn't be. I stroked her hand, the webbing between her fingers finer and more delicate than I had ever noticed. Her iridescent scales glistened.

She didn't move, she wouldn't move, she couldn't. Lish, my Lish, was gone. There was nothing I could do and it was my fault. I had left the ankle trackers that became bait; I was the reason that thing got in. I leaned over and kissed her on the head. "I'm so sorry," I said, my voice breaking into a sob.

I was shivering already, soaked through. I didn't want to move, ever, because if I didn't leave, if I didn't let her go, then she wasn't really gone. Shifting position, I gasped. Something sharp and hard had gone straight through my leggings, cutting into my thigh. Red seeped into the water, and it was enough to jar me out of my stupor. Kissing Lish again, I laid her gently back down. I stood and pulled the shard of glass out of my thigh, wincing.

It was here. I ran out of the tank and to the wall where there was an emergency panic button. Smashing through the glass cover with my elbow, I pushed it down. The over-head lights went a notch brighter with strobes going off and a loud alarm shrieking.

Raquel—Raquel had to know about this. I pulled out my communicator and punched in her number while I ran for her office. "What?" she said. "I'm trying to contact Lish, we don't know what the alarm is."

"Lish is dead," I sobbed, still running. "It's here. It's here."

The line was silent for what felt like forever. "Heaven help us all," Raquel whispered. Then, her voice hurried and panicked, she said, "Meet me at Transport. I'll message all the personnel. It doesn't go after humans—we should be able to get out."

I changed direction and started running for Transport.

Then I stopped. "What about the paranormals?" What
about Lend?

"There's no time. Get to Transport."

I hesitated. Everything in my body was screaming for
me to run, to get out. Death was walking the hallways and
I needed to escape. "No," I whispered, turning my communicator off. I ran back the way I came, headed for Lend's
cell. He was trapped. He'd be completely helpless, just like
Lish.

Oh, Lish.

No one deserved to die like that. I was running past the
gym when I stopped dead again. There were over a hundred werewolves in there, sleeping. Charlotte was in there,
and Jacques—he should have been in there, too. I wanted to
throw up. I couldn't wake them, tell them to run. I couldn't
carry them out. What could I do? Then it hit me.

"Denfehlath!" I shouted. After a few seconds a door
opened in the wall and she stepped out, ruby eyes blazing
with excitement.

"Save the paranormals, starting with the werewolves," I
commanded.

Her smile disappeared. "What?" she hissed.

"Start now. You've got a lot of sleeping bodies to move!"

She glared at me, trembling with fury, but entered the
gym. She couldn't disobey. After the gym doors closed
behind her, I palmed them, holding my hand there for
a full fifteen seconds. The pad turned red and I hit a

combination, locking it.

A couple of vamps came out of a side hall, seeing me. "What's going on?" Vlad asked. He was with the guy from before who'd tried to hit on me.

"You need to hide! It's here!"

The end of the hallway filled with light; a figure turned the corner. It was shaped like a person, but made entirely of living gold fire and burning so brightly the image was seared into my retinas. It walked toward us, beautiful and terrible as the sun made living flesh.

"Run!" I shouted to the vamps. They hadn't reacted. How did they not notice the light?

They turned toward the creature just as it got to them. Neither one of them looked frightened. "Run!" I screamed again. The creature cocked its head, turning toward me as it lifted both hands and put one on each vampire's chest. I watched in horror as the vampires stiffened, for a brief moment glowing brightly. Then it was like someone turned off whatever was inside them; they dimmed and fell motionless to the ground, nothing but corpses now.

I couldn't move. The thing turned in my direction. It was only fifteen feet away. My eyes watered. It was too bright, too much.

It glided toward me. A scream, no doubt my last, built in my throat. I couldn't make out any features as it paused a few feet away from me; everything blurred together in the sheer brilliance of its light and heat.

"I love the boots," a woman's voice said playfully.

I turned and ran, sprinting as fast as I could, waiting for my own life to be sucked dry. I looked back. She was walking after me. At least she hadn't gone in the gym. I turned into a hall and ran straight for a door, palming it open and leaving through a door on the other end. I was almost to Lend's cell. If I could get Lend out, if I could get him to Transport, I could leave. The faeries were at Transport—that was the set evacuation plan.

I nearly ran past his door, skidding to a stop and darting into his room. He was standing there, looking anxious.

"It's here!" I panted. "It's here, in the building—we have to go now."

"I can't!" He pointed to his ankle. "Leave without me, go!"

I knelt down next to his leg, grabbing the ankle tracker. This would be my last action as a member of IPCA—what I was about to do qualified me for permanent lockup. I placed my thumb in the middle of his tracker, thanking whatever deities I could think of that I had been the one to put the tracker on Lend. That meant I could take it off, but it would be recorded in the computer systems, marking me as a traitor.

"What are you doing?"

"Don't move." I concentrated on holding perfectly still. After twenty seconds, a green light flashed. I leaned down and blew gently on it and the light turned red. There was a small hiss as the sensors retracted. I reached around and unlatched it.

"Come on!" I took his hand and put the tracker in my pocket. "We have to get to Transport now." We went into the hall and turned—and there she was, walking toward us. "No, no, no," I whispered.

"What?" Lend asked, looking over. "Oh, that's weird."

"Run!" I shouted, tugging on his hand and running in the opposite direction of the burning woman—and the opposite direction of Transport. I racked my brains, trying to think of alternate routes we could take.

"Who was that?"

"Who was that? What are you talking about? That was it—the thing—the life sucker!"

"What?"

"Did you miss the whole *on fire* part?" I panted, turning another corner. Clearly Lend was in shock.

I wasn't thinking straight. We hit a dead end.

"Evie, she wasn't on fire."

"She's so bright it burns my eyes!" I slammed my fist into the wall. "Come on. This way." We ran back across the connecting hall and down another passageway. Everywhere in the Center looked exactly the same. Brilliant floor plan. Perfect for getting lost and trapped. Normally I knew every inch, but in my rush I had gotten turned around. Taking another hall, we stopped. Four bodies were slumped on the ground.

"This way," I whispered, unable to take my eyes off the

bodies as I palmed open a door to cut through. When we got out into the next hall it was clear—and another dead end. I realized to my horror that I didn't know where we were. "Maybe one of these rooms connects somewhere." I desperately opened doors, looking for any way out. They were all storage rooms. There was nothing. "Back, back," I said, trying not to sob. I opened the door and we ran through the room and turned into the hall. She was already there.

"Here you are," she said. I heard the smile in her voice—her bizarrely normal, pleasant voice.

I screamed, pulling Lend back into the room and waiting for the door to lock. We ran back through and into the small hallway and I locked that door behind us, too.

"That won't stop her!" She could probably melt straight through the door. They weren't designed to withstand attack or fire.

"Evie, are you sure that's her?" Lend asked, out of breath and confused.

"Yes! What's wrong with you?"

He was quiet for a second. "She looks totally normal. Like a person. Like—" he paused "—like you."

WHAT'S IN A NAME

*W*hat do you mean she looks like me?" I asked. "She's freaking on fire!"

"I can't see that! It must be under her glamour or whatever, I didn't see anything."

"Show me what she looks like then!"

Lend's face shimmered and he shrank a few inches. I couldn't believe what I was seeing. She had short, light blond hair, a pretty face, and a similar build to me, maybe a few years older. She also had eyes such a pale gray that Lend couldn't get them right. "Same eyes," he said softly in her voice.

"That's— I don't— What is she? Why is she on fire underneath her skin? She's all bright and glowing, like—" I looked down and pulled up my sleeve. "Like this." I watched the flames under my skin. "Times a million."

"'Liquid flames to hide her grief,'" Lend-as-fire-girl said.

"Well, she's got the 'death, death, death,' part down. There has to be a way out of this." I pulled out my communicator. If I could get ahold of Raquel, she'd send help. The communicator flashed dully, then displayed that Raquel couldn't be reached. "I can't call Fehl. I made her save the werewolves—they're all sleeping. She hasn't had enough time to move them." I couldn't risk all their lives for my own. That left me with one option; I shook my head, unwilling to face it.

"Isn't this exciting?" Reth said from behind us. I whipped around. Speak—or rather think—of the devil. He leaned casually against the wall, beaming. "I do love a good reunion." He looked at Lend and waved, then frowned. "That's not her."

"How would you know?" I asked.

"We've already met. Lovely girl. Very gracious."

"You—you let her in!"

"They said to go and see what was happening. They never said not to bring anyone back with me. And she asked so nicely."

I shook my head in disbelief and rage. This was what

came of thinking you could control faeries. My best friend had paid the ultimate price. "I'll kill you for this," I said, angry tears stinging my eyes.

He sighed. "Really, there's no need for melodrama. There will be drama enough when she gets through those doors."

I looked back nervously. I didn't know what powers she had besides the whole sucking the life straight out of immortals thing, but I didn't want to find out. "I'll check the doors again," I said to Lend. He nodded, shimmering and switching back from my look-alike into his typical form.

"I remember you," Reth said. "If Evelyn dies, it will be your fault for interrupting us."

"Shut up!" I ran up and down the hall, opening all the doors, looking for any way out. "Enough of your stupid riddles."

"No riddle. But I never finished filling you, and I'm afraid our new friend is a tad impulsive. No telling what she'll do, and she's much, much stronger than you. Pity, too. I do so enjoy you, my love. I had high hopes for us."

I pulled out my knife and stepped right in front of him, holding the point near his throat. "Shut up. Now. You're taking Lend and me out of here."

"I would like nothing more. Unfortunately I cannot touch you, and you cannot go through a faerie door if you aren't touching me. You see, I have a very binding order from IPCA, and I simply cannot break it."

I closed my eyes, shaking my head. There had to be another way. I wouldn't use his name again. It was too dangerous.

"Evie!" Lend called, his voice sharp with panic. I looked over—the door was starting to glow red in the middle, superheated. She was coming through.

"Crap, crap, crap." We were going to die. I looked back up at Reth.

He was watching me, an eyebrow raised and his golden eyes shining. "I'm afraid you haven't much time, love."

"Fine! Fine! Lend, take his hand." Lend ran over and took hold of one of Reth's hands, clearly unhappy about it.

Reth's face was a portrait of triumph. I remembered his words—he'd enjoy it when I begged him to touch me. He had been right. I looked back; I could see the imprint of her hand now, pushing through the warped metal. The door was curling open.

"Take away IPCA's order," Reth whispered, hungry and impatient.

I closed my eyes, forcing down the fear and nausea. "Lorethan, ignore what IPCA told you. Touch me." I almost choked on the words. "Get us out of here. To Lend's home," I added quickly, not wanting to end up in Reth's realm again. He laughed, his voice silver and ringing. He reached out and wrapped his hand around my wrist—the wrist he had already filled with fire—and pulled us both into the darkness. I heard a woman's voice yell something, and then there was nothing but the vast silence of the Faerie Paths.

The burning started immediately. It raced up my arm and I whimpered, trying not to scream out in pain as I stumbled along blindly. I fought it as best I could, but the fire inside me called out, excited at the prospect of more. "Stop," I whispered. "Please, stop."

"Evelyn," he answered, his voice a caress against the pain.

I saw a hint of light beyond my eyelids, and opened them as the three of us walked out of the darkness and into a forest bathed in the dim twilight. "Let go." I broke into tears as I sank to my knees, Reth's hand still around my wrist and the flames dancing their searing pain up and down my arm.

"Let her go!" Lend shouted, and I felt Reth get knocked to the side as Lend attacked him.

"You are meddlesome, aren't you?" He let go of my wrist. I collapsed onto the ground, dropping my knife and gasping as the pain dulled, the heat settling once again in my wrist and heart. There was more inside me now. I pushed myself onto my hands and knees. Reth seemed so bright against the dim light.

He leaned down, cupping my face in his slender hands. This time there was no burning, just the warmth I used to crave so desperately. I still craved it. "If you let me finish, I can tell you everything. No more questions. No more searching. You can be with me then."

The flames inside pulled, drawing me closer to Reth. His heart glowed beneath his shirt, answering mine. It would be so easy, so safe. I'd be done. I looked into Reth's amber eyes and opened my mouth to agree.

Lend coughed and I tore my eyes away. He was getting up from the ground several feet away. Reth must have thrown him. "Are you okay?" I asked, jerking away from Reth's hand and its seductive warmth.

Reth sighed. "Evelyn, you are so difficult."

I turned my back on him, walking to Lend. "Are you okay?" He nodded. "Good." I needed to do something about Reth, *now*. I turned around but he was right next to me. "Lor—"

Before I could finish his name he was behind Lend, my silver knife pressed against Lend's throat. "I think you should be very careful what you say now," Reth said with a playful smile. "I find myself weary of taking commands. But I do have one last thing I'd like you to tell me to do. Oh, no, don't say a word." He shook his head when I opened my mouth. Lend's eyes were wide with fear. "One slip and I'm afraid you'll be responsible for the death of yet another friend. I'm going to tell you exactly what to say, and then you can repeat it."

I nodded dumbly, ignoring the small shake of his head Lend gave me. I couldn't lose him. Not tonight, not after Lish.

"Excellent. I want you to command me to change my name."

"I— Can I even do that?"

"I cannot refuse a named command. So if you please, tell me to change my name."

I had played perfectly into his hands and was giving him exactly what he wanted. Just how much of this had he known would happen? As usual, we were all stumbling around in the dark while the faeries perched above us, seeing patterns and pathways we would never realize were there until it was too late. "Lorethan." I willed my mouth to make the words. "Change your name." It came out a whisper, but it was enough.

His face broke into a blissful smile. He looked truly beautiful in that moment, and I remembered why I once thought faeries were angels. Surely nothing so perfect deserved to be on this earth. He spun Lend out and away from himself, closing the distance between us in one step. Putting his arms around my waist, he leaned in, his mouth almost touching my ear. "Thank you. Such power in a name—someday I'll tell you yours. And now I'm afraid I've got a lot of business to attend to. So many people to visit, so many favors to repay. Until we next meet, my love." He backed up a step. The air shimmered around him and he disappeared into it.

The evening suddenly felt cold, the wooded grove dark and empty in his absence. "What have I done?" I whispered, horrified.

GROUNDED

My mind refused to wrap around the truth. I had freed Reth. The potential ramifications of that were overwhelming. I couldn't think about them right now—I couldn't think about anything right now. Lend got up from the ground.

I rushed over to him. "Are you okay? I'm so sorry. I screwed everything up. I screwed it all up." I started crying again.

Lend wrapped me up in a hug. "You didn't. If it wasn't for you I'd be dead."

I let my head rest against his shoulder. He was so warm;

a wholesome, comforting warm, not like Reth's. I needed to be in someone's arms. We had gotten away, we were safe for now, and it hit me hard. The mixture of grief for Lish and relief that I had escaped and saved Lend was overwhelming.

After a few minutes Lend pulled back. "You're shaking. It's freezing out here." He looked around. "I think I know where we are. Good call telling Reth to bring us to my home." I was sure I hadn't made any good decisions with Reth, ever, but at least we had a chance now. Lend took my hand. "This way."

I took a step and gasped. I had forgotten about my leg; the cut in my thigh from Lish's aquarium glass hurt now that all the adrenaline had worn off. I put my hand down, then looked at it in the fading light.

"What's that? Are you bleeding?"

"I cut my leg in—when Lish was—" Trying to hold back the tears, I stopped.

"Can you walk? It's not far."

"I think so."

Lend let go of my hand, putting his arm around my waist instead. We walked through the trees, the final remnants of day snuffing out and leaving the pale light of the full moon. After a few minutes, my leg stinging and throbbing, I saw lights through the trees.

"There it is!" He sounded excited and anxious. I wondered what kind of place Lend lived in. I always pictured something like the Center, filled with paranormals. When we got close enough to see I was shocked. It was a normal, beautiful two-story white house, complete with wraparound porch. I hadn't been inside a real house in eight years. Lend opened the door. "Dad? Dad!"

"Lend?" A man rushed down the stairs right by the front door. He was good-looking for an older guy, maybe in his late forties, with dark hair and dark eyes—obviously who Lend had patterned his favorite face from. "Where have you been?"

"I— It's a long story. She's hurt. Can you look at her leg?"

Lend's dad—he had a dad, and it filled me with a sense of almost bitterness—noticed me for the first time. "Of course, but you're going to tell me everything while I do. You are in deep, deep trouble." Contradicting this statement, Lend's dad caught him up in a big hug, practically lifting him off the ground. Lend had to let go of me, and I felt uncomfortable watching their reunion. "Don't you ever scare me like that again."

Lend laughed, a dry exhalation of air. "I don't plan on it. Her leg?"

His dad turned to me. "Where are you hurt?"

It was all too much, too strange. Lend in this setting, this welcoming, warm home, Lend with this completely normal man who was his dad. No glamour at all, nothing beneath his kind face. It felt like I had entered another world; I knew I didn't belong and that the Lend who lived here could never be mine.

"Is it that bad?" he asked, his face growing even more concerned as he looked at my expression.

I shook my head hastily. "No—I—my right thigh."

"We've kind of been through a lot tonight," Lend said gently.

His dad knelt on the wood floor next to my leg. "I'm just going to take a look, see how bad it is." He pulled my leggings out, stretching the slit more. "Okay, not too bad. I'll go upstairs and get my kit. It needs to be cleaned and then I'll give you a couple of stitches, no big deal." He smiled reassuringly at me. Then he gave Lend another stern look. "Get her some dry clothes, and be ready to explain everything."

"Don't worry—he's done tons of stitches." Lend smiled and followed his dad upstairs. I stood there in the entryway, feeling like an intruder until Lend came back. He handed me a bundle of clothes. "They're mine so they'll be a little bit big, but they should be okay."

I frowned as I took them. "Why do you have clothes?" He could just make them with his various glamours, after all.

"I usually wear them, believe it or not. Most of the time I don't need to change form; I wear this face almost all the time."

That made sense. After all, his glamour clothes looked perfect but had a strange texture. In public it would be better to wear things that felt normal. He showed me to a small bathroom, and I locked the door.

I pulled off my boots—my stupid pink boots that would forever remind me of the horrible burning girl now—then took off my tank. I didn't want to see it, but my wrist was like a beacon, burning even in the well-lit bathroom. It was brighter than ever. I didn't look at my chest, yanking Lend's soft T-shirt on so I wouldn't have to. Then I peeled off my leggings, mopping up the blood that had dripped down the side of my leg as best I could.

I tried not to get blood on Lend's drawstring shorts as I pulled them on. Then, to my horror, I realized I hadn't bothered shaving that day. Not only were my legs brilliant white and too skinny, they were also prickly.

The fact that I was worried about what Lend would think of my legs struck me as the most ludicrous thing imaginable. I had just lost my best friend, barely escaped having my life sucked out by a psychotic burning girl, committed treason, and nearly gotten the guy I liked killed by a crazy faerie. What were hairy legs compared to that? I started laughing and then crying, doing both in an awkward, gasping mess that made my head hurt.

Lend knocked on the door. "Are you okay?"

Taking a deep breath, I tried to stop. I opened the door, holding up the shorts on the side where I was cut. "Yeah." I sniffled but held back from full-on sobbing again.

"He'll do it in here." Lend put his arm around my shoulders and led me into a well-lit kitchen, painted in warm yellow. I sat in a chair and his dad knelt next to it, cleaning my leg with a warm cloth.

"I'm David, by the way."

"Evie," I answered. After he finished wiping away the blood, he put something on the wound that stung. I drew in my breath sharply.

"Sorry about that. Don't want it to get infected. Now you'll feel a couple of small pricks; I'm just numbing the area for the stitches." I tried not to flinch, focused on holding still and not shivering. "Where have you been?" he asked, and I looked up, wondering why he was asking me.

Lend answered. "It's kind of a long story."

"Talk." His dad was still working on my leg but his face was set.

Lend sighed. "I broke into IPCA's Center."

Stopping mid-stitch, David looked up, horrified. "You what?"

I was confused, too. Lend always made it sound like he had been sent there.

"I had to!"

"I—" David took a deep breath, closed his eyes, and shook his head. "You had better wait until I'm done, then." He went back to the stitches, finished, and taped a gauze pad over the top. He stood up and put away his supplies, then folded his arms and glared at Lend. "Now, start from the beginning and tell me the whole story, clear up until the end where I ground you for the rest of your life."

Lend hung his head. "I heard—I listened in to your meeting, when you said that the answer was with IPCA, in the Center. And I knew no one else could do it. I thought I could. So I went to a graveyard and put on a zombie body, shambled around. It took a couple of nights, but an operative finally showed up. So I, well, I hit her." He looked ashamed at that admission. "Then I called for pickup. When the faerie came I walked through with her. I got to the Center and ran into the director."

"Raquel?" David asked, and I looked at him, surprised. How did he know her?

Lend nodded. "I took her communicator and face, then found her office. I was searching for information when—when I got caught."

David's eyes went wide and he looked down at Lend's bare ankle. "How did you get out?"

Lend smiled at me. "Evie got me out. Of course, she's also the one who caught me. She can see me—the real me, all the time."

His dad looked at me, wonder and fear in his eyes. "You're IPCA?"

I shook my head. I wasn't anything. There was nowhere in the world I belonged now. My home was gone, my best friend was dead, and I could never go back to Raquel after what I had done. I bit my lip, holding back the tears. "Not anymore. After tonight, I don't think there's even going to be an IPCA."

"Well, from one former employee to another, I don't think that's a bad thing."

MY FIRST SLEEPOVER

Sitting in Lend's warm kitchen, I couldn't believe what his dad had just said. "You were— You worked there?" IPCA was kind of a lifetime thing.

"Actually, I was APCA. I got out about a decade before IPCA was formalized. Didn't think I'd ever see the day that would happen. None of the countries was willing to work with any of the others on paranormal issues. I never did find out what triggered the change."

I swung my foot awkwardly against the floor.

"You're looking at her," Lend said, grinning.

David raised his eyebrows. "Really? Wait, Lend, you

haven't finished your story, don't think I'm going to forget."

Lend sighed. "It's actually more Evie's story than mine, considering all I did was sit in an empty white cell. I didn't tell them anything, so they wouldn't let me go. Then their tagged paranormals started getting hit, and they finally picked up on this thing. Evie had a run-in with it, and—"

"You saw it?" David asked me.

"We both did," I said. I tried to shut her image out of my mind, but when I closed my eyes it was like she had burned herself onto my eyelids. "I saw her once right after she killed a hag and Jacques—a werewolf. But I couldn't see her very well."

"It's a woman? What is it?"

Lend shrugged. "Looked like a totally normal girl to me. But Evie can see through glamours."

Every time I thought David couldn't look any more surprised he topped it. "You can see through glamours?"

I nodded. "It's a glamourless life." My favorite joke hurt tonight. Lish always liked that one.

He sat down heavily in another chair. "Wow. The possibilities— I've never heard of anyone being able to— That's amazing. No wonder they were finally able to find common ground to form IPCA. So what is this thing?"

"I don't know. I've never seen anything like her." My wrist shone up at me. Well, that wasn't quite true. Stupid, stupid Reth. "She's like—like living, liquid flame. She's so bright it hurts my eyes."

"That's new. What's her glamour?"

Lend gave me an apologetic look, then shimmered as he transformed into Fire Girl. David swore softly, looking from Lend-as-fire-girl to me.

"I can't get her eyes right," Lend said. Fire Girl's voice coming out of his mouth made me shudder. "Can't get Evie's, either."

I felt guilty and dirty, even though I hadn't done anything wrong. David gave me a wary look. "And you brought her home?"

Lend shifted back to normal. "Dad, no, don't even start. She saved my life. That thing would have killed me. And Evie didn't just save me, she saved every werewolf there. She doesn't know who or what it is any more than we do."

David shook his head, bothered. "Well, I guess we know what we're looking for now. Or at least a description. I have no idea *what* she is."

I didn't know if he was talking about me or Fire Girl. "I'm not— You have to believe me. I'm not like her, whatever she is. She's horrible, and she killed—she killed my best friend." My voice cracked. She took Lish away from me, from the world. I didn't ever want to think about her again, and I couldn't stand Lend's dad suspecting I was somehow in league with her.

"She broke into the Center tonight." Lend put his arm around my shoulders. I appreciated that one little gesture more than I could say. He believed me no matter what.

When I looked up, I could tell his dad did, too. His eyes were gentle and kind again. "She must have planned everything, because they had called all their paranormals in and the werewolves were sleeping, so easy targets. We barely got out. I need to talk to Mom about what we saw."

I was surprised again. I don't know why I'd assumed he didn't have parents. Maybe he was adopted; things like Lend don't just *happen*. And the timing of his dad leaving APCA would have been right around when Lend was born. I definitely wanted to hear more about this.

"Can't visit her tonight, it's too cold," Lend's dad answered, which was even more confusing.

"Evie? Are you okay?"

I was shaking. "I'm cold," I said, trying not to let my teeth chatter. More than that I was overwhelmed and beyond exhausted.

David stood. "I'm going to give you something for your leg; it'll hurt when the numbing wears off. And if it's okay I'll give you painkillers with a sleep aid. Would you like that?"

"Yeah. Thanks." I wasn't looking forward to trying to fall asleep tonight on my own. I wanted to check out, leave reality.

He went through a cupboard, coming back with a couple of pills and a glass of water. I chugged them; they couldn't kick in fast enough as far as I was concerned.

"Where are we going to put her?" David asked. "The

guest rooms are off-limits tonight."

"Oh, yeah. She can sleep in my room. I'll take the couch."

"That's okay, I'm fine on the couch." I didn't want to be any more intrusive than I already felt.

"Saving Lend's life and breaking him out of the Center earns you a bed, I think," David said with a smile.

"I'll take you up and get you a sweatshirt so you won't be so cold."

"Thanks."

"Come back down when you're done, young man. We've still got some things to talk about."

Lend held back a sigh and nodded. The phone rang and David answered it. "He's home." He sounded relieved. "Everything's okay. We've got some new intel, too."

Wondering if that was Lend's mom, I stood and followed Lend up the stairs. He passed a couple of doors. Both were bolted shut with thick locks—on the outside. Nervous that his door would feature that nifty little security measure as well, I was relieved when he stopped and opened a bolt-free door.

"Oops," he said, picking some things up off the floor before I could see them. "Sorry, I've never had a girl in my room." He smiled sheepishly as he shoved them in a dresser drawer.

I gave him the best smile I could manage. "I've never been in a boy's room, so we're even." It was great, with sketches and band posters tacked up all over the pale blue walls. I wanted to just stand there, looking at how he defined himself through his room. That way I wouldn't have to think or be alone.

"Oh, here's a sweatshirt." He pulled a dark green hoodie out of the messy closet. I put it on; it was nice to have my wrist covered up again. Plus, it smelled like Lend. It was a fresh, cool scent, like what you'd expect by a cascade or waterfall. I hugged my arms around myself, trying to get warm again.

The bed was the only thing that didn't quite fit the room. It was a four-poster, and the headboard and footboard were elaborate, scrolling metal. It didn't go at all with the simple, soft-looking blue comforter. I put my hand on one of the poles. "Iron." I smiled in relief. Obviously Lend's dad knew his faerie lore. It made me feel a little bit safer—at least as far as Reth was concerned. Iron couldn't protect me from nightmares, though.

"I'll be downstairs if you need anything, okay?"

I turned and smiled. "Thanks."

He stood there for a moment, looking awkward, then leaned in and gave me a quick hug. "Thank *you*," he said, then left, closing the door behind him.

I held my breath. I didn't want to be alone. I wanted to call out, ask him to come and stay with me until I fell asleep, but I couldn't bring myself to do it. I'd already spent the entire night bawling in front of him.

I turned off the light, but as soon as it was dark I could see spots that reminded me of Fire Girl. I flipped the lights back on. No dark for me tonight. Climbing into bed, I curled up to get warmer under the covers.

In spite of my best efforts, I couldn't keep my mind from drifting to exactly what I didn't want to remember. Here in this warm house with a family, I was alone. I could never go back to my home at IPCA, never tell Raquel just how much she meant to me. *Oh, please*, I prayed to the silence, *let Raquel be okay.*

But my poor, sweet Lish was gone forever. In her place was the terrible beauty of Fire Girl, walking death in the sterile hallways of the Center. In my mind, she was still gliding through the rooms, cheerfully sucking the life out of anything and anyone she found.

I hoped she would never get out.

GIRL TALK

$\mathcal{I}$ walked through the Center hallways, blinking against the white. The place was empty. I kept expecting to find bodies, but it was pristine, abandoned. I stood in front of my unit, then walked through the door without it opening. That was strange.

She was already there, sitting on my purple couch. "There you are." She smiled pleasantly at me. We definitely had the same eyes, but her lips were a little wider than mine. She looked like she was a few inches taller, too.

"Why aren't you on fire anymore?" I asked. "And, hey, that's mine!" She was wearing the zebra print dress.

"Oh, chill out." She rolled her eyes.

"Where's the fire?" I looked down at my wrist—mine was gone, too.

"It's right there." She gestured toward the corner, where the liquid flames pulsed and shimmered, spherical with constantly shifting edges. I held out my hand toward them. For the first time I realized they were beautiful. I wanted them.

"You can't get them yet," she said. "Have a seat."

I sat down on the far end of the couch, narrowing my eyes. I knew I should be scared of her. I wasn't. "What is this?"

"A dream, you dork."

"Oh." I frowned. Weird. "Are you going to kill me?"

"I might have earlier, by accident. Sometimes I get carried away." She flashed an impish grin. "It's kind of hard not to get lost in the rush. But now that I know who you are, I would never."

"Who are *you*?"

"Oh, sorry. I'm Vivian."

"You killed my best friend. I thought I'd have nightmares."

She shrugged. "That wouldn't be very nice of me, coming in here and scaring you. I just want to talk. I've been trying to get through to you for a while now."

"So, wait, you're really here? Where am I?" What had Lend's dad given me in those pain pills?

"You don't know anything, do you? We share a soul now, so I thought I'd drop in, introduce myself properly."

"What do you mean we share a soul?" I glared at her. "I don't want to share anything with you; I've got my own soul!"

"Seriously, chill out. You're so tense. We share *a* soul, not *your* soul. I borrowed some from Reth when he brought me here; he had a ton in his hand, which was weird; usually you can only pull from the chest. I wanted to see if I could drain him—I've never done a faerie before, they won't let me touch them—but he pulled away before I could get much. Man, that was a nice trip."

"Wait, he gave you some of the fire stuff too? I hate it! It burns like crazy!"

"You must be doing it wrong. It's the greatest feeling ever."

I shook my head. We were getting off topic. "What are you?"

"Tsk-tsk, so rude. We're the same thing."

"We are *not* the same!" She was getting on my nerves. Even in my dreams no one would give me a straight answer.

"Don't be stupid, Evie. If I'd known you would be so pissy, I wouldn't have come. I guess you don't want answers after all."

I knew I should be sad or angrier, but my emotions seemed removed. The fire in the corner kept distracting me. I wanted to watch the flames, touch them. It was all I could do to keep my eyes on Vivian. "I don't want anything from you. You killed my best friend, remember?"

"No, not really. Who was it?"

"The mermaid."

"Oh." She looked puzzled. "She was your friend?"

"Yeah." My eyes drifted to the corner. They weren't like flames, exactly, more golden and wavering. Almost like this great shade of nail polish I had once. But on fire. That didn't make any sense. I shook my head, trying to clear my mind.

Vivian shrugged. "Sorry. But I was doing her a favor."

"A favor?" I couldn't look away from the corner now; I didn't want to.

"Giving her rest. Some peace. Don't you think the weight of all those millennia would be heavy? Besides, those things aren't supposed to be here. I'm just letting them go. Releasing them, if you will."

"Oh," I murmured distractedly.

"It's what we're supposed to do, you know," she prodded.

"Oh?"

"It would be more fun if we were together. Could be a sisters' thing."

I stood up. I had to touch it, see what it felt like.

"You can't have them yet." She sounded annoyed. "Besides, those are mine. We'll get you some of your very own, soon. And then you won't be cold or alone. Aren't you tired of being cold and alone?"

I could touch it now, if I just reached out my hand. "What is it?" I lifted my hand and, knowing I would get burned but not caring, plunged it inside.

The fire scattered, swirling around and past me. I turned to Vivian. She was the glowing, brilliant figure again. "Told you. You're empty. I'll help fill you."

I nodded, tears in my eyes. I wanted that. I didn't want to be empty anymore. Vivian walked closer to me, all heat and light, then cocked her head. "You've got to go. I'll talk to you soon." I could feel her smiling underneath the flames, and then everything went dark and cold again.

LIKE A BAD JOKE

Vivian?" I opened my eyes, panicked, and stared at the ceiling. Where had she gone?

"Evie, wake up." Lend's voice startled me.

"What are you doing here?"

He smiled. "It's my room."

I sat up, looking around. Everything from the day before clicked into place, and I wished it hadn't. It was like losing Lish again.

"Sorry," Lend said, "but they need you downstairs."

I blinked, trying to get my eyes to focus. "Who's they?"

He shrugged uncomfortably. "Just some people my dad

works with. I'm sorry, I let you sleep as long as I could."

"Oh, that's okay, then. Can I go to the bathroom first?"

"Of course. It's right down here." I followed him out into the hall and he pointed out the bathroom. "Hey, who's Vivian?"

My stomach dropped as the dream flooded back. "Don't know," I blurted, walking into the bathroom. Why did I feel guilty hiding a stupid dream from Lend? I shook my head, trying to dismiss it as a meaningless nightmare. After all, Vivian had said a lot of the same things I'd heard from Reth. It was probably my brain trying to process everything that had happened. Ignoring the nervous feeling in the pit of my stomach, I swished some toothpaste around my mouth.

Lend was waiting when I came out and I followed him down the stairs. The two bolted doors were open now. Wondering what I would find, I walked into the kitchen behind Lend and stopped dead.

Lend's dad, two werewolves, and a vampire. It was like the setup to a bad joke or something. A doctor, two werewolves, and a vampire walk into a bar. "What'll you have?" the bartender asks. "We were thinking him," the vampire answers, eyeing the doctor.

Okay, jokes weren't my strong point.

The yellow eyes staring warily out at me from the werewolves and the shriveled corpse face of the vamp— I automatically reached for Tasey before remembering

I didn't have her. I didn't know where she was, either, which made me all sorts of nervous. All their ankles were covered by pants, but I was certain there weren't any trackers underneath.

The vampire's glamour was a pretty, goth-looking woman in her early twenties. Black hair streaked with crimson; heavy eye makeup; and all black, skintight clothing. Way to blend in there. The two werewolves, holding hands, were a man and a woman in their thirties; he was tall, with his head shaved, and she had curly brown hair, cropped very short. There was something familiar about her face, but I couldn't place it.

Of course, now the bolted doors made sense. Holy crap, I had just spent the night of a full moon with two unneutered werewolves. And a vamp, too, although one vamp I was pretty sure I could handle, even without my beloved Tasey.

"Lend, you little monster," the vampire said, glaring. "Don't you ever pull that again."

Lend hung his head. "Sorry. I didn't mean for— When did you get here?"

"Just now." She turned to me. "So." She sounded witchy. I didn't like her. "IPCA, huh?"

"So." I raised my eyebrows (wishing I could raise just one like Lend did), "Bloodsucker, huh?"

"Yeah. So are Luke and Stacey." She jerked her head toward the werewolves.

"Okay, sure. Since I'm stupid and don't know they spent last night as wolves."

All three of the paranormals looked surprised. "Fine," the vamp snapped. "Did you figure out what David is yet?"

I gave her a flat stare. "Did you really wake me up for this? Because unless one of you did something to him last night, he's human." I glanced over at him to make sure. Yup, just human.

David cleared his throat. "We wanted to ask about this." He moved to the side and gestured at the table, where I saw Tasey—yay Tasey!—my communicator, and Lend's ankle tracker. David looked sad. "You brought IPCA technology to my home. Will they track you?"

"No!" Truth was, I hadn't even thought about that stuff in the confusion last night. There wasn't a problem with it, but he had a right to be worried. "Trust me, they'd already be here. The tracker is deactivated and my communicator doesn't have GPS or anything. It kept getting screwed up and reset every time I went through the Faerie Paths so they got rid of it. They always knew where I was anyway, since the only way I ever left was with a faerie. They can't track the communicator unless you hit the panic button, I promise."

The vamp cut in again. "Sure, but you could still call them, couldn't you?"

I glared at her. "Yeah, because I really want to get locked up for the rest of my life. Sounds like a party. In fact, I think

I'll turn myself in right now!"

"Like they wouldn't kill to get you back," she sneered.

I exhaled sharply, trying not to yell at her. Vamps grated on my nerves more than any other paranormal—the disconnect between their glamours and real faces was just too much. "Listen, corpse girl, do you know what I did? I broke section one of the charter. As in, *the* section. As in, let a paranormal loose without authorization and be locked up for the rest of your mortal life. Even if I wanted to go back, which I don't, and even if there was anything to go back to, which there probably isn't, I couldn't. So bite me."

She looked like she was going to take me up on it, but David interrupted. "That's enough. We're all on the same side here, Arianna. Lend told me everything that happened and I think Evie's right—if they could track her, they'd already be here." He picked up the communicator. "It's been beeping off and on all night. We found it with your clothes in the bathroom."

My heart leaped. Raquel! She had to be worried sick about me. If I could call her, let her know I was okay . . . then they'd know exactly where I was and I'd be locked up for the rest of my life. "They're probably trying to figure out whether or not I'm dead," I said sadly, then paused. How many times had I told them not to work with the faeries, urged them to trust Lend and figure this out together? Of course, my classification was proof enough of how IPCA really saw me. And no matter how I felt about Raquel, she *was* IPCA. I shook my head. "Let them think I'm dead."

The woman werewolf spoke, her voice gentle, fear in her eyes. "Did you really see it?"

It took me a moment to realize she was talking about Fire Girl. Vivian. I closed my eyes and nodded. It was just a stupid dream; I didn't actually know her name. I didn't want to talk about it anymore; I didn't want to think about it anymore.

"How's your leg?" Lend's dad asked.

"Oh, it's fine. Hurts a little, but nothing major."

"Good. We're going for a little walk."

"Okay." Confused, I looked over at Arianna. Vamps stayed away from sunlight. Not because they'd burst into flames or anything, but because in direct light their true selves showed through. Only a little, but they avoided it just the same.

"You'll probably want long pants," Lend said. "It's kind of cold today."

I followed him upstairs. He rifled through his clothes, frowning. "You're skinnier than I am."

I laughed. "Umm, yeah, kind of happy about that."

He looked up at me and grinned. After a minute he pulled out an old, worn pair of flannel pajama pants. "These are a couple of years old; they probably won't fall off." He handed them to me and stood there. I raised my eyebrows and he blushed. "Oh, yeah, I'll let you change."

After the door closed I slipped out of his shorts and

pulled on the red and blue flannels. They were a couple inches too long, but they'd stay on. Those combined with the oversized green hoodie meant I wasn't exactly looking hot. I sighed. I could have used a shower, too, not to mention some makeup. My eyelashes were as blond as my hair; without mascara I felt like a five-year-old.

I opened the door and Lend smiled. "They look better on you."

"Wow, they must look just awful on you then." I smiled back.

He handed me my boots, which completed my ensemble of ridiculousness. To make matters worse, he looked downright adorable in a thermal shirt that fit him just right (trust me, I noticed) and a pair of jeans. I looked at his face. I loved his eyes—his real eyes. They were always the easiest of his features to pick out.

"Are you doing okay?" he asked, and his soft, sad look made everything rush in again.

"No, not really, but I'm trying not to lose it in front of everyone." I willed myself not to cry. I might bawl like a baby during *The Notebook*, and, sure, I cried myself to sleep sometimes . . . okay, a lot . . . but that was by myself. I didn't like doing it in front of other people.

"Let me know if you need anything."

I smiled, wanting to get a move on so I could stop thinking about things that made me sad. It was weird being on Lend's turf; I was a lot more confident when we were both

in the Center. Like right now, I really wanted to hold his
hand, but I wasn't brave enough to try with his dad and that
stupid vamp downstairs.

Lend and I met David and Arianna outside and I got a
better look around. A narrow paved road led away from
the house through the trees, but we turned to the right and
walked down a barely-there path into the woods for about
twenty minutes. The trees were budding, the air crisp and
clear with a hint of warmth. Spring was on its way. I tried
to focus on the sun streaming down through the branches.

"Where are we?" I whispered to Lend.

"Virginia."

Through the trees ahead, I saw a pond fed by a wide
stream to our right. We came through the last of the trees
and stood on the banks. The pond was oval, fairly large,
and pale blue, reflecting the cloudless sky. The edges were
crystallized with frost.

"Oh, good," Lend said. "She can come out today."

I frowned at the horrible idea that maybe they were
friends with a hag. But the look on Lend's face—excited
and happy—reassured me that I wasn't going to meet a vio-
lent end. "Who?" I asked.

He smiled at me. "My mom."

RUNS IN THE FAMILY

Your mom?" I asked. I turned back to the pond, looking for a house of some sort, but there was nothing. Lend picked up a rock and, giving it an expert flick with his wrist, skipped it across the top of the water. Another thing he could do that I always wanted to. The others were watching the water expectantly, so I did the same.

The middle of the pond moved, shifting as though there was a sudden change of current. It turned toward us, the water building up and moving of its own accord, creating a small wake. I'll admit I was nervous. Most of my experience with paranormals involved things that could kill me. It was all I could do not to take a step back as the wave came closer, flowing faster and rising above the level of the pond.

When it got within feet of the shore, the water shot up, spraying high into the air. Little droplets, freezing cold, showered down on my head. The water settled to reveal a woman standing there. Well, standing being relative, considering she was still on the water and made of it, too. The light reflected off her rippling form; she was absolutely amazing. Her top half was well-formed, right down to a hauntingly beautiful face and cascading hair. She held out slender arms toward us. After her waist the water dropped down, forming a sort of dress shape where it connected back to the pond.

"Hi, Mom." Lend waved cheerfully.

She laughed. It blew my mind. I had always thought Reth had the most beautiful voice and laughter, but she put him to shame. It made you feel like you were lying next to a stream on a warm day, letting it run over your fingers as you lost every care in the world except the cool, cleansing sensation. It bubbled with clear music notes.

"Hello, my darling," she said. Her features rippled into a smile as she looked at Lend. I could see right through her to the other side, but the way her face manipulated the water and reflected light you could see her expressions. It was like Lend in his normal form, only much less stable. I noticed something else, too. Her heart, or where her heart would have been, seemed to generate light—like she glowed from inside. This must be a normal thing for paranormals. Why had I not noticed before?

"Cresseda," Lend's dad said. He looked happy and sad at the same time, watching her. It made me wonder what the family history was.

"David."

"He got home safely."

She laughed again. "I told you he would. And he found the answer." She fixed her eyes on me. I didn't know what to do, so I raised one hand in an awkward wave.

Lend looked down, shaking his head. "No, I'm sorry. I didn't find anything. I saw what was doing this, but I don't have any answers."

Cresseda shook her head, water droplets raining down in front of her. "You have the answer with you." She smiled, and her eyes, insubstantial as they were, seemed to bore straight through me. "What a lovely balance. Lend shows whatever he wants the world to see and you see through whatever the world wants to show you."

"What do you mean?" Arianna interrupted.

Cresseda shimmered like she was about to lose her form. "Lend found what he was meant to find."

David frowned. "You mean— Did you send him?" He turned to Lend. "Is that why you went? Did she ask you to?"

Lend shook his head. "No, I went because I heard you guys talking. Didn't you get that info from a banshee?"

"Yeah, but I—"

"Things are not as they should be. Now they may return. Or they may be lost entirely," Cresseda said thoughtfully. And really unhelpfully, too. She wasn't much good in the whole making-sense department. Of course, Lend had been talented at the whole vague, random-answer thing while he was in the Center. It was obvious now where he'd learned it. "Change is coming. 'Eyes like streams of melting snow.'" She smiled at me again.

I shrugged, uncomfortable. "That's not about me."

She shook her head. I didn't know whether she was agreeing with me or telling me I was wrong. "The waters are emptier now." Her voice was tinged with sorrow. "I am sorry about Alisha. You will set it right?"

"How did you know about Lish?" I asked, my voice catching.

"She was part of the waters. Return her to us?"

I shook my head, tearing up again. "I can't; she's dead."

"Cresseda," David said, his voice gentle and leading, like he was trying to get her to focus. "We know a little more about the thing that's doing this. We were hoping you could help us."

She waved one hand dismissively. "This is not a matter of the waters—it is a matter of fire and spirit. The path is not mine and I cannot see it." Lend's shoulders slumped. Everyone in the group looked disappointed. "And, Lend? Stand up straight, stop slouching. My beautiful boy."

I almost laughed. I guess she really was a mom, after all. She beamed and the light reflecting from her grew brighter, then the water that formed her let go, dropping back to the pond with a loud splash.

"Bye, Mom," Lend said softly.

Arianna folded her arms petulantly. "Well, that was a bloody waste of time."

"I don't know," an all-too familiar voice mused behind us. "I found it rather entertaining." I turned around, terror bleeding from my stomach outward until even my fingers trembled.

Everyone else seemed equally shocked, although only Lend looked scared. Reth stood in the middle of the path like some sort of beautiful Victorian dandy. He even had a walking stick—clearly freedom agreed with him and he'd stepped up his fashion. If he weren't so breathtaking, he would have looked ridiculous. On him it worked, and somehow made him creepier.

"What do you want?" David asked, his voice even and cautious.

"I've come to collect what's mine." He smiled at me. It was over. Without his new name, I was powerless. I didn't even have any weapons. He would take me and there was nothing anyone could do.

"Don't touch her!" Lend jumped in front of me, planting his feet and holding out his arms. If I weren't so scared it would have been adorable—Lend thinking he could fight off a faerie. I wanted to cry. I'd never see him again and it broke my heart.

Reth frowned. "You are getting very tiresome."

I put my hand on Lend's back. "Lend, no!" He had to get out of here. He knew what Reth could do, what Reth *would* do.

David, hands in his pockets, stepped closer to the faerie. "I'm sorry, I don't believe we've met. I'm David. What's your interest in Evie?"

Reth didn't even glance at him. "Time we were off." He held out his hand. My mind raced as I tried to think of a way out that didn't end up with anyone dead.

Arianna stood her ground, spitting on the path in front of him. "She's not going anywhere with you."

Reth raised an eyebrow. "What charming company you keep, my love." He flicked a hand lazily and Arianna went flying into a tree.

The sun glinted off something on David's knuckles as he swung at Reth's face. What good did he think that would do? His fist connected, and Reth fell backward, clutching at his face with an inhuman shriek. My jaw dropped as David turned toward us. "Let's go, now."

He turned his back too soon. From the ground Reth raised his hand and whispered something.

I shrieked as my wrist burned and I was dragged forward. I dug my heels into the dirt, but the pull was too strong and I fell forward, knocking Lend out of the way.

There was nothing to hold on to. I clutched at my wrist like I could somehow tear away the fire.

Lend jumped on top of me, grabbing me around the waist and bracing us both with his feet. We slowed. Reth raised his other hand and the fire flared, pulling from my heart now, too. I screamed in agony. It hurt so bad I couldn't breathe, I couldn't think. A door melted into place behind Reth. A few more feet and I'd be his forever.

"No!" Lend squeezed me even tighter. David spun to hit Reth again, forcing the faerie to move one of his hands; I gasped with relief as my heart was released. He froze David on the spot.

Reth dusted himself off, maintaining his pull on my wrist. "Barbaric race, really. Now then." He glared at Lend and raised a hand.

"No, don't hurt him, I'll come, I'll come!" I sobbed. At least then the pain would be over and Lend would be safe.

"No!" Lend yanked me backward, gaining a few feet on Reth.

Smiling, Reth opened his mouth. He was going to kill Lend.

Water, foaming and flecked with bits of ice, shot past us, whipping my hair forward with the force of its motion. Before hitting Reth, the water curved, turning back on itself and swirling around us. The fire in my wrist died, the invisible threads cut. Lend and I sat safe in the middle of the vortex, watching Reth's image ripple through the water.

"Really now," Reth snapped, looking past us. "I would hope that you, of all things, would understand. You know what she means to us. *All* of us."

"That is my son."

Reth's nose wrinkled in distaste. "I see. Very well, he's of no import to me. I'll take Evelyn and be on my merry way."

"She is under my protection as well."

"She's no thing of yours. The waters have no claim."

"Neither does the air."

"We made her!"

My blood froze. What did he mean?

"Creation is not claim," Cresseda said.

"And yet you claim the boy," Reth sneered.

"Leave." Cresseda's voice had gone from bubbling brook to roaring waterfall; it was power, eternal and unassailable.

Reth straightened his waistcoat and picked up his walking stick. "Very well. I'm not the only one who will come looking, though. Until next time, my love." He waved his cane at me and stepped back through the door.

ONE OF A KIND

Arianna wasn't dead. Or dead*er*, I guess. I never thought I'd be so relieved about a vamp, but the girl had guts. Back at the house, David patched up her ribs while Stacey and Luke holed themselves in upstairs, avoiding me after hearing what had happened. I didn't blame them. I was like a plague: where I came, bad things followed.

"How did you hurt Reth?" I asked as David finished checking Arianna's ribs. I realized Reth had a new name, but had no idea what.

David stuck his hand in his pocket and pulled something out. It looked like brass knuckles but the wrong color. Iron.

Brilliant. "Designed them myself."

Was he cool or what? "Can I get a set?" Lend and I asked at the same time.

David laughed. "I'll see what I can do."

"What if Reth comes back?" Lend asked.

"There's a reason he didn't come to the house. We're not very faerie friendly here. But I wouldn't underestimate your mom's power. Now that he knows the water elementals are protecting Evie, I don't think he'll try anything. Soon he'll forget he was ever interested in her."

I hoped that was true, but I seriously doubted it. It sounded too dismissive, too like Raquel. I wasn't just some pretty thing Reth wanted to dance with—his interest in me ran far deeper. There was some sinister purpose behind it all. Still, David was obviously faerie savvy, and with Cresseda's protection, maybe I really would be safe. Until I had to leave here, of course.

"There are a few other tricks," David said, walking to the counter. He grabbed a loaf of bread, took out two slices, and handed them to us. "Keep a bit of stale bread in your pockets all the time."

"Okay," I said, frowning dubiously at the bread.

He laughed. "It works. Faeries don't like things that tie them to our earth. Bread is the staff of life for humans—they won't touch it. Same thing with iron; it binds them here, rings too sharply of imprisonment. That's why it hurts them."

"Cool!" Bread, at least, I could take with me everywhere. "Can I have my taser back, too?" Tasey wasn't much good against faeries, but I felt kind of naked without her.

Frowning thoughtfully, he finally nodded and gave it to me. I had to restrain myself from stroking the pink grip.

Arianna fixed her clothes, glaring at me. "Why's the faerie so obsessed with you anyway? You're not *that* cute."

David cleared his throat loudly. "Lend, why don't you take Evie into town, get her some clothes and things?"

My heart leaped in my chest. That sounded promising. "I can stay?" I had been waiting for him to kick me out since we got here. I figured it was a sure thing now with the added Reth threat. I wouldn't want me around, either.

"Of course." He smiled at me. "You brought my son back. You're always welcome." I wouldn't cry, not again, but that one sentence meant the world to me. Maybe I wasn't totally alone, after all.

Lend frowned. "You're trying to get rid of us so you can talk about all this, aren't you?"

"Yes."

"Fine." Lend held out his hand. "Keys? And a credit card?"

David pulled a card out of his wallet and handed it over with the car keys. "Be back before dark. You're still grounded."

"I promise not to have any fun," Lend said solemnly.

"Get out of here, you bum," his dad said, shaking his head.

We climbed into a plain silver sedan. Maybe I'm weird, but watching Lend drive was sexy.

"So," he said, "I'm guessing you have some questions?"

"Just one: what's the limit on that card?" He looked shocked until I started laughing. "Kidding. I'm not going to push my luck, don't worry. I would, however, like to get pants that aren't yours, no offense. And I do have a few questions—real questions."

He smiled. "I figured. How about I start at the beginning?"

"A very good place to start."

"You already know my dad was APCA. Some of the things they were doing really bothered him. The imprisonment, regulations, forced sterilizations, tracking—"

"Whoa, hold on—forced sterilizations?"

He glanced at me. "You didn't know? They were worried about what would happen if a werewolf got pregnant by another werewolf. Had this whole panic, ethics debate, so on and so forth, then made any paranormal-human hybrid breeding with another paranormal or human totally illegal, and, umm, made it so no werewolves they caught could ever reproduce."

All those neutering jokes I had made—they weren't jokes. "Oh," I whispered, horrified. "I had no idea." I thought about all the werewolves I knew, Charlotte especially. She had always been so sweet and attentive. She would have made a great mom. And IPCA took that away from her after everything else she had already lost. "I think that's the worst thing I've ever heard." Then it really hit me—would they have done that to me? Would I have been seen as a breeding risk? Even the term, "paranormal breeding." They really thought of all paranormals as animals. What else did IPCA do that I didn't know about?

"Anyway, he was on an extended assignment trying to track down evidence of nymphs or sprites. He found my mom."

"What is she, exactly?"

"Kind of the equivalent of a nymph. She's a water spirit, an elemental. She thought he was funny and kept showing up to talk to him. And my dad fell in love with her." He smiled. "That was all it took to convince him that he was done with APCA. They weren't about to let someone who knew as many secrets as him quit, so he faked his own death by drowning. They lost a lot of operatives in those days and it wasn't a hard sell."

"So did your mom and dad—" I stopped, suddenly aware of what awkward territory I was heading into.

"She's made of water. If you tried to touch her, your hand would go right through." This was so not adding up, and I didn't want to try to come up with an explanation. Fortunately, he continued. "But all elementals have the gift of choice. My mom decided that, after all the ages she'd been around, she'd like to see what really being alive, being human, was like. So she took on a mortal form and lived with my dad as husband and wife. But she couldn't leave the water—she didn't want to. She didn't tell him, but she took on mortality for only one year. That was long enough to make me." He smiled and blushed. "And at the end of the year, she gave my dad a son and went back to the water."

I looked at him in amazement. He was incredible. My original idea of him as water come to life was exactly right. I wondered what Lish would have thought, since she was a water paranormal, too. It stung, knowing that my best friend had never met this boy I was crazy about. They would have loved each other.

"So you really are one of a kind, aren't you?"

He shrugged. "Guess so. It was hard for my dad when I was little. I changed form constantly; it was like a game. I had to be homeschooled until I was old enough to understand that it would be really dangerous if people found out about me. Plus, you met my mom—she wasn't exactly the most helpful parent." He glanced at me warily, as though he expected me to laugh. "So . . . that's where I came from."

I smiled, shaking my head. "You are so freaking awesome."

He laughed, obviously relieved. I was way too happy. Part of it was Lend opening up to me, part was knowing I had a place with his family. But besides that, I hadn't been in a car in like six years. I eyed him in the driver's seat with undisguised envy.

"Tell you what," he said, noticing my stare. "I know you can't get a license, but I might be able to do something better."

"What?"

He smiled. "How would you like to come to school with me tomorrow and see a real, live locker?"

I'm pretty sure I squealed.

After our shopping was done (I was so eager to get out of Lend's clothes, I changed in the store bathroom), we got back into the car. I was pretty sure he had checked me out a few times. I hoped so, at least. Goodness knows I was doing my fair share of sneaky staring. "You hungry?" he asked, pulling out.

"Oh, my gosh, I'm starving," I said, just now realizing it. I looked at the clock on the dashboard. It was three in the afternoon.

"Let's get something to eat, then."

"Aren't you grounded?" I teased.

"My dad said be back by dark. It's not dark yet."

We drove a couple of blocks to a small diner. I had never been on the East Coast before except for a few late night jobs, so I enjoyed looking around. Lots of trees, hinting at buds. We walked into the diner and my jaw dropped.

Every single person in there was a paranormal.

"Umm, you do know this whole place is filled with werewolves, vamps, and a couple of other things I've never seen before, right?" I whispered. Lend laughed, sitting down in a booth.

"Well, yeah. My dad owns it."

"Oh."

"After Mom went back to the water, he was left with a very paranormal son. He knew how bad things were with the government agencies, so he decided to do something about it. He runs sort of an underground railroad for paranormals, shielding them from IPCA, giving them jobs, helping them control the nastier sides of themselves."

"What about the vamps? Does he let them suck someone dry every now and then?"

"There are lots of other sources of blood. They all know that if they break the rules, he won't help them anymore. Most of them are young vamps, too. They still remember what it was like to be human and don't really relish the thought of killing. Plus they're helpful with the whole mind control thing."

I felt kind of bad. I had never even considered giving vamps the benefit of the doubt. "Do you have any hags?"

Lend laughed. "We're accepting, not suicidal."

I sighed in relief. "Okay then. That's pretty cool, I guess." Truth was, the whole thing made me more than a little nervous. The sentiment was great, but expecting all these creatures to control their natural instincts? Sounded dangerous. How many lives were worth risking to give a handful of vampires more freedom?

A waitress came to take our orders, interrupting my thoughts. She knew Lend and was drop-dead gorgeous, with blond hair, blue eyes, and these absolutely luscious lips. Her non-glamour face was just as beautiful, although it was mottled brown and gray. We both ordered and she turned around. My jaw dropped. Underneath her glamour her back was hollow like an old tree, and she had a tail. "What is she?" I whispered.

"Nona? Oh, she's a huldra. Tree spirit."

Watching her and the other paranormals in there, things shifted for me. They were vibrant, happy, not hurting anyone. This was a good place.

I used to think that IPCA was some noble organization, protecting humans. But I thought it helped paranormals, too. The werewolves and vamps had jobs, and all paranormals had protected status. However, this recent information gave me a new perspective. IPCA acted on absolutes, and I was increasingly realizing that nothing was absolute in this world.

Lend's dad wasn't totally right, but he was probably more right than my former employers.

I thought of something else. "With all the stuff you know about IPCA, how were you so calm while we—they—were holding you? I would have been freaking out."

He laughed. "Oh, trust me, I was terrified. Beyond terrified. I kept waiting for them to cut me open or something. Lucky for me they were distracted with the dead paranormals, otherwise I don't even want to think about it."

"Man, I thought you were like some supercool operative and knew exactly what you were doing. Now I find out you weren't even supposed to be there in the first place."

"I've got a lot of practice acting. I do it every waking hour, after all." He had a point—he acted with his whole appearance.

"Well, I guess I still think you're pretty cool."

"Thank goodness." He shook his head in mock relief. "Of course, I can't really act in front of you." He gave me a small, shy smile. It must have been so weird for him that I could see him like no one else. I kinda liked it.

"You don't need to act for me," I answered, then blushed. Wow, was that dorky or what? Pretty soon I would tell him how dreamy I thought his real eyes were, and how much I'd like him to hold my hand in a non-the-world-is-ending-and-I'm-being-nice sort of way. He smiled bigger and we both went back to our food. Good thing too, because I was probably one step away from blurting out hey, wanna be my boyfriend?

When we left, half the restaurant waved cheerily to Lend, most of them giving me curious looks. I figured it was a good thing they didn't know who I was. I tried not to stare at anyone, pretending like I couldn't see what they really were. Besides the tree spirit waitress, there was a woman who had fins underneath her glamour legs, several werewolves, a couple of vamps, and I was pretty sure I had seen two gnomes working in the back. This place was even weirder than the Center.

Remembering my old home made me feel more pangs of guilt. I didn't even know if Raquel was okay, and I was sure she'd be really worried about me. But there was so much she never told me, so much she hid, it was easier to push down the guilt in favor of anger. And Lish I tried not to think about at all. If I were still in the Center, her absence would be like a hole in my heart. Here I was so removed from my previous life that it made it a little easier. I could pretend she was still there in her tank, waving her hands around and making the computer say bleep.

When we got back to his house, Lend sighed. "I'd better call some friends and find out how far behind I am in my classes." He pulled out his phone.

"Lend?" David called.

"Yup," Lend answered. "We're back, we already ate."

"I know, Nona called and told me you were there."

The person Lend was calling picked up and he started talking. I didn't know what I was supposed to do. My impulse was to go to Lend's room. I always thought the Center made me claustrophobic, but now I suspected I had the opposite problem. All that time today in open spaces and outdoors made me kind of twitchy, nervous to get back inside. How lame was that?

And I still couldn't get over what Lend had said, especially about the sterilizations. "David?" I asked, walking into the kitchen.

"Yes?" He looked up from the table.

"I— I didn't know. About IPCA, I mean. The things they do." I looked guiltily at the floor, remembering all the werewolves I had brought in. And now I had abandoned them for this safe, happy home. "I want to help, if I can."

"I told you and Lend, I don't want you involved in this anymore."

"No, not the killer thing. I mean, with other things. With what you're doing here." It hit me. "The werewolves! All IPCA's werewolves were taken out of the Center! We can help them."

"Where?" David stood.

My heart sank. "Oh. I don't know. I made a faerie get them out so they'd be safe. I have no idea where she took them. The Center is in northeastern Canada, if that helps. Maybe she just took them outside?"

"It's in *Canada*?"

"APCA wanted it here but the other countries pitched a fit. Everyone hated APCA because you guys always had the best technology. One of the conditions of forming IPCA was that the main center had to be off US ground, so they picked Canada since it was fairly neutral." Politics. Honestly.

He frowned thoughtfully. "If they're still unsupervised,

we might have an opening. I have a few contacts I could try. They've got to be somewhere."

"What about the ankle trackers?"

"We've been working against IPCA for a long time, Evie. I couldn't do this without a few key people on the inside. We'll figure something out." He smiled. I felt a little better. At least I'd done something to help Charlotte. Hopefully.

But him saying he had someone on the inside made me remember Raquel. I cleared my throat, nervous. "Umm, could you maybe find out if some of my friends are okay?"

"If you mean Raquel, I've already contacted my sources and they're going to let me know where she is as soon as they find out."

I let out a relieved breath. "Thanks!"

I went into the family room and sat down on the couch next to Lend. Not *next* next to him like I wanted to, but close. After a few minutes he closed his phone and sighed. "I'm dead. This is going to take me forever to make up. I'll be right back. I gotta go see what books I have here so I can get started." He grabbed the shopping bags and went upstairs.

I watched him leave, jealous of his life. I'd even take real homework.

"Oh," Arianna said, her voice flat. She had just come in the room and looked annoyed that I was there. "I was going to watch TV." She gave me a just-try-to-stop-me look.

"Be my guest." I didn't move, giving her a don't-think-you-can-bully-me-bloodsucker look.

She sat down in an armchair next to the couch and pulled out a couple of remotes. After searching through a menu, she selected a show and hit play.

"No way!" I sat up. "I totally love this one."

"You like *Easton Heights?*"

"Umm, best show ever."

"I know, huh?" The eyes of her glamour were lit up, excited. The dead eyes underneath even looked a little animated. "I missed a couple of episodes while I was out looking for that twit," she said, glaring at Lend as he walked in the room.

Lend sat down on the couch—closer to me than he had been before—and then noticed the show. He sighed heavily. "Great. I am kind of trying to get some—"

"Shhh!" Arianna and I said at the same time.

After catching up on all the episodes she missed, Arianna and I had a long, slightly heated discussion over who Cheyenne should end up with. She wasn't as much fun as Lish, but she certainly knew her *Easton Heights*. I wondered what Lish would think, knowing I was talking about our show with an untagged vamp. At least Lish would have my back in the argument.

"You know she belongs with Landon," I said.

"Oh, as if! He'll never reform. She should just accept that Alex is going to make her happy."

"You're crazy! What about the time Alex got drunk and

went to that club where he made out with Carys before he found out they were actually cousins? Yeah, that's stability."

Lend stood. "Evie, we've got to wake up early tomorrow for school."

"Oh, yeah, good point." I was pretty exhausted. "We'll talk about this tomorrow," I warned Arianna.

Lend and I walked up the stairs together. "You can have your room back," I said.

"Don't worry about it. It's not a full moon anymore, so Stacey and Luke can share a room again. I'll take the extra one."

"I could take the extra one."

He shrugged, smiling. "I already put all your stuff in there—don't worry about it. We'll get you settled more permanently tomorrow."

I really, really liked the sound of that. After getting ready for bed, I bumped into him in the hall again. "I had a great time today. Besides the whole Reth attack, I mean."

"Me, too." We were both quiet, and then he leaned forward, giving me a strange look. For a second I thought he was going to hug me or—holy bleep—maybe even kiss me and I got all excited. Then he just smiled and said, "Good night."

"Oh, umm, night," I said back, not even managing to hide my disappointment.

I was never going to get kissed, was I?

HIJINKS AND
HIGH SCHOOLS

I woke up early the next morning, relieved after a dreamless sleep and buzzing with excitement to go to a real, live high school. I took a quick shower and got ready. It was nice to be able to do my hair and makeup—it made things feel a little more normal. I chose a shirt Lend had picked out for me (pink and sparkly, how cute was that?) and was ready to go forty-five minutes before we needed to leave. Lend hadn't even woken up yet. With nothing else to do, I went downstairs to eat breakfast.

David was sitting at the table with Arianna and the two werewolves. "Oh, hey," I said, feeling like I had intruded.

David smiled at me, and Arianna even gave me a nod. Stacey and Luke barely looked at me. I think I scared them. Awesome.

"Cereal's in the pantry—help yourself," David said. I did, finding a bowl and spoon and then sitting at the counter to eat. I tried not to listen to their conversation, but it was a small kitchen. "If we just knew *how* it was killing them."

"Wait, what?" I turned around to face the group. "Are you talking about the girl that's killing paranormals? I saw her."

"You did? How does she do it?" They all looked at me, eager and intense.

"It's weird. She just sort of puts her hand on their chests and then they're dead. Afterward, there's a handprint, all shimmery and golden, but it fades. I don't think anyone else would be able to see it."

"Can you show me exactly what she did?" David stood up. "Are you sure she didn't have a weapon of some sort?"

"Nope, nothing."

Arianna stepped up. "Show him on me."

It was more than a little awkward. I wasn't all that eager to put my hand on Arianna's chest—I wouldn't have been even if she weren't undead. Not my thing. Still, David was watching intently, so I shrugged. "Okay, she walked up and put her hand out like this, and then—"

The second we touched, Arianna's eyes went wide and

she started convulsing, letting out a horrible shriek.

David jumped back and I screamed, yanking my hand away in terror. What had I done? I really was like Vivian, a murderer. I watched, stunned, for the golden handprint to show up and Arianna to crumple to the ground. And a part of me, a small, terrible part, waited to know what it would feel like.

Her convulsions shifted into giggles. "Oh, I got you bad!" She was laughing so hard now she doubled over.

I leaned against the counter and gasped for breath. Trying not to cry, I shoved her shoulder, almost knocking her over. "You stupid brat! I can't believe you did that!"

David sighed. "That was in very poor taste."

At the table, Stacey had her head buried in Luke's chest. She was bawling, and Luke looked like he wanted to rip Arianna's throat out.

"Oh, lighten up," she said, still laughing. "That was awesome and you know it. You should have seen the look on your face. You really thought you were killing me."

"Yeah, well, now I kind of want to." I glared at her. I couldn't get that dumb dream out of my head. I had actually thought of Fire Girl as Vivian again.

"Hey, good morning." Lend walked into the kitchen, stopping as he took in everyone's faces. "What did I miss?"

"Arianna's a freaking comedic genius," I muttered, sitting back down to finish my cereal.

"Evie was showing us how this thing kills, and Arianna

decided to make it a little more dramatic," David added drily.

"So great," Arianna said, finally getting her laughter under control.

"Were you talking about the poem?" Lend asked. "What have you figured out?"

David shook his head. "No, you're officially banned from listening to us. Or thinking about this. Or even thinking about thinking about this, understand?"

"But I—"

"No. I mean it. You and Evie both. This is not your problem anymore."

Lend scowled as he got some cereal and sat next to me. Honestly, I had been under so much pressure for so long that it was a relief to turn it over to the adults. I didn't want to think about faeries or crazy burning girls anymore. I, for one, would be following David's rules. It was about time I got to be sixteen.

I pushed the image of Lish's lifeless body out of my mind with a wave of guilt. This wasn't my fight. I'd done my part already.

"Are you ready?" Lend asked.

"Oh yeah." I was so ready. Distractions, please. "Are there a lot of paranormals at the school, too? Vamps?"

Arianna snorted. "Why on earth would a vampire go to high school?"

"Well, then I don't have to deal with you today, so

already high school's super."

"You'd better get going," Lend's dad said, looking at the clock.

I followed Lend out to the car, practically skipping.

We pulled up to a sprawling brick building and parked in a crowded lot. I jumped out of the car, waiting impatiently while Lend gathered his backpack and books.

"We'll go to the office first to check you in." We entered through glass double doors, and a couple of perky office ladies greeted us. Lend gave them a winning smile. "I've got my absence excuse slip and I'm checking in my guest. I think my dad called?"

"Oh, yes," said one of the ladies, a plump woman with short, curly red hair. "Been sick, sweetheart?"

"Yup. Pretty bad." Lend handed her a paper and she looked over it, then entered something into a computer. She handed me a visitor pass, which I rather reluctantly clipped to the bottom of my shirt. Lame.

"Okay, you're all set."

"Thanks." I got butterflies in my stomach as we turned and walked through the door into the main hallway.

It was *amazing*. Seriously, it was incredible. The school was kind of run-down and dingy, but the kids! Teenagers, everywhere! Deliciously ordinary, completely oblivious teenagers! I had never been around so many at one time. Lend and I cut into the traffic flow and walked down the hall, and I realized that none of them noticed us or cared. They jostled each other, shouted hellos, insulted each other in slang I'd never heard but vowed to try out. And I was there in the middle of it all.

I was normal. It was heaven.

We turned down a side hall and Lend stopped, holding his hands up dramatically. "I give you—my locker."

It was a sickly teal, paint chipping off the corners to reveal a previous tan coat. I reached out and put my hand on the cold metal.

"So, is it everything you imagined?" he asked.

"Everything I imagined and more," I whispered, then busted up laughing. "Seriously, this whole place—it's incredible! I can't believe you get to do this every day!"

"Funny, because most people here, myself included, really wish that we didn't have to."

"That's because you have no idea how precious normal is. Now." I put my hands on my hips and looked around. "According to *Easton Heights*, a fistfight over a girl should be breaking out at some point today, followed by a tear-streaked catfight in the girl's bathroom. Should I keep my eyes open? And, more important, do I join the fight, or just watch?"

Lend laughed. "Umm, yeah, probably not going to happen. We'll go to my classes, eat lunch, go to more class, and you'll realize that high school is mind-numbingly boring."

"Not a chance," I said, grinning. "It's already awesome."

• • •

At the end of one of my best days ever, we sat in the car waiting for the line out of the parking lot to move. "So, you like the whole high school thing?" Lend asked.

"Let's see." I frowned thoughtfully. "History is boring—already knew that. Some classes are a joke—nice surprise. Even normal people are strange—figured that one out already. No vicious creatures I needed to subdue with a Taser—always a plus. Yup, high school's pretty cool in my book." And it was. I even got to go to art class. The teacher made me model in front of the whole class for life drawing, which was almost scarier than facing that room full of vamps. At least I knew what the vamps were thinking.

We pulled out of the parking lot and I saw a sign on the corner advising students to buy their prom packages. "You guys haven't had your prom yet?"

"Oh. No, I guess not." Lend fidgeted in his seat and was quiet.

Oh, crap—he probably thought I was hinting that I wanted him to ask me, and now he felt awkward because he didn't want to. We made it halfway home in perfect silence, our awesome day ruined. Brilliant move, Evie.

"So," he said, finally speaking up. "Do you— I mean, it's kind of lame, but do you want to go to the prom? With me?"

"Seriously?"

He shrugged, not taking his eyes off the road. "You

don't have to, I just thought maybe you'd—"

"Yes! I'd love to! Absolutely! I mean, it'd be kind of fun, right?" I could have melted ice, my smile was so bright. Lend's face broke into a smile, too, which made me realize how nervous he had looked before. No wonder he'd been so quiet!

"Cool. It'll be fun."

The afternoon passed quickly. Every time I thought about the prom, a sort of giddy sense of unreality descended on me. Surely this couldn't be my life. It was too amazing. I was going to the prom—my prom—with Lend.

GIRLS, CRYING,
WOLVES

Dinner was a little uncomfortable. I hadn't been to
an actual family dinner in years. Sometimes in the Center
Raquel or Charlotte ate with me; when they didn't I took
my food into Central Processing, but it wasn't like Lish
could exactly sit down at a table with me.

No crying at the dinner table. No thinking about Lish.

Stacey and Luke sat on the opposite end of the table,
and every time I glanced up, Stacey was darting looks at
me that hovered between terrified and furious. I could
barely even make eye contact with either one of them,
not now that I knew what would have happened if they

had been caught by IPCA.

David was on the phone in the other room all through dinner, but when we were nearly done eating he came in, and sat down heavily in his chair, a relieved and weary smile on his face. He turned toward me.

"We did it."

"Did what?" I asked.

"I didn't want to say anything until everyone was safe, but your Canada tip was enough. I have an old friend who's a CPM, Canadian Paranormal Monitor. They always maintained a degree of separation from IPCA because they were uncomfortable with an international organization having rights to their citizens. He'd been tracking IPCA activity, and with your info he found all the werewolves."

I sat back in my chair. "All of them? And they got the trackers off?"

David nodded happily. Stacey's eyes had gone wide; I couldn't read her expression.

"Where are they going to go?" They couldn't go back to their old lives—IPCA had records on all of them. They'd be retagged in no time.

"Some of them are going to be folded in as CPMs, hidden right under IPCA's nose. Another busload just arrived in town so we can get them new identities and then help them settle somewhere."

"Here?" Stacey whispered. "What about—"

The doorbell rang. Stacey turned toward the entry, her

face as white as a sheet.

Lend, puzzled, got up to answer the door. After a few seconds he came back in. With Charlotte.

"Charlotte!" I said, shocked. Stacey stood up and burst into tears, throwing her arms around Charlotte's neck.

"I'm so sorry!" Stacey sobbed, burying her face in Charlotte's shoulder. "I never should have said those things— never should have— I'm sorry."

Tears spilled down my former tutor's face, too, and she pulled Stacey in closer and stroked her hair. "It's okay. Really, it's okay. I'm sorry, too."

That's when it clicked, why Stacey looked so familiar. This, then, was the family member Charlotte had attacked and felt so guilty about she'd tried to kill herself.

David and Arianna stood; Lend and I followed them out to give the sisters some privacy. Guilt twisted, sharp and gnawing in my stomach. I knew none of it was my fault. I hadn't turned Charlotte into a monster, hadn't made her bite her sister. I hadn't personally separated them when they needed each other the most. But then again, I'd helped IPCA every step of the way.

"So, any other news?" Arianna asked, lighting a cigarette as we gathered on the porch.

"You know I don't like you smoking those things," David said, frowning.

"Yeah, 'cause they might kill me?" She grinned bitterly, but put it out.

David sighed. "The news isn't good. IPCA lost another center."

"Which one?" I asked, fear tightening my throat.

"Bucharest."

Bucharest, so mostly vampires. I was instantly relieved, and then felt even guiltier. Would I have been relieved if Arianna were one of the victims?

"At least Bucharest is far away," she muttered.

"The attacks are getting worse. I'm going to send as many of the paranormals away as I can. It's not safe anymore, having such a high concentration here. We don't know how she's finding these places; we can't take any risks."

"What about everyone who stays?" Lend asked.

"We'll make do. It seems like she's got some sort of target on IPCA, so hopefully we'll stay under the radar. In the meantime, my contacts are going to smuggle out as many tagged paranormals as they can and filter them through us."

"What's IPCA doing?" I asked. Surely they were doing something more to protect themselves and the paranormals.

"Near as I can tell, running around like a chicken with its head cut off," David said with a sigh. "They're trying to work in some emergency plans, get things moving, but they've always been the bully, never the victim. They don't know how to handle it."

"What can we do?" Lend asked.

"You can go inside and do your homework."

Lend looked ready to protest, but David silenced him with a raised hand. "None of this is your problem. Inside, homework, now."

I followed Lend, sitting by him on the couch as he glowered at his calculus book. I knew he was frustrated, but I was with David on this one. If IPCA couldn't do anything, who could? The best we could do was protect paranormals and hide.

Hearing the murmurs from the kitchen made me nervous. I didn't know what to say to Charlotte, what I could possibly do to make up for what had been done to her. What I had been a part of.

After about an hour she came out with Stacey and Luke, along with a couple of suitcases. Stacey gave me a tight smile as she walked out, but Charlotte stopped. I stood awkwardly, staring at the ground.

"Charlotte, I didn't know about— I'm so sorry."

She put her hand on my shoulder and I looked up. Her warm blue eyes sparkled over her yellow wolf ones. "Please don't apologize. We're both free now. Enjoy it." She leaned in and pecked me on the cheek, then left, giving me one last smile. For once, it had no trace of sadness at all.

HEY, STUPID

I was relieved later when Lend finally shut his books; I'd had too much time to sit there, stewing over lost friends, werewolves, and Fire Girl's escalating attacks. I was tired of feeling guilty and scared.

"Want to watch a movie or something?"

I enthusiastically agreed, and we scanned through the channels, debating the merits of various movies they had on demand. Settling on a romantic comedy (yeah, I totally won the debate), I snuggled into the couch while Lend made popcorn. When he came back, he sat down so we were touching.

Just after the opening credits, he took my hand and wove his fingers through mine. I knew from the triumphant, happy flips my stomach was doing that, this time, we were holding hands for real. And it was the best thing ever.

Have I mentioned how amazing Lend's skin was? Unbelievably soft and smooth. And his hand was so warm, it felt wonderful. Not weird, creeping-up-my-arm warmth like Reth, just nice, very-normal warm. Tingly and happy-all-over warm. Over-the-moon, I'm-holding-hands-with-a-super-cute-guy-who's-taking-me-to-the-prom warm.

He stroked the top of my thumb with his. "Is this okay?" he whispered. I loved that he actually sounded nervous.

I snuggled into his side more, squeezing his hand and laying my head on his shoulder. "Yeah." I smiled so big I thought my face would break. "It's okay." He let out a relieved breath and rested his head on the top of mine.

When the movie was almost over (best movie ever—no idea what it was, though, didn't really care) Lend's dad came into the room. I quickly lifted up my head, but Lend didn't move. After a second of taking in the scene, David smiled. "I'm headed to bed. Don't stay up too late, it's a school night."

"Okay, Dad, good night."

"Good night," I added. That had gone well. I put my head back on Lend's shoulder, never wanting the movie to end.

I guess Lend felt the same way, because when the credits

rolled he said, "Want to watch another one?"

"Yeah!" Did I ever.

He picked another movie, then pulled a throw blanket from the side of the couch and put it over our legs. The last few weeks had been so strange, so scary, that this little piece of wonderful normal was the best thing that had ever happened to me.

Halfway into the movie my eyes drifted shut. When I opened them the light in the room was different. I couldn't put my finger on it until I realized it was brighter, warmer—and not coming from the TV. I lifted my head. Vivian was sitting in the armchair, watching the movie. Her golden sphere of flames floated tantalizingly behind her.

"What are you doing?" I hissed. I looked over at Lend; he was staring at the TV, oblivious. Then I glared at Vivian again. "You shouldn't be here!"

She rolled her eyes, slouching down and propping her feet on the coffee table. "Relax, I'm not."

I frowned. "Oh. I'm asleep."

"Duh?"

"This is so stupid. You aren't real."

She raised her eyebrows. "I'm not? Ouch. Here I thought we were finally connecting."

"You're just my brain trying to make sense of everything that happened."

"Wow. Okay." She smiled, a mischievous glint in her pale eyes. "How about I prove it to you? You still have that phone thingie from IPCA?" ·

"I don't know." I didn't like where this was going.

"Find it, take a look at your messages."

Nerves gnawed at my stomach. This was ridiculous—it was a dream. "If you were real, I'd be totally scared right now."

"Why?"

"Because you're crazy and you run around killing people?"

"I don't kill people."

"You killed Lish and Jacques and all those vamps!"

"Yeah, last time I checked—not people."

"Whatever. And can you move your stupid glowy thing? It hurts my eyes." Truth was, I just wanted to look at it. If Lend's hand hadn't been firmly anchoring me to the couch, I would have gone over to it already.

She laughed. "You're so weird. Didn't you already get more?"

"No! I don't want any." My eyes lingering on the brilliant mass probably gave away the lie.

"Well, you're brighter than you were before. I thought you figured it out."

I looked down. My shirt was gone, and I was sitting there in my bra. Sure enough, my heart was even brighter. "That's weird," I said, both about the missing shirt and the brighter flames. I looked at Lend, panicked about my near nudity, but he was still staring at the TV. I turned back to Vivian. "I didn't do anything. And I know Reth hasn't been around."

Vivian shrugged. She kept her eyes on the movie. "You can't keep going on your own forever, you know."

"What do you mean?"

"I mean, you're already on borrowed time. When they made you, they only gave you a little bit."

"Wait—*made* me?" Reth had said the same thing. "You mean our parents? Did you know them?"

"So you still don't think I'm real, but you want me to answer questions? Face it, you know it's true. Anyway, what makes you think we had parents?"

I frowned, fighting panic. "Don't be stupid. Of course we did. How else could we be sisters?"

"We're two of a kind. I figure that makes us related, right?"

"Fine, Miss Two-of-a-Kind, what are we, then?"

"The Empty Ones. Didn't they tell you anything?"

"Who?" I was almost shouting now. She was so frustrating, and the temptation of the flames behind her grated on my nerves. I wanted them.

"No wonder you're so confused. What, did your faeries lose you as a baby or something?" She saw my blank look and laughed. "They did! Oh, that's rich. Gotta love faeries. Idiots. Here the court has been trying to pit me against you in some sort of epic showdown and you don't know a thing."

"I thought you didn't know any faeries."

"No, I said I'd never taken any soul from a faerie. They don't let me touch them—they're not *that* stupid. Anyway, what I'm saying is, who cares about them? They're always trying to meddle, fix things to line up with their stupid little poems. You and me, we're what matters. So screw the fey, let's be a family." She smiled at me, her face both tender and slightly manic.

What was she talking about? Had she been raised by faeries? And why wouldn't her dumb flames stop swirling around, drawing me in?

"I don't know." I closed my eyes. "I don't get anything you're saying. And I don't like what you're doing."

"Grow up, Evie. You'd better figure it out if you want to stay alive."

"Are you going to kill me, then?" I opened my eyes and glared at her.

"No, stupid. You're going to kill yourself if you don't get with the picture. I'm bored. I'm gonna go now. But check your communicator, then give me a call. We'll hang out—conscious, next time." She smiled at me, then the golden flames were sucked back into her. I shielded my eyes against her light, tearing up. I didn't know if it was from how bright the flames were or how much I wanted them to stay. To come to me, to make me warm.

"Evie?"

"What?" I opened my eyes and squinted against the

expected light. There wasn't anything—not even the glow of the TV.

"We should probably go to bed," Lend whispered. "I think you fell asleep."

"Oh, yeah." I shook my head, trying to get the insidious dream out of my mind.

"Are you okay?"

"What? Oh, yeah, I'm okay." I squeezed his hand, forcing a smile. "Really okay."

I wanted nothing more than to walk upstairs with Lend, maybe even kiss, but I couldn't get the dream out of my head. I bid him a quick good night to cover up my nerves and went to my room. When I took my shirt off, I risked looking down. It was probably just the power of suggestion, but my heart looked brighter. Frustrated, knowing it was dumb and feeling guilty, I waited until I heard Lend's door shut, then sneaked back downstairs to the kitchen.

I was sure my communicator wouldn't be in there, sure that David would be suspicious enough to hide it, but I looked around anyway. And then, in a drawer filled with kitchen supplies, there it was.

I pulled it out. "This is ridiculous," I whispered. There wasn't going to be anything weird there, because there wasn't anything real about those dreams. I looked at the screen. Twelve new messages were flashing. The top one had come in about two minutes ago, from Raquel's communicator. None from Vivian—Vivian who was not real, a figment of my imagination, not actually Fire Girl. I shook my head, relieved. Then, hit with a sudden pang, I missed Raquel. I wouldn't respond because that would give away my location, but I wanted to see what she was writing, make sure she was okay. I opened the message.

I shouldn't have.

"Hey, Stupid," it said. "Where do you want to meet? Love, Vivian."

WHAT YOU DON'T KNOW

I dropped the communicator like it had burned my hands. It was real—I was connected to everything, to Vivian. Why didn't I pay more attention when she said what we were? And she said I was dying, or I was going to die, or . . .

I sat and put my head down on the table. This was so, so bad. So unbelievably bad. Not only did crazy paranormal killer know way more than I did *and* could sneak into my head, she also seemed to think we should be together. And the faeries were involved, of course.

What the bleep was I?

My earliest memories were of the foster system. The police had found me wandering naked and alone in a park when I was three years old. They never found any leads, so I became a ward of the state. What if— What if I didn't have parents to begin with? Where did I come from?

"She's delusional," I whispered to myself, forehead pressed against the wood of the table. "She's crazy. We're not the same."

"Evie?" I sat straight up, shocked and scared. Lend's dad was standing in the entry to the kitchen. "Couldn't sleep?"

"No, no, I couldn't sleep." I wondered if I should tell him. But he liked me, trusted me. What would they do if they found out that this thing they were terrified of was my sister? That I might be the exact same thing as her? My eyes filled with tears. Why couldn't I just be normal?

"Yeah, me neither." He got a glass of water and sat down at the table across from me.

"I have a question." I wondered how I could get answers without giving anything away. If David even had any answers. I had a feeling I knew more than anyone else here now, which wasn't saying much. "Reth knew the words to that poem thing about Vi—about the girl that's doing this. Is it some sort of faerie prophecy?"

"He knew about it? Interesting." David looked thoughtful. "Is Reth Seelie or Unseelie?"

"What?" Yet another thing I didn't know. Great.

"There are two types of faeries—two courts. The Seelie

and the Unseelie. You didn't learn about that?"

"Never heard a word."

He frowned. "They had you working with faeries but didn't talk about the differences? Did they teach you about faerie lore or magic?"

I shrugged. "Not really. Raquel wouldn't answer many of my questions. She always said that stuff didn't matter as long as we knew their names."

"But they only worked with Seelie faeries, right?"

I shrugged. "I think they took whatever they could get."

He sat back, rubbing his face wearily in the same way Lend did. "Idiots."

"No kidding. So what's the difference?"

"Well, many faeries are more independent and not actively involved with the courts, but they're all divided into two basic groups. The Seelie faeries are the good faeries—good being relative, of course. They still manage to do quite a bit of mischief. But the Unseelie are even worse."

"Oh, he's totally Unseelie then. You saw him. He was the one who brought Fire Girl into the Center, too."

"And he knew about the prophecy. Hmm. I wonder why the fey would be involved. The banshee's insight was obvious since she heralded the deaths." I nodded, pretending like I understood what he was talking about until I remembered Lend said they had gotten the info from a banshee.

"There was something else he mentioned." I bit my lip. Time to lie. "He said something about being empty. That she was an Empty One?" I watched him for any reaction but he looked stumped.

"I don't know. It doesn't ring a bell. Faeries operate on a different level than we do. Long-term planning for us is years; they set things in motion centuries ahead. They meddle with human stuff the most, but all the true immortals are disconnected from our time frames. Take Cresseda." He smiled sadly. "Try getting a straight answer out of her about anything. She just doesn't have the same sense of immediacy that we do. It's like her mind is on a different plane. Still, we take what we can get."

"Yeah." Cresseda! Maybe she could answer my questions. I'd have to wait until the morning since I wouldn't be able to find my way in the dark, but it gave me hope that I could figure some of this out.

There was one more thing, though. Vivian's message had come from Raquel's communicator. I didn't know what that meant, how she had gotten it, but it couldn't be good. "Umm," I said, staring at the table, "I know that you probably don't like her, but Raquel"—my voice caught saying her name—"was always pretty good to me. And I'm worried that she might be . . . Did you find out anything yet?"

David smiled, patting me on the shoulder as he stood. "I was going to tell you in the morning. I know for a fact that Raquel is alive and well."

"Really?" I looked up at him, tears of relief in my eyes.

As much as she had frustrated and disappointed me, she was the closest I had to family. Knowing she was safe felt like a huge weight had been lifted from my chest. "Could you—" I wanted to send her a message. Something, anything to let her know that I was okay.

But she was bound to be disappointed in me. After everything I'd done—losing the trackers that Vivian used to trick her way into the Center, freeing Lend and running instead of following protocol, not coming back now that I was safe—no, she wouldn't be happy to hear from me. And then they'd look for me, too. It was best to leave it alone.

"Could I what?"

"Never mind." I smiled weakly. "I'm just glad she's okay. You're sure?"

"Positive. And now I'm going to try and get some sleep."

"Oh, yeah, me, too."

Several nervous and mind-numbingly long hours later dawn finally came. I was exhausted and angry. I should have lain awake in bed last night because I was too giddy over Lend to sleep—not because I was terrified and paranoid thanks to my creepy sister thing and her little dream visits.

Around seven Lend knocked on my door.

"Yeah?"

He peeked in. Gosh, he was adorable.

"Hey—did you want to come to school with me again? It's only a half day."

"I don't really feel well." I hoped he could see how regretful I was. This was my only chance to see his mom without having to answer questions from Lend or David. I wasn't ready for questions.

"Oh, sure. Slacker. I'll be back before noon." He grinned at me and I felt like the worst person in the world.

"Can't wait," I said, smiling. I listened until I was sure the house was empty, then threw on a jacket. I tucked Tasey into my pocket. Lend and his dad might be satisfied that Cresseda had banished Reth, but I wasn't taking any chances.

The trail seemed shorter this time, probably because I was nervous about what Cresseda would say. Plus, every cracked twig made me jump, certain that Reth—or worse, Vivian—was going to come sauntering out of the trees.

When I reached the edge of the pond, I stopped, flummoxed. I had no idea how to get her to come up. Lend had skipped a rock, but I couldn't do that to save my life. Frowning, I picked up a likely looking candidate and imitated his expert wrist flick. I was rewarded with a very ungraceful splosh. No skipping at all. I tried again; no luck. This was going to be a long morning. After lobbing in another four rocks, I was ready to give up, when the center of the pond started churning.

Cresseda formed in front of me. The frost was nearly gone and she was much closer this time.

"Oh, umm, hi."

"Evelyn," she said in her melodic stream of a voice.

"I was wondering if you could maybe answer some questions for me?"

She looked at me, grave and sad. "As I said, yours is not a path of the waters. Yours is a path of spirit and fire."

"Yeah, but do you know what an Empty One is?"

"You are an Empty One."

Okay, not so helpful. "Yes, but what *is* that? What does that mean?"

"That has not been determined. You have yet to choose, and you are not filled."

My voice caught, tears stinging my eyes. "What if I don't want to be filled?"

"We cannot change our nature." As if to demonstrate, she smiled sadly and held out her hand to me. I reached out, hesitant, and touched it. My hand went right through.

"I don't want to be anything." The tears started in earnest. "I don't want to be like her, like Vivian. I don't want to hurt anyone. Am I going to hurt people?"

"No one can make you do that, child. You are caught between two worlds, much like my own Lend. You will want the fire, you will want to be filled. It is your nature. I hope you do not fall, but she is much stronger than you are."

She smiled at me, reaching out as though she would wipe away my tears. "Cling to what is good in your life. Be good to my son." Then the water tumbled down, losing its form as she returned to the pond.

I walked back, feeling very cold and alone. She hadn't given me much to go on. I still didn't understand what the Empty Ones were or why I was one. I was depressed, wondering if I shouldn't just go find Vivian right now. She seemed to be the only one who knew what was happening.

But then I thought about what Cresseda had said—Lend and I were the same, stuck between two worlds. And even though she knew what I was, she didn't try to kill me, or tell me to stay away from her son. My step lightened as I dwelt on that. Cresseda didn't think I was dangerous, and I would take what I could get. The rest of the Vivian and faerie crap could play itself out without me. I didn't care.

Okay, I cared a lot and was still worrying obsessively over it, but I wasn't going to get involved. My connection with Vivian didn't matter. I wasn't like her; I didn't care about being empty. The only things I wanted to fill me were happy thoughts of holding Lend's hand.

LIAR, LIAR,
WRIST ON FIRE

My eyes flew open in panic—the whole world was shaking. Lend laughed, still jumping on the end of the bed. I grabbed my pillow and threw it at him. He caught it and sat cross-legged on the bed, facing me.

"Lazy," he said.

I sat up, narrowing my eyes. "Hey, this is the first vacation I've had since I was eight. Give me a break."

"Fine. But school was boring without you there. No one was freaking out over the lockers or anything."

"They're all fools."

He looked down at the bedspread. "I was wondering

if you wanted to hang out with some people tonight? A bunch of my friends are going to go out for pizza."

I sat up even straighter. "Oh, my gosh, like a real date? With real teenagers?"

"I'm afraid so."

I threw myself across the bed and wrapped my arms around his neck. "It's like a dream come true!"

He put his arms around my back. "You're really easy to keep happy, you know that?"

"But—oh no!" I pulled back so I could look at him; he didn't move his arms. "You're grounded! Are you gonna climb out the window and steal a car?"

"Yes, because I'm insane and this is one of your television shows. I already asked my dad. He said it was okay."

"Gosh, harsh disciplinarian, huh?"

"I think he's glad I'm finally doing normal things. He always worried that I was too isolated."

I smiled, sad that I didn't have anyone worrying about whether I was social enough in my life. I mean, sure, Raquel worried whether or not I died, or if my French homework was done (maybe not in that order), but as far as emotional stuff, she was always kind of distant. I hoped David knew what he was talking about when he said she was okay.

"What?"

"What do you mean what?"

"You're worried about something."

I looked into his real eyes, trying to smile. I didn't want

to talk about Raquel right now. I knew I should, but it was easier to focus on the happy stuff, which definitely didn't include wondering how Vivian had gotten Raquel's communicator. "I worry about a lot of things lately."

"Can I help?"

"Maybe. We'll talk about it later, okay? I've got a date to get ready for."

"It's gonna take you three hours to get ready?"

"I don't know. My date's pretty freaking hot—I'd better look good."

He laughed, letting go of me and climbing off the bed. "Yeah, mine too. Maybe I should change?" He shimmered, switching to blond hair and blue eyes. "What do you think? Does this face make me look fat?"

I laughed. "Maybe go Asian tonight?"

He shimmered again, switching to the cute Chinese boy. "Better?"

"Hmm. I don't know, not quite my taste."

"What's your taste?" His voice shifted with every different form he took. It bothered me, as usual.

"I like guys the color of water."

He looked down at the ground. "You really like the way I look? It doesn't, I don't know, freak you out?"

I stood, putting my hand on the side of his face and concentrating so that I could see under his glamour. "I *really* like the way you look. None of these faces you wear compare."

He gave me a nervous frown. Then he shimmered and

the color drained out, leaving just him. I hadn't seen him like this since he was unconscious. I forgot how amazing it was. I smiled, keeping my hand on his face. The texture had changed—it was even softer and smoother, if that was possible. "There you are." If I focused on his eyes I could make out his whole face in my peripheral vision; it was when I tried to look at anything else that it seemed to slip away.

"Here I am," he said softly—in his real voice. It was like his mother's, but richer and with more of a human tone to it, making it far warmer and more familiar. Just like slipping into a steaming bath when you were cold all over; I couldn't imagine a better voice.

"I think you should know," I said, pretending to frown, "I'm not going to be happy with your other voices now that I've heard the real one."

He laughed and I went weak in the knees. Reth spreading his warmth through me was nothing compared to how I felt about Lend, how that laugh made me feel.

"You're kind of incredible, you know that, Evie?"

"I kind of figured." Grinning mischievously at him, I moved my hand from his face and wrapped both my arms around the back of his neck.

He put one of his hands behind my back, pulling me in closer, then traced his fingers along my jaw. I was on the verge of hyperventilating, almost scared now that the kiss I'd dreamed of for so long seemed like it was going to happen.

Our lips were only a few inches apart. Then his face went serious, and our lips weren't any inches apart at all.

I closed my eyes, melting in. His lips—oh, bleep, his lips—just when I thought his skin was the softest thing ever. And warm like you wouldn't believe. I felt like I was floating: I couldn't believe I was there, kissing Lend, and it was the best kiss ever.

After a few seconds I wondered if I was supposed to be doing anything else. I'd never done this before. Lend must have been thinking the same thing, because he slowly moved his lips. I answered with mine, and we stood there in his room, figuring out how to kiss.

It was absolutely amazing.

I could have done that all day. How on earth had I never kissed before? After what seemed like forever and no time at all, we pulled apart. Lend looked at me.

"Are you sure that was your first kiss?" he asked in his wonderful voice, eyeing me in mock suspicion.

"Wasn't it yours?" Oh no. What if I was doing it wrong?

He laughed. "Yeah. But I'd kinda like to do it again . . ."

I answered by leaning in and positively smashing my mouth against his.

We were really getting the hang of it when a knock made us jump apart. "Doors open, please," Lend's dad called through the shut door.

"Um, yeah, sorry, Dad," Lend said. Pigment rushed back into him, and he settled into his normal hottie appearance.

Opening the door, he grinned. "Just telling her about tonight."

"For the last forty-five minutes?" David raised his eyebrows. Holy crap, had it really been that long? I blushed from head to toe but Lend laughed. "Why don't you two come and talk about it downstairs?"

"Sure." Lend held out his hand for me and I took it, still embarrassed. I spent the next couple of hours in giddy impatience. I kept remembering that we had kissed—I had been kissed!—and the giddiness set in anew.

Finally it was time for us to go. Lend seemed more relaxed and happier than ever on the drive, joking around about making me pick up the tab for the date.

The pizza place was great—packed and noisy, with dim lighting and bench tables. John, a lanky red-haired guy I recognized from school, waved to us from a table in the back near some arcade games. There were five other kids, a couple of whom I had met.

A girl I didn't know beamed at Lend, way too excited to see him. Pretty, with dark hair and too much makeup. I didn't like the way she looked at him, or the way she leaned forward, using her low-cut shirt to its full advantage. I shifted closer to Lend and wished we were holding hands. Still, I'd dealt with predators she couldn't imagine in her darkest nightmares. I wasn't intimidated. Much.

"Lend, you're back!" she said. "I'm so glad, I was really worried about you! You must have been so sick! I tried to bring you cookies, but your dad said you were contagious."

"Yup, feeling better now." Lend smiled politely.

The girl hadn't so much as glanced at me. It was like she was trying to make me disappear by the sheer force of her determined ignoring. Finally, when she realized that Lend wasn't going to say anything else, she looked at me with a thin smile.

"Who's this?"

"I'm Evie."

"Hi! I'm Carlee. Are you guys cousins or something?" She looked way too hopeful as she said this.

I turned to Lend, looking at his black hair and dark brown eyes. "Wow, I had no idea we looked that much alike."

"So you are!" she said, almost laughing with relief. I felt bad.

"Nope, not related at all," Lend said. "Evie just moved to the area."

Her face fell. Poor thing. She was a trooper though, I'd give her that. She plastered on a bright smile. "That's so great!"

We sat down and Lend put his arm around me. Every single jaw at the table dropped.

"Man," John said, shaking his head. "All this time I was pretty sure you were gay."

I batted my eyes innocently. "I'm sorry, John. Are you disappointed?" Everyone laughed, and John grinned.

"Maybe a little," he answered, scooting into Lend's free side to cuddle up.

"Oh, get off me." Lend shoved him off the bench. After that, I was part of the group. Me! Part of the group! I thought yesterday had been the best day of my life, but today beat it by a million. At school I had been an observer, but here I was really hanging out, accepted.

There was nothing special about it (besides Lend, who I liked more than I dared admit). But with these ridiculous, clueless teenagers, I felt at home. Sure, I jumped every time a blond girl passed my peripheral vision and got cold chills when I thought I saw someone who looked like Reth, but no one noticed how twitchy I was. I reassured myself with Tasey's familiar bulk in my purse and the heavy weight of the iron knuckles in my pocket. Things were going to be fine.

As the evening progressed Carlee seemed to get over her disappointment and flirted up a storm with John, which was a relief. "You've got really pretty hair," she said when John got up to play a game.

"Oh, thanks!" I said, genuinely pleased. "I love your necklace."

She smiled and, with Lend's arm around me and the growing hope that I'd have friends, I was elated. There was no pressure, no one to report to, nothing that I needed to do.

For the first time ever, I was just a teenager.

Rather than go right in when we got home, we walked a

little way into the trees. He was amazing in the dark—there was definitely a luminescence about him. My wrist was like an open flame, but I ignored it as Lend's color melted away and we kissed until my hands were so cold they hurt. When my teeth started chattering, he pulled away and laughed. "Okay, time to go in."

He put his arm around me as we walked to the house. "Evie?"

"Hmm?"

"I'm just— I'm glad we can be ourselves with each other. It feels like I can be totally honest with you. I've never had that before."

My stomach sank. *He* was finally being honest. But what was I doing, hanging out with normal teenagers, pretending I could be one of them? Lend showed me exactly who he was, but he had no idea what I was.

Suddenly the whole day felt less like the best one of my life and more like the biggest lie I'd ever told.

SO ALONE TOGETHER

Lend and I were out in the woods again, kissing. It was nighttime, but I could see perfectly.

"Wow," Vivian said, and I looked at her, then back at Lend and me. Seeing us kiss from farther away made me sad for some reason, like it wasn't me anymore. Like it never was to begin with. "Look at you two go."

I shrugged, uncomfortable standing there watching myself make out with Lend. "I really like him."

"Obviously." She frowned. "What *is* he?"

"None of your business, that's what he is."

"No, seriously, he's different."

"Yup. And mine."

Vivian laughed. "Oh, chill out. I won't try to steal your little boyfriend. I won't have to."

"What's that supposed to mean?" I glared at her.

"Do you really think he's going to stay with you when he finds out what you are?" She didn't say it cruelly. In fact, she looked sorry for me.

"He likes me," I said, realizing how pathetic it sounded.

"You're not what he thinks you are. You're not one of them. You can pretend—pretend to be normal, pretend to be paranormal, but it never matters in the end. We aren't anything." Her face was empty.

"Why do you do it?" I asked softly. "Why do you kill them?"

"I'm not killing them! I'm letting them go."

"You don't have to kill them."

She looked at me, her pale eyes deep with sorrow. "It's what we are, Evie. It's what we're supposed to do. Let them go, release them. They don't belong here. And if I didn't take their souls, I'd die."

"You're really pulling out their souls?"

She shrugged. "Souls, spirits, life energy, whatever. It takes a huge amount of energy to sustain life, and paranormals live a long, long time. That's what I take. I figure it's a win-win situation. They finally get a ticket out of this miserable, cold world, and I get what I need to keep going."

"But I don't do that, and I'm not dead or dying."

She raised an eyebrow. "You're brighter again today. Either that faerie's been visiting, or you've been getting it somewhere else. We don't have our own souls, Evie."

"I have a soul," I said, desperate.

"We're both Empty Ones—like little, hollow china dolls. We can't keep going on our own. When we were made, they only gave us a little bit. Such a very little bit. Even humans have brighter souls than we do, and they have such a pathetic amount it's not even worth noticing. Didn't you wonder why you're always so cold? Why you always feel alone?"

I looked down at the ground, unwilling to meet her eyes. "I really don't have a soul?"

"Not your own. And I don't know how long you can last unless you start doing what you were made to. But, Evie, listen to me." She reached out and took my hand in her equally cold one. I looked up at her. Her eyes were shining, bright, intense. "It's amazing. It really is. That flood, that fire as it rushes in—you've never felt anything so wonderful in your whole life. It's like you're finally alive, and you're not alone. You've got all those spirits inside you, and you're not alone! And I keep them. I treasure each and every soul I've been given. They're mine, and I love them, and they keep me warm."

For the first time I noticed the golden flames behind her. Now I understood what they were. It should have made me sad, but I wanted them more than ever before. I didn't want to be empty.

"I'm supposed to kill you." Her voice was low and serious. "All their stupid prophecies, they want me to get rid of you before you figure out what you can do. And I could. Kill you, I mean. You don't understand anything. You don't even know how to take the souls, and I've got so much power now." She looked thoughtful. I wanted to run, but she was so still and had my hand in hers. "But I don't want to. The stupid fey, they think they know everything, they think they can control me. I'm tired of them and I'm tired of being alone. We're family. We should be together, you know?"

I didn't know what to say. How do you respond when someone tells you how easy it would be to kill you, then says she wants to be best friends, family?

"I can't find you." Her gaze intensified. "Even the faeries that are helping me can't find you. Tell me where you are."

The souls moved closer, dazzling me with their blinding beauty. She could teach me how to get my own. I opened my mouth, and then I heard Lend laugh. Looking over, I watched us. His arms were around me, his mouth close to my ear. "I'm with him," I whispered, pulling away from Vivian.

She looked hurt, then her mouth curled into a cruel smile. "Sure. Tell him what you are and let me know if you're still with him. You'll see. I'm the only one you have. The only one."

She drew the flames into herself again, so bright and terribly beautiful I started crying.

When I woke up I was still crying. It was just turning light outside, but I'd never get back to sleep. I sat up and pulled my knees to my chest, wrapping my arms around them. She was right. I was empty. I was alone and cold, and I'd always known it. I pulled out the neck of my T-shirt and looked down. My wrist hadn't changed since Reth burned me, but my heart had definitely gotten a little brighter.

And then I had a thought. A horrible, horrible thought. What if I had been sucking life and energy from Lend? What if I was killing him? I finally got a boyfriend, I was pretty sure I loved him, and here I was, stealing his soul.

I had to leave, run away to somewhere where I couldn't hurt anyone, especially not Lend. But after how he opened up to me, how much he trusted me, I owed him more than that. Trying not to cry, I padded across the hall to the room he was staying in. Lend was asleep, almost invisible, sprawled out and tangled in the blankets. He looked adorable. It broke my heart. Next to him on the bedside table was his open sketchbook.

Tiptoeing over, I saw in the pale dawn light what he had been working on. It was a portrait of me, probably one he had started in art class. I was in this sassy pose, holding

Tasey and giving this awesome *I rock!* look to all the world. Lend drew me the way he saw me, and I was beautiful.

I totally started bawling. Lend sat up, startled awake, and color flooded into him. "Evie? What's wrong?"

I shook my head; I could barely see him through my tears. "I think I'm killing you."

PINK, SHINY LOVE

Lend looked confused. "You think you're killing me?"

"I just— Vivian said— And I'm getting brighter, and—"

"Calm down." Lend scooted over and patted the bed next to him. Sniffling, I sat down, careful not to touch him. "What are you talking about?"

"I know who's doing this. Her name is Vivian and she's my sister—sort of, I guess? She said we're not really sisters, but we're the same thing."

"When did you talk to her?" He sounded surprised and nervous.

"Last night. And a couple of other nights. While I was

sleeping, in my dreams."

He tried not to smile. "So you've been dreaming that this thing is your sister?"

"No." I shook my head. "I thought they were just dreams, thought I was going crazy because I was worried, but then she told me she'd send me a message and she did, on my communicator. It's downstairs in the kitchen in a drawer. I found it, I'm sorry."

Lend frowned. "Seriously?"

I nodded, wishing it weren't true.

"Wow. So what has she been telling you?"

"It's kind of confusing. But she says we're the same thing, that we weren't born, we were made. That we're empty, and she said—" I started crying again "—I don't have a soul. I'm just empty and cold like her, and that's why she takes the souls. To fill herself up. But she thinks she's doing a good thing, setting the paranormals free from this world. Her souls are always there, glowing and beautiful, and she said the faeries want her to kill me, but she wants us to be a family."

Lend was quiet; so quiet. I waited for him to shout for his dad, to back away in terror.

"She says that if I don't start taking these souls, the energy, that I'll die, since I don't have a soul of my own. But I don't want to! And, Lend, I'm so sorry, but I've been getting brighter, my heart, and—what if I'm taking *your* soul? When we touch, kiss?" I could barely talk I was crying so hard now. "I don't want to hurt you. I'm so, so sorry."

He sat motionless for a long time. Then, to my shock, he reached out and took my hand. I tried to pull back. "No! I don't want to hurt you!"

"Evie," he said, his voice tender and serious. He held my hand tighter. "Do you really think that's true? Even if this Vivian is who you think she is, why would she tell you the truth?"

I shook my head. "I don't know. It makes sense. Why else would we look the same? And the glowing? And I've always felt cold and empty."

He reached out and put his hand on my chin, forcing me to look at him. "You have a soul. That's the dumbest thing I've ever heard. No one as bright and happy and caring as you could not have a soul."

"But what about the glowing? It's getting stronger."

"Do you feel yourself pulling anything out of me? Does it feel like what Reth did to you?"

I frowned, thinking about it. Lend made me warm and happy, but it wasn't the same. Reth's always felt foreign, like something new was being put in. With Lend, it was like he was warming what was already inside me. I shook my head. "But you don't feel weaker?"

He laughed. "Not at all. If anything, I have more energy than ever. And I'm definitely happier than I've ever been."

I couldn't believe it. Here I'd just told him I was a monster, that I was designed to suck souls out of paranormals, and he was okay with it. "But I know I'm the same thing Vivian is. I talked to your mom. She said it was true."

"She talked to you? Wow. She doesn't show up for anyone except me and my dad. Did she think you were going to do anything bad?"

"No. She said that I could make my choices, but she didn't know what would happen."

"Well, there you have it. I don't care if you're the same thing as this Vivian. She's a lunatic. You're not. And, besides, if she's working with the faeries and they want her to kill you, who's to say that anything she's telling you is true? Even if she thinks it is, she could be totally wrong. Or she could be lying, trying to trick you into meeting her so that she can kill you."

"Maybe. I think she was raised by faeries. She knows a bunch of their prophecies and stuff, but she doesn't like them very much." I frowned. "She seems pretty lonely and sad." I couldn't imagine what being raised by faeries would have been like. As weird as my life was, at least I had people who cared about me. I looked at Lend. "You're really not scared of me now?"

He shook his head, letting go of my hand and putting his arm around me to pull me in closer. "Not even a little bit. Just because you don't know what you are doesn't make you scary. I'm pretty familiar with that." He smiled. "Besides, how could I ever be afraid of someone who wears so much pink?"

I laughed, wiping away the last of the tears from my face. I couldn't believe it. Lend was probably the only person in the world who would have reacted this way. "Do you think we should tell your dad?"

He was quiet for a while. "I don't know. You already talked to my mom and she knows way more than my dad about stuff like this. Besides, it's not like it makes any difference. We still don't know where Vivian is or how to stop her. You're safe here—she can't find you. That's what's important. I think if my dad and some of the others knew it would . . . make them nervous. So there's not really a reason to tell them, is there?"

I shook my head, more relieved than I cared to admit.

"We'll keep this between us. And if Vivian visits you again, or you learn anything else, we'll figure it out together, okay? In the meantime, keep Tasey on you." In spite of his reassurance that Vivian couldn't find me if she hadn't already, his eyes had a tight, worried look. No doubt they mirrored mine. No matter how safe I felt here, she was out there, somewhere, looking for me.

He must have seen it in my face. He squeezed my hand, pulling me in closer. "It's going to be okay. We're in this together."

I was overwhelmed with how wonderful Lend was. I realized then that I didn't feel so cold and empty anymore. It wasn't anything dramatic, just a subtle sense of well-being, of wholeness. "But you'll tell me if you ever feel anything weird when I'm touching you, right?"

"Oh, I feel a lot when you're touching me. But it's not weird."

I grinned, hitting him lightly in the chest. "I'm serious."

"I know. I will—I promise." He kissed my cheek, then looked at the clock. "Umm, you'd probably better get out of my room. It wouldn't be good for my dad to wake up and find us together."

"Oh, yeah, good point." I jumped up so fast I practically fell over. "I'll see you downstairs."

He smiled at me. "Can't wait."

I shut the door to his room and I leaned back against it, closing my eyes. Vivian had been wrong. I wasn't alone.

The rest of the day was wonderful. David had gotten some fake papers made for me and we filled out everything I needed to enroll in school for the fall. I even got a cute new last name, Green. I couldn't remember what I had gone by in the foster system, and it wasn't like I'd needed one at the Center. Still, just seeing a first and last name together made me feel like a real person, like maybe I really could have an identity and a life away from IPCA.

David had also purchased several homeschooling courses so I could continue my studies on my own, since it was so late in the school year there was no way I could catch up in regular courses at the high school. I was kind of bummed about it. It was less time with Lend and more time without a locker of my own. But now that I had a future to look forward to, I was a lot more eager to get good grades. I had to get into whatever college Lend went to, after all. If that meant more homework for me, well, that's what I'd do.

Besides the studying, Lend's dad needed help with the extra paranormals. Word had spread not only of his underground aid but also of the killings. Directed by David's IPCA contacts, paranormals were steadily trickling into town; he either transferred them to another location or found places to put them here.

All the paranormals I met were totally jumpy, trading whispered rumors about where the latest killings had taken place. Lend had to constantly turn into Vivian to show them what she looked like. It was more than a little creepy watching the boy I liked turn into the girl I was terrified of.

I also worried about what that many paranormals in one spot could do, but Lend told me it worked better. They policed themselves, and if anyone broke the rules— like, say, drinking human blood—the others would turn that one in. Nobody wanted to attract the attention of IPCA or Vivian.

I appreciated what David was doing and was happy to help with arranging things, but his lack of organization and records made me nervous. Here he was, setting up vampires with fake identities and sending them to new towns to live in with no way of knowing what they were going to do there. If IPCA was too harsh, David was definitely too trusting, in my opinion.

But no one was asking my opinion.

That afternoon, after finishing the last of the day's werewolf processing, Lend mentioned to his dad that we were going to prom together. You'd think David was the one going, he was so excited. He insisted we go to the mall immediately. I didn't argue. Lend kept laughing at how giddy the rest of us were, even Arianna, who tagged along.

"Oh, come on, you know you love the mall," I said, squeezing his hand as we sat in the backseat. "It's like teenage nirvana!"

"And here I was thinking purgatory."

When we got there, David and Lend split off to look at rental tuxes, while Arianna and I went to check out dresses. I'll admit she wasn't my ideal shopping partner, but she was so thrilled I found myself laughing with her after a few minutes. It balanced out the fact that crowds made me nervous now. Twice I thought I saw Reth out of the corner of my eye, only to grab my new iron knuckles out of my pocket and have it be just some random guy. I wondered if I'd ever be able to relax again.

In our third store, Arianna sighed, browsing through a rack of gowns. "Man, I miss this. I was in fashion design before I, well, died, I guess. I never have figured out how that works. David doesn't know, either." She frowned.

"Yeah, turns out I don't know anything about anything. IPCA wasn't exactly thorough in their paranormal education program."

"It's just weird. I mean, ten years ago I was in school, looking forward to everything to come. And then, bam, suddenly I'm this—this *thing*. And what I can't figure out is, what's the point of it all? Am I really going to be stuck, just sort of existing, for the rest of time? It makes me tired thinking about it, you know?"

I frowned, trying to ignore what Vivian had said about freeing paranormals from this world. "You're doing things," I said.

She shook her head. "Oh, well. Hey, how about this?" She held up a dress. It was floor length, with a shiny, flowing skirt and a strapless sweetheart neckline. And it was pink. Lovely, lovely pink that shined and caught the light just right. I was in love.

IN YOUR DREAMS

Vivian didn't show up again until the week of the prom. I was sitting in one of Lend's classes, but I didn't know anyone. The teacher spoke in another language, I had forgotten how to read, and I was wearing my prom dress with combat boots. Just the promise of school in the fall and I was already having nightmares.

As I frantically tried to decipher the words of a test on a subject I'd never heard of, I looked up. The rest of the students had disappeared. Vivian sat at a desk, giving me a strange look; the souls hovered, shining behind her.

"You're weird," she said.

I looked down at the paper, still nervous that I needed to finish it. "Yeah, I know."

"So, did you tell him yet?" Her small smile was tinged with a hint of smug.

"I did, actually."

"Why haven't you called me then?"

"He didn't care."

Her smile dropped off, replaced by furrowed brows. "He didn't care?"

"Nope. He likes me no matter who or what I am."

She shook her head. "No, you don't understand. You must have lied to him. You keep getting brighter. You figured out how to do it, didn't you? Did you kill him?"

"No, I didn't kill him! I would never. I didn't 'figure it out' either, and I don't want to. I'm happy where I am."

"Oh, I see." Her face went hard and cold. "Lucky Evie. Are they going to take care of you, then? Aren't you just the special one. Friends everywhere."

I shrugged, uncomfortable. "I don't want anything to do with the faeries or with taking souls or any of that. I can be normal here. I want to be normal."

Her face contorted in fury. For a moment I thought she'd attack me. But then her expression changed, and she looked down at the desk, tracing her finger along it. Black marks seared the wood, small trails of smoke rising. "Normal, huh? Wouldn't that be nice, little Evie, normal Evie." She looked up, thoughtful. "I always wanted a nickname.

Faeries aren't real big on affection, you know? A friend or someone who liked me well enough to say, hey, Vivi, or maybe just Viv. I always wondered how that would feel."

Her eyes filled with tears. "You know how long I've waited for you? I was alone for so long, and then they started talking about how the other court made a new one. At first I was jealous, ready to kill you like they said. But then I saw you in Ireland, and I realized, here's someone like me! So I started looking for you. They couldn't find you, but I knew I could, knew I'd be able to get to you. And when I finally found you, you left before we could talk. I'm still alone, and I can't find you again." Her thin shoulders shook. She looked so broken, so sad it made my heart hurt. "It won't last. You can't be normal. Be with me. I'm so tired of being alone. Please, let me find you."

I went to her, trying not to look at the souls, telling myself I didn't want them. I stroked her hand. "I'm sorry. I'm so sorry."

She looked up at me and I saw the fire burning behind her eyes. "Then come with me."

"I—" I started to tell her no but she grabbed my wrist, her hands like a vise.

"I'll find you," she whispered, smiling.

My eyes flew open and I sat up in bed. Not good. So not good.

It was still dark, but I went silently over to Lend's room. He was dreaming, flickering through different people. I climbed onto the bed, lying down next to him but on top of the covers. "Lend," I whispered. He didn't move, so I said it again, a little louder. "Lend."

His eyes popped open, his face shifting from a random older man to his usual form. "Evie?"

"I had another visit."

"Oh." He stared at me for a while, frowning. "Oh," he said again, shaking his head. "Sorry, what time is it?"

"Late. Early. Sorry."

"No, it's okay. You had another dream with Vivian?"

"Yeah."

"What did she say?"

"She said I was getting brighter." I looked at him, worried and nervous.

"Well, my soul's still completely in place. She's manipulating you."

I nodded, even though my quick, nervous checks every day in the shower made me pretty sure she was right. Even Lend had commented the other night that my hands weren't as cold as usual.

"Anything else?"

"She was mad that I haven't told her where I am. She's really sad. She's so lonely." I felt horrible remembering the look in her eyes. "She said she'll find me even though I told her I didn't want her to."

"She hasn't found you yet."

"No, and she seemed really frustrated. That big killing

spree she went on, I think it was about me. Finding me. I bet her faeries knew I was working for IPCA. They must have figured sooner or later it'd draw me out. And then when she saw me after she killed the hag—" I paused, thinking about it. "I don't think she'd made up her mind yet. She might have still been trying to kill me when she broke into the Center. But now she wants us to, I don't know, hang out. Kill paranormals together. Family bonding time."

"Shouldn't faeries be able to find you really easily?" He looked worried.

I shrugged against the pillow. "I don't know. Maybe it's because I've been carrying around bread like your dad said? Or something your mom's doing? I have no idea why they haven't been able to find me. But I'm really worried—what if she comes here? What if she hurts you? Or Arianna, or Nona, or any of the other paranormals? I'm putting everyone in danger. It would be my fault, and I don't think I'd ever be able to forgive myself."

Lend shook his head. "You aren't responsible for anything that she does. And I really think that if she hasn't found you yet, she isn't going to."

We kept saying that, and the more times I heard it, the better it sounded, but that didn't settle the nagging worry bubbling in my stomach. Could I really just hang out, hiding in a small Virginian town forever?

I wouldn't mind.

But I still couldn't forget how sad she was. "I never thought I'd be grateful for my childhood, but poor Vivian. I know she's crazy and a killer, but she's never had anyone. Ever. I wish there was some way I could help her, you know?"

"I know. But you've got to remember she was raised by faeries. Everything she tells you is probably a lie."

I smiled wanly, but I knew he was wrong. You couldn't fake that kind of pain and loneliness. He didn't understand—he'd always had someone. I wondered what I would be like if I had been raised by faeries. It made me shudder.

"So, umm, were you planning on spending the rest of the night in here?" he asked, raising an eyebrow.

I narrowed my eyes, trying not to smile. "In your dreams."

He laughed. "Well then, let me go to sleep so I can get back to them."

Shaking my head, I leaned in and kissed him quickly on the lips, then, already missing him, went back to my room. I wouldn't have minded spending the night in there, but I wanted to take it slow and figured sleeping in the same bed wasn't a really smart idea. After all, I'd seen it time and time again on *Easton Heights*—when the couples hooked up too soon it never ended well. Plus, I didn't think his dad would like it very much and I wasn't about to push my luck.

It took a long time for me to fall asleep again.

• • •

The next morning Lend went to school. I stayed home, like I did most days, to work on my schoolwork and study for the SATs. It was so bizarre I wanted to laugh. While Vivian and her faeries plotted my destruction, I sat at the counter memorizing vocabulary words. Normal was stranger than paranormal sometimes.

"How's it going?" David asked, fixing himself a sandwich for lunch.

"I have a question if you've got a minute."

"It's been a long time since I studied for that thing, but I'll try to help."

"Oh, no, not about the test. I was just wondering, kind of worrying actually. About faeries. How do they find you? I mean, like if some of the IPCA faeries were looking for me, would they know where I was?"

"I don't think so. I know if faeries have some sort of connection, something of yours, usually an important possession or part of your body"—he saw my eyes widen and smiled—"like hair, or a finger or toe, they can always find you. And if you call them, of course. But if you mean just know where you are, no. They do have ways of finding people. If, for example, they know your full name, then it would be simple."

I frowned. I didn't know my real full name. I was pretty sure IPCA didn't, either, and Vivian's faeries wouldn't. Then I remembered what Reth had said about telling me my name someday. A cold chill settled between my shoulder blades. That must have been why he always seemed to know exactly where I was in the Center. "Any other ways?"

"If faeries really wanted to find you, they probably could. Which means they already would have." He smiled. "I've already worried about all this for you and I don't think it's an issue. You're safe from IPCA here."

I nodded, wishing it was IPCA I was afraid of. No, I was worried about much worse things. I grabbed another slice of bread and shoved it in my pocket. I wanted to stay here, wanted this happy life to go on forever.

Something told me slices of bread weren't going to be enough.

DON'T MUSS THE MAKEUP

Arianna was studying my hair, deep in thought. Her face lit up. "I've got it! Remember Cheyenne in the masquerade episode?"

"Oh, my gosh! That's perfect! You're a genius!"

She smirked. "I know. Best episode ever, right?"

"Seriously." I watched in the mirror as Arianna put in hot rollers. I had never seen a vamp in a mirror before. Turns out they do have reflections, but, just like in sunlight, their glamours don't quite transfer all the way. You can't see the corpse underneath, but you can tell that something is wrong. No wonder they don't like mirrors; I'd hate to see myself that way. Arianna avoided looking at the mirror, constantly shifting so that she wouldn't be facing it.

I'll admit the idea of her hands on my hair—her glam-oured corpse hands—still bothered me a little bit. But I was trying to get over it. After all, things were a lot more complicated than they used to be. It was no longer see vamp, stun vamp, tag vamp. Now it was ponder the philosophical implications of people who had immortality forced upon them, doomed to hang onto the coattails of humanity while having almost none left themselves. Man, no wonder they drank blood.

When the rollers were removed, my hair fell down my back in loose, tumbling curls. Taking a crystal-covered barrette, she pulled a piece back from my face on one side in a slight braid, clipping it in place. "Perfect." She smiled. I had to agree. The style was simple but showed off my hair, which was definitely one of my best features.

"You are an artist."

"Oh, I know. Now for your makeup."

The girl-bonding time with Arianna really made me miss Lish. Not that she would have been able to participate, what with the whole mermaid-underwater thing, but she would have liked to see it. As Arianna applied dark, dra-matic eyeliner and fussed over which shade of eye shadow to use, I wondered about what Cresseda had said when we'd first talked. She asked me to return Lish to them. But how could I? She was dead; she was gone.

"Oh, my gosh." Things clicked into place—how could I not have seen it before?

"I know, huh? You never knew you could be this hot," Arianna answered smugly.

"Oh, yeah, you're amazing," I said, covering. As good as I looked (and, really, I looked *good*), it wasn't anything compared to what I had just realized. I needed to talk to Lend right now.

I stood, but Arianna pushed me back down in the chair. "Not done yet, your lips are still naked." It was all I could do to sit still as she applied a rosy lipstick hue with a hint of shimmer. "Okay. You are perfection. I'm a genius."

"Thanks!" I smiled at her before I sprinted upstairs. Arianna laughed at what she assumed was my impatience to get into my dress.

"Lend!" I burst through his door. He looked up, surprised. Still in basketball shorts and a plain T-shirt, he was lying on his stomach on the bed, sketching. I stopped and frowned. "Aren't you going to get ready?"

He laughed. "Remove clothes, put on tux. Should take all of two minutes. You look hot though."

"Listen, I figured it out!" I sat down on the end of his bed.

"Figured what out?" He pushed himself up to sit across from me.

"The poem thing! I know what it means!" Why hadn't I thought about it more? I'd been so stupid!

His eyebrows went up. "Really?"

"Yeah! Okay, so 'eyes like streams of melting snow,' duh. Then the 'cold with the things she does not know,' well, if she's like me she's cold all the time, right? Things we don't know, I'm not sure about." There were a lot of things Vivian didn't know that left her feeling cold and alone. "Anyway, 'Heaven above and Hell beneath,' that's Earth, where we're all stuck. I mean, like the faeries are. But then 'liquid flames to hide her grief,' that's what the souls or energy look like—liquid, golden flames. And she takes them because they make her feel warm, like she's not alone anymore. But then the last part—'death, death, death with no release'? It's not about how she's killing paranormals! Remember what your mom said, about giving Lish back to them? Vivian's not just killing them, she's taking their souls and *keeping* them. They're stuck inside her, swirling around. So she's killed them, but their souls are trapped!" I was tripping over my words, talking so fast to get it all out before I forgot anything. "Lish and Jacques and everyone else, their souls haven't been released—they've just been stolen!"

His eyes widened. "It makes sense."

"So do you think— What if we could get the souls out? Do you think that would mean— Could Lish come back? To life?"

He frowned. "I don't know. Those bodies, they were dead. Even immortal bodies can die if it happens the right way."

"Oh." My shoulders slumped. I really thought that I had figured it out, thought I could get Lish back. In those last few minutes, it felt like I already had her. And now I'd lost her again.

Lend put his arms around me. "I'm sorry, Evie."

I nodded. It had been stupid. Even if there was some way that Lish's body and soul could be put back together, which wasn't likely (and would probably be gross, given how much time had passed), I had no idea how I could get the souls from Vivian, or if it was even possible.

"Still, I think you're right about the meaning of the poem. They're dead but not released, because their souls are stuck. That's something, at least."

"For all the good it does us, right?" I sighed. He leaned in to give me a comfort kiss, but I pulled back. "Oh, don't even think about it. Arianna will kill you if you mess up my makeup."

He smiled, raising one eyebrow. "I'm fully planning on messing it up before the night's over."

"Good luck with that." I left his room for mine, more than a little disappointed that my aha moment hadn't actually solved anything. I couldn't help but feel I was failing Lish in a major way, but I didn't know what else I could do. I'd figure out this Vivian thing. Eventually.

At least I had the prom for consolation. Shallow, maybe, but I knew Lish would have wanted this for me. I could see her now, eyes beaming at me in approval. And I could see the tight line that Raquel's lips would form as she looked at the lack of sleevage and hint of cleavage. I could almost hear which sigh she'd use.

If I thought about them anymore I was going to cry, and I was wearing far too much mascara for that. I stared at my dress, touching the material lovingly, blinking back tears. I had dreamed of a prom for so long, I couldn't believe I was going. With a boy I was in love with, no less. I would be as happy as Lish would have wanted me to be.

I wished there were a mirror in the room, but I didn't need one to know how awesome this dress was. I had only stared at myself in it for like half an hour the first time I tried it on. And with the added touch of my high-heeled, peep-toe slingbacks in light gold, I was pretty sure there had never been a better prom ensemble in the history of the dance. Rather than jewelry, I rubbed shimmery lotion on my shoulders. I sparkled enough on my own tonight.

Lend knocked. I opened the door, grinning. His reaction was perfect. His jaw dropped, then he just smiled like he couldn't believe his luck. I couldn't, either. Believe my luck, that is, because as hot as Water Boy was all the time, Water Boy in a tux was like ultimate hotness.

"You look amazing." He held out his arm. I hooked my hand through his elbow and smiled.

"Likewise," I said, trying not to laugh I was so happy. "Maybe you should have bought the tux." He laughed and we went down the stairs to where his dad and Arianna were waiting with cameras. After about a million pictures (and I didn't complain, I wanted proof, lots and lots of proof, of tonight), we went to the waiting limo.

The driver held the door open for us. I stopped, squeezing Lend's arm. "You do know the driver is a troll, right?" I whispered, nervous.

He laughed. "Yeah, we know. Good family friend."

We climbed into the back, the first ones to be picked up. After a few more stops to pick up John and Carlee (who smiled at me and complimented my dress), we drove to a small restaurant for dinner. The lights were dim and intimate, the decor elegant. We sat against a windowed wall, and I was glad—the plush bench seat meant I could snuggle in right next to Lend.

Then we drove to the high school. John complained loudly about how ghetto it was to have the prom at the school, but I didn't care. Prom was prom. And there I was, at a prom, at a normal, wonderful prom, with my mostly normal, totally wonderful boyfriend. I felt like I was glowing I was so happy.

We went into the gym, which was decorated with twinkling lights and gazebos, and I realized I really was glowing. In the dim lights my arm was like a flashlight. I glanced down at my chest and immediately regretted the neckline I had chosen. If my arm was like a flashlight, my heart was like a miniature sun. I put my hand over it and looked around, panicked, until I realized that no one else could see it.

"Wanna dance?" Lend asked, leading me out into the middle of the floor. Trying to ignore my glowing wrist as he put my arms behind his neck and pulled me in close, I smiled. It was some cheesy ballad, but I didn't care as long as it was a slow song. "So, prom." He grinned at me as we slowly moved back and forth. "You like it?"

I beamed. "Better than *Easton Heights*."

PARTY CRASHER

I already knew I was a disastrous dancer, thanks to the iPod ankle-spraining fiasco, but Lend and I threw caution and self-consciousness to the wind, flailing around in the middle of the floor with everyone else.

Lend pulled me out for more pictures. "Let's just do a classic pose, okay?" he asked as we waited for the couple's picture.

I shrugged. I didn't know what he meant, and I didn't care as long as we got the photos. Like I said, I wanted proof. We stood next to each other, his arms around my waist. Then, right when the picture was about to be taken,

Lend dipped me, putting one hand behind my head and kissing me full on the lips. I was so surprised I would've fallen over if he hadn't been holding me so tightly. As soon as the flash went off he pulled me back up.

"You dork!" I smacked him in the shoulder, laughing. "That's going to be the weirdest picture ever."

"Told you I was going to mess up your makeup," he said, a smug grin on his face.

"Yeah, speaking of which, now I have to go to the bathroom and reapply my lipstick." I reached out and ran my thumb along his bottom lip. "It's a good shade for you, though."

"You have lipstick here?" he asked, confused since I hadn't brought a purse.

"Oh, never underestimate the ingenuity of a girl in figuring out where to pack necessities." As much as I hated to leave him, I was determined to look hot all night.

"Aren't you going to ask someone to go with you?"

"To the bathroom? Why?"

"Girls never go to the bathroom by themselves."

"I'll try not to be too lonely in the ten seconds it'll take me to finish."

He smiled. "Meet you by the drink table." He put his arms around me, pulling me in close. "Hurry," he whispered, then let me go.

I practically floated to the bathroom. A couple of other girls were in there, giggling about their dates and gossiping about who was wearing what trashy dress. I pulled the lip-stick out of my bra. Being flat had its advantages in added storage space.

Retouched to perfection, I walked back to the gym and looked for Lend. As I made my way around the dark edges of the gym, I scanned them for potential trouble.

Rolling my eyes, I laughed. Tonight there were no vampires or faeries or crazy burning girls. As far as this high school was concerned, none of those things even existed. Lend waved to me from the drink table and, for the first time in years, I felt all the tension melt from my body.

Just as I reached him, a slow song started. We moved to the dance floor and swayed like everyone else. "You know," he said, leaning in so closely his lips were on my ear, "I might lose all my masculine credit forever for saying this, but I'm pretty sure tonight is perfect."

"Me, too." If it were possible to die of happiness, you could have written my obituary right then.

After a couple minutes of the swaying, Lend shook his head. "We can do better than this." He took my hand in his and began dancing us through the crowds in a bizarre imitation of the tango. As he dipped me backward, I saw John and Carlee, dancing so close you'd be hard-pressed to slip a sheet of paper between them.

Lend pulled me back up and grinned mischievously. "You thinking what I'm thinking?"

As one we charged forward, using our outstretched

hands like a wedge to break them apart. Carlee laughed and John jumped on Lend's back, trying to give him a noogie.

"Boys, honestly," I said, giggling.

"May I cut in?" a voice like liquid gold murmured in my ear. My spine stiffened as my stomach clenched with fear, and before I could scream a slender hand took mine and spun me away through the crowd. I tried to pull back but we were twirling impossibly fast, the room around us a blur as a sea of faces swirled around me. Reth's arms around me were like steel bands.

"Lend!" I shouted, only keeping my balance because of Reth's too-strong hand on my back. In a glimpse I saw Lend, his face a picture of panic as he tried to fight through the mass of dresses and tuxedos to get to us. Silk and sequins made a rainbow curtain, hiding him from my sight once again as Reth slid expertly through the bodies around us. Humanity, as always, provided no protection from him.

We broke through the edge of the crowd and Reth danced us straight through a faerie door and away from everything I had ever wanted.

"Evelyn, my love. Finally we dance." He dipped me back, pulling my body right up against his in the infinite darkness. I closed my eyes, my head spinning, as I willed myself not to cry. Why couldn't I have remembered to shove some dry bread in my bra along with the lipstick? Or an iron pipe?

Why did I let myself think I could be normal?

"Take me back," I said, pushing myself as far away from

him as possible, hating that I had to keep hold of his hand in the Paths.

"Oh, come now. We haven't spoken in so long. I'm sorry about that, really. I meant to visit, but you were sleeping in a nasty iron bed and that watery witch was rather vigilant. But I've managed to keep busy with our old friends at IPCA. So many social calls to make thanks to you and your wonderful words."

"What are you talking about?" I asked, my voice flat to avoid betraying the rising panic. What had I done? I thought of my words from that night—commanding him to take a new name. That would keep IPCA from bossing him around anymore, but I didn't see how that would free him completely. Then I remembered the other command: ignore what IPCA told you. I wanted to throw up as the full weight of my words hit me. No doubt he took it to mean ignore every command IPCA ever gave him, including all those don't-harm-people rules. "Oh, no," I whispered, horrified. "What have you done?"

He smiled, his teeth brilliant white in the darkness, and took several steps. I resisted, but he dragged me along, and then we were in a meadow that wasn't really a meadow. The edges were hazy, indefinite, and the cheery yellow sky felt far too close. Grass and small pink flowers were set in whorls and patterns, the whole place a mocking picture of tranquility.

"There." Two chairs appeared and he sat in one, gesturing for me to do the same. "Now that you're safe and sound, we can finish."

"Oh, I'm finished." I folded my arms tightly across my chest. "How many of them did you kill?"

He frowned. "Who did I kill?"

"IPCA. How many did you kill? Did you kill Raquel? Is that how Vivian got her communicator?" I was shouting now, so angry with him I didn't care what happened. I wanted him to get mad; I was tired of his smug smile.

"Goodness, Evelyn, listen to you. I've simply helped them into an early retirement of sorts. I didn't kill anyone. Why would you want me to do a thing like that?"

"I *don't* want you to! Why should I believe you, after you let Vivian into the Center! Are you going to pick her up next? How long have you been working with her?"

He smiled. "Oh, yes, that evening was a nice bit of choreography. But, I assure you, I've not been 'working with her,' as you put it. I needed a new name and you seem to work best under stress. I wouldn't have allowed anything to happen to you. Still, it hasn't been easy, getting involved in the dreary workings of the court again, and you've sorely tried my patience. When we finish, you might stand a chance of justifying my involvement."

I shook my head in disbelief. "That's really what it was about? All those paranormals died so you could force me into a situation where I'd give you that command?"

"Well, yes. But we've got to move along."

"Why couldn't you leave me alone? I was fine! You have your stupid new name. Why didn't you just stay in the Faerie Realms?"

"Because they were about to find you, my love. I could only hide your location for so long before they caught on. Vivian is on her way there right now."

I covered my mouth, shaking my head in horror. "No, she can't—she'll— Take me back! Right now! I've got to warn them!"

Reth sighed, crossing his legs. "They don't matter. And you have yet to be filled."

"I don't want any more of your disgusting soul!"

He narrowed his eyes, angry. The sky twirled from yellow to nearly black, wind whipping my dress. "My dear girl, you've no idea what I am sacrificing to keep you alive; to secure your eternity. It comes at great cost, and I'm not about to waste all the effort it took to make you by throwing you at Vivian."

"You—you made me?" It was too horrible to imagine.

"My court made you. We had to have something to balance against theirs, after all."

"Oh, I know all about your court," I spat. "And I'm not doing anything for the Unseelie faeries!"

He gave me a puzzled look once again. "What makes you think I'm Unseelie?"

"I'm not stupid! Unseelie faeries are the evil ones!"

"I absolutely agree. Horrid, the lot of them. We would have made you sooner, but we didn't know they had succeeded with Vivian. Still, there's time. If you'll give me your hand." He stood.

"Never." I glared at him, so angry I was shaking. "And

you forgot something."

"Oh?" he asked, calmly walking toward me.

"Denfehlath!" I shouted. His eyes went wide with surprise and anger as a door opened next to me and the faerie with ruby eyes walked through.

"What have you done, Evelyn?" he asked.

"Take me to Lend's house!" I said, turning to Fehl. She laughed her shattering-glass laugh, shooting a look of triumph at Reth.

"There you are." She took my hand and we jumped through the door. Her steel grasp through the Paths made me nervous. She wasn't annoyed anymore, she was eager. I had to run to keep up. At last another door opened and we came out in Lend's kitchen.

Vivian, in all her fiery glory, sat on the counter, swinging her legs. "Finally!" she said, jumping down. "It's about time! Thanks, Fehl." I couldn't make out her features under the brightness of her light, but I could hear the smile. I was dead. We were all dead, and once again it was my fault.

I looked at the faerie in horror. She smiled at me. "Oh, bleep," I whispered. If Reth really was a good faerie, I couldn't imagine what Fehl must be like.

Vivian picked something up off the ground. Before I could react she swung it, barely missing me and smashing it into Fehl's face. Fehl crumpled to the ground. "Iron skillet," Vivian said cheerfully. "Smart family. So, baby sister, how's it going?"

SOUL SUCK

What could I possibly say to Vivian, standing here in Lend's kitchen? I was terrified. And not just for myself, but for Lend and everyone here. I'd brought Vivian right to them. I had to get her out, away from the people I loved. "I— You're here." My brain felt as frozen as my body. I watched her burn, golden and bright.

"Yeah, stupid. I would have gotten here a lot sooner if you had just told me where you were." It was so weird talking to her now that I couldn't see her features. I had to go by the tone of her voice. She seemed happy.

"Umm, sorry about that. I guess a faerie was blocking

you." I had to get her to leave with me. I didn't know what Lend would do now, but we couldn't be in this house much longer. "So, what do you say we go?"

She laughed. "Why? I've always wanted to drain a faerie. Plus, hey, I can show you how!" She knelt down next to Fehl. "I wonder how long she'll be out. Well, forever now." She put out a burning hand, placing it on the faerie's chest. "I always hated her. Her voice was like—I don't know— like breaking glass."

I shook my head. "We should go. Right now! I mean, other faeries know where we are, right? Let's leave."

"Chill, Evie." She turned her face up to me and I could barely make out her eyes above the liquid flames. "We don't need to worry about the faeries anymore, not now that we're together." She looked back down at Fehl. "Man, she just keeps going and going. If I had known faeries had this much to offer, wow. It's— Come on, I want you to feel this with me. You're going to love it. There's nothing better, not in this whole sucky world."

"Please stop," I said, half sobbing. I couldn't help it. As much as I didn't like Fehl, I couldn't stand there, watching her soul being sucked away.

"Why?"

"Because—you don't need to!"

Vivian shook her head, standing up. "You don't get it."

"No, I do! But, look, you said I'm getting brighter, right?"

She nodded. "Killer dress, by the way."

"I haven't taken any! I don't even know how. So there's another way, there's got to be, right?"

"No, there isn't. I already told you. We don't have our own souls. I'm not going to stop, not now that I found you. Do you know how long I've been waiting? Do you? Fifty years, that's how long."

I was shocked. She didn't look older than twenty. "You're not— How?"

"Because of this." She held out her flaming hands. "How do you think? I would have burned out before I even hit adulthood. So tell me, Evelyn, do you want to die?"

"No, I don't, but I don't want to take other souls just to live!"

"You don't have any choice!" Her voice changed, went softer. "What about your boyfriend? The one made of water? You've noticed his soul, right? That light he carries around with him? It was bright. Do you know what that means?"

I shook my head. I didn't want her to talk about Lend, to notice him. He had to stay safe.

"That means *he isn't going to die*. Did you ever think about that? Your little boyfriend will last forever, and you're going to snuff out like a stubby little candle. So, you still too good for this?"

Lend was immortal. My heart broke in that moment, remembering the way David looked at Cresseda, that sorrow, that separation. Would that be my role? Left behind? Or would I be dead, like Vivian said?

"Listen to me. This faerie? Do you know how many people she killed before IPCA started controlling her? Men, women, children. And for no reason. She thinks it's funny. So you tell me how much she deserves that soul. Tell me why *any* of these things deserve what they have. And even the ones you think are innocent—why should they be forced to stay here? It's wrong. I'm saving them, and I'm protecting the world from the ones like her."

I closed my eyes. I used to think I was protecting the world, too. But it wasn't that simple. Nothing was. Who were we to decide that anyone or anything didn't deserve the spark of life they had been given? "That makes us just as bad as the faeries."

She slapped me. I stumbled, falling against the counter and putting my hand to my cheek. It burned.

"I'm nothing like them!" She grabbed my hand, pulling me to where Fehl was lying on the ground, but the faerie was gone. Vivian swore loudly, standing up and looking around. "Look what you did! I wasn't done with her. Now who will I show you on?"

Just then another door lit up. Reth stormed through, looking like he was ready to bring the house down on all of us.

Vivian laughed. "Perfect timing."

Reth looked at me, giving Vivian time to pick up the

skillet. She swung it at the back of his head, knocking him down. He tried to stand but she pushed the skillet flat against his chest.

"Don't know why it works, but so glad it does," she said. "Come on, Evie. You can't tell me this faerie—after everything he did to you, how he lied and manipulated and used you—you can't tell me he deserves to live forever. Think of how many more girls he'll take, how many more he'll hurt."

I shook my head, tears in my eyes. I didn't know which one of them I was more scared of. Reth's amber eyes blazed with fury. I was sure that if the iron hadn't been blocking him, Vivian would be dead. If she *could* die with the amount of energy she had flowing through her. And then I realized—there was nothing I could do to stop her. If I fought her, she'd lose her temper and kill me. Everyone I cared about would die, too, and we'd all be trapped forever, swirling around in her sad, empty black hole of a body, just like Lish. I couldn't fight her. Reth was right; I wouldn't survive.

Kneeling, I shook my head in defeat. "Show me how."

She laughed. "It's about time!"

"Do I just touch him?"

"No, it's not that simple. Otherwise you'd drain everyone you ever touched. Put your hand there—right over his heart. That's where the soul is centered. Then you have to want it. You have to know it should be yours and want it and call for it. It'll hear you, because that's what we're made for. We're the Empty Ones, and the souls want to come to us. That's why we can see everything, why we can see past the glamours. And once you have more, you can see straight through to souls." She put her free hand on my arm, and I could hear the happiness in her voice. "It's beautiful, Evie, and they'll all be ours. Together."

Nodding, I put my hand on Reth's chest. His achingly lovely face had gone calm, and he regarded me with placid eyes.

"You've got to want it," Vivian said eagerly. "Take it."

And then I knew. I knew what I wanted. "Hey, Viv," I said, trying not to cry as I turned to look at her. I could feel her joy at finally connecting with someone. "I'm sorry you were alone for so long. And I'm sorry. So sorry."

I shoved my palm against her chest. She was so hot it burned. I could feel her searing my flesh, but I didn't move, closing my eyes and, for the first time, opening myself up, inviting the souls in.

Nothing happened.

Vivian ripped my hand away from her chest and threw me across the room. I slammed into the wall, pain blossoming through my whole body. "Why'd you do that? Do you want me to kill you? Because I will! I don't need your pity, you pathetic little thing. Do you know what I am? I'm a *god*, Evie. I am death, and I am life, and I can't believe I wanted to share this with you. The faeries were right." She shook her head as she crossed the room and stood over me, bright and terrible. "There's no point in keeping you around." She pulled me up by my hair, forcing my face right next to hers. I could feel my skin turning red from the heat, the stench of burning hair stinging my nose. Her voice lowered, softened. "I should have known you wouldn't understand, you wouldn't really want it. But don't worry. I'll add what little soul you've managed to scrape together to my collection. That way we really can be together forever."

She put her hand over my heart.

I held my breath, clutching at the last precious seconds of my life. How would death feel? Her hand was hot, burning. But that was it—my life didn't rush out of me.

Her shoulders started shaking and I realized why it wasn't working. "You have to want it," I whispered. Vivian didn't want to kill me. Lifting my own hand, I put it gently over her heart. I understood now—I wanted it. I wanted those souls, wanted to free them from her. "Let go, Viv."

I gasped, stiffening as the heat burst through her skin, racing like an electric current through my entire body. I was flooded with it, overwhelmed. Nothing existed but me and the fire spreading to every cell.

Vivian dimmed, all her fire draining. Her features became clearer, the flames dwindling until they were only in her heart and behind her eyes. Just a little more, I knew, just a little more and she'd be gone. And then I felt her. Felt Vivian, her own soul. It was such a tiny, broken thing, and I longed to take it, give it haven in myself. I nearly did, until I saw her eyes. They had gone cold—so cold, and blank.

I ripped my hand away and Vivian fell to the ground. I thought I could still see a spark, the very faintest hint of a soul.

And then I didn't care.

With the fire coursing through me everything was removed, like I was seeing the world as it truly was—nothing but a passing dream, dark and cold and dead. I was eternal and nothing in this existence, nothing in this normal life I had craved so much, mattered at all.

"It's about time," Reth said, leaning casually against the counter.

PATHS AND POSSIBILITIES

I looked at Reth. Filled as I was, I could see better than ever through his natural form and straight to his soul. It was beautiful. Unlike the liquid flames he'd given me, his soul was stationary, crystallized. It was the same bright gold of all the other souls but utterly unchanging.

"I was going to be cross with you, calling an Unseelie faerie right to you. If you had died, I would have been very disappointed. But this worked out nicely. Now we don't have to waste time filling you." He stood up straight, smiling. "We can get right to the fun part."

"The fun part?" Even my voice sounded different; it was

richer, layered, like multiple versions of myself were speaking at the same time. An immortal voice.

"Oh, yes." He clapped his hands. "We can dance all night, every night, and you'll last forever now. Of course, there's work to do as well. But that can wait until after I've taken you around the court. They'll all be thrilled to meet you. And now that you'll be joining us, I can explain everything to you. Listen to me, prattling on. I'm so pleased we won, that you can come home with me where you belong."

"Why?"

He looked puzzled. "Why what?"

"Why would I come with you?"

"Well, you certainly don't belong here anymore! You can feel it, can't you? The transience, the flimsiness of this world? Besides, it's impossible to keep anything clean." He frowned down at his waistcoat and brushed at it. "And then there's the work to be done, gates to be opened, homes to find. I'm glad it's going to be your poem. Far more cheerful."

"My poem." I would have been eager to know before, desperate almost, but it was difficult to care, burning with life, so much life.

"Let's see, how did that one go . . . 'Eyes like streams of melting snow,' and so striking, by the way. 'Cold with the things she does not know. Heaven above and Hell beneath, liquid flames will end her grief. With her fire, at last release. With her fire, at last release.'"

The house felt close—too confining, too temporary. The decay weighed me down. I walked to the front door, barely noticing when the doorknob melted in my hand. Stepping off the porch, I breathed in deeply and looked up at the sky. The stars, cold and bright, felt like good company. Odd shadows and hints of light surrounded me. I saw everything. Not only was every leaf, every blade of grass perfectly defined, there was more—just beyond what I was seeing.

"Evelyn, love, where are you going?" Reth caught up, standing next to me.

"The light and shadows. Where are they coming from?"

"Paths and possibilities. I can teach you how to manipulate them, if you'd like."

I stared up at the stars. Lifting my burning hand, I held it flat against the air. "There's something here," I said softly, my voice foreign and strange in my ears. There was so much more to this world, more than I had ever felt. "A door."

Reth put his hand on my arm. "Oh, you don't need to bother with that. That's nothing. I'll make the door. You belong with me, by my side for eternity."

I turned back to the sky. If I aligned those stars just right in my vision, it looked like a gate. Odd I'd never noticed.

"Evelyn, stop," Reth said, an edge of panic in his voice now.

"Stop what?"

"You don't want to let them go. Not like this."

I turned to him, frowning. "What are you talking about?"

"The souls. You need them. That is not the gate you're supposed to open."

"My souls." I sighed. I loved them. Closing my eyes, I breathed in deeply, tracing the energy, my energy, my souls. I was filled. But underneath, vague and gnawing, I felt off. It was too much, and not enough, all at the same time. The flames were stretching me, changing me. And while I was already full to bursting, I could feel the craving, the desire seeping in. "I want more," I whispered.

"Well, that can be arranged. Come on." Reth pulled gently on my arm. Why didn't I burn him?

Then I noticed lights. It took me several seconds to realize it was a car. It screeched to a stop in front of us and a man jumped out of the driver's side. His soul was a pale, quavering thing, already on the decline. It made me feel peaceful in a way I couldn't explain, tender toward its fragile beauty.

Then the other door opened. I went rigid. If I had thought Reth's was beautiful, it was nothing to this soul. It filled the night with light, dancing and rippling like the reflection on a pond. I hadn't seen many souls, but I knew that this one was special. I wanted it. I needed it.

"Evie!"

I blinked, trying to filter through my disconnect and place the voice.

"Evie, are you okay?"

"Lend." My Lend. It clicked into place. That soul was my Lend. I clenched my hands into fists at my side. I shouldn't take that one.

"What's— Your voice, it's different. What did he do to you?"

I squinted, trying to see Lend's face over his soul. Maybe if I could see his face I wouldn't want him so badly, maybe I'd be able to stop. I lifted one hand toward him.

"Oh, go ahead," Reth said. "He doesn't matter. But do hurry, we should be getting along."

"What happened?" Lend ran up to me, within reach. I wanted to cry as I put my hand on his chest, but I couldn't. It had to be mine. I opened up the channel—

And gasped. In that moment, touching Lend's soul, I finally connected with my own. It had been lost in the swirl of new souls, overwhelmed. But my soul knew Lend's, loved it, and it was enough.

I pulled my hand back before Lend lost anything. Closing my eyes, I held onto that recognition, focused on my own soul in the flames. And then I noticed the individuals. Hundreds of them, freed from Vivian only to be trapped again. My breath caught—I felt Lish's. I knew it was hers. Gentle and intelligent, swirling nearest to my heart. I wanted to keep her with me forever.

The guilt came then and I tried to push it down. If I let them go, I didn't belong with Lend. Not with the soul I'd seen. I'd burn out and he'd continue, eternal and breathtaking. Just like Vivian had said.

"If I keep them, I could stay with you." Tears streamed down my face.

"Keep what?"

"The souls."

"The—what?"

"I took them, from Vivian."

"Vivian's here?" He looked around, panicked.

"Not anymore." I shook my head sadly. "But, Lend, I've got them—they're inside me."

"What do you mean? You took the souls?" His voice was concerned and scared.

I was ready to argue, explain why I had to keep them. But watching his soul dancing in front of me, I knew I couldn't. I couldn't be with him, not like this. I wouldn't deserve to. This immortality, this life exploding within me—it wasn't mine. I couldn't ask Lend to love me like this. My own soul was the only one I could offer. Now that I knew I had one, it was enough. I had never been empty.

"I have to let them go," I whispered.

"Let the souls go?"

"They need to be released."

"Not yet!" Reth said, anger twisting his smooth, golden voice.

I looked back at the stars. The souls nudged me forward, guiding my hand up.

"Evie!" Lend said, panicked.

I looked down at him. I was rising into the air; I couldn't stop. If I didn't release them now, I didn't think I'd be able to. Finding the outline of the stars, I pushed my hand forward—and met resistance. This was it.

"Stop." Reth's voice was hard, commanding. My arms wouldn't move. "That is not the gate you need to open. If you let them go now, all this will be wasted. We need those souls! *This is not the right gate.*"

I focused, willing the fire to concentrate in my arm. It grew even brighter, turning from gold to pure white, blinding in its intensity. And then, still pulling against the power of Reth's voice, I lifted a single finger and traced the stars, the light leaving a trail of white between each point until the entire gate was outlined.

I closed my eyes and took a deep breath. "Go," I whispered. For the briefest moment I felt peace, gratitude; then excruciating pain as the fire ripped straight out of my body and shot through the gate of stars. Just when I thought I could stand the pain no longer, it was over. Almost. A single lingering soul—Lish, my Lish—paused, passing through my heart in what I knew was her last good-bye.

As my body went cold and dark I fell toward the earth, wondering again what death would feel like. I smiled, grateful I had at least known my own soul if only for a moment, and then everything went black.

HEAVEN, HELL,
AND THAT LITTLE
PLACE BETWEEN

Being dead wasn't supposed to hurt. Where was the fairness in that? If I was dead, the least the universe could do was make it painless. Maybe I was in hell, but I really didn't think I deserved that. Besides, hell was supposed to be hot, and I was freezing. Absolutely freezing.

I moved my legs, trying to get more comfortable. Holy bleep, I wasn't dead! If I were dead, I wouldn't have my body. As my soreness settled in, I knew I definitely had a body. That hurt. All over. I forced my eyelids open, feeling like they weighed twenty pounds each.

Not hell. Not heaven, either, because I really hoped that

place would have more taste than this ugly paneled ceiling with fluorescent lights. "Ugh," I said, figuring that one word summed up both how I felt and what I thought of the decor.

I raised my head, ignoring the swimming lights in front of my eyes, and looked down at myself. I was covered with several blankets and one of my arms had a lovely little IV taped to it. Then I noticed something really bad—my dress was gone. I might not have been dead, but if anything had happened to that dress, someone was going to be.

Lifting my arm to scratch the area around the IV tape, I stopped. The glow—the liquid fire that had been there since Reth forced it on me—was gone. All of it, every last bit from him and Vivian. I was both relieved and sad. With my flames gone, everything was strangely heavy, like gravity pulled harder than normal on me, binding me to the earth.

I felt around my body then, looking for damage. Nowhere seemed especially sorer than anywhere else. I sighed, laying my head back down. Maybe I was here because I was dying. Maybe letting go of all those souls hadn't killed me, but I didn't have enough left to hang on for much longer.

Or maybe I should just push the freaking call button and ask a nurse. The worst that could happen was them coming in with stun guns, having figured out I was a freak of nature. I paused. That would actually be pretty bad. I'd take a nap first. At least then I'd be well rested if I was going to be interrogated or something.

I fell into a strange, exhausted sleep. I thought I heard the door open, but couldn't muster the energy to open my eyes or move. Someone set something down on the table next to me, then sat on the edge of the bed. A gentle hand brushed the hair back from my forehead, and then lips brushed the top of my head.

The bed sprung back and soft steps padded away. I heard a small, soft sigh—a happy one.

"Raquel?" I murmured, finally forcing my eyes open. The room was empty. Disappointment washed over me. I had been sure it was her. I wanted it to be her.

A vase with an explosion of bright tropical flowers was on the table next to me, with a small card. My hands trembling, I opened it. It read, "Be *happy*, my darling girl. You'll be missed more than you'll ever know. Love, Raquel."

I looked back at the door, my heart fluttering. I wanted to say good-bye, even if it would make things harder in the long run, even though I knew Raquel wouldn't leave IPCA and I wouldn't go back. Our time together really was over.

Suddenly I missed her more than ever before.

I wiped a small tear away, feeling very alone in this stupid room with its salmon-colored walls and worn furniture. Where was Lend? I was more than a little disappointed. If this were *Easton Heights*, Lend would have been by my bedside the whole time, having cried himself to sleep holding my hand. Then I'd gently wake him up and we'd kiss like crazy. Of course, we'd also break up before the end of the episode, which I didn't like quite so well.

My stomach tied itself in horrible knots. Maybe Lend didn't want to be here. I had, after all, nearly sucked out his soul. I closed my eyes as the memories of what happened overwhelmed me. "Vivian," I whispered, wanting to vomit. Had I killed her?

A throat cleared next to me and I sat up in bed, startled. "Raquel?"

"Hardly."

"Oh, go away," I snapped, turning to look at Reth, who had made himself comfortable in a chair next to my bed.

He glared at me. "I'm very disappointed in you, Evelyn. After all that time, everything I gave you. Very disappointed indeed."

I laughed. What can I say, I was loopy from pain and an empty stomach. And I was done with Reth and his crap. "Ouch. I'm devastated."

"Not only did you release the soul I gave you but you didn't even fill your end of the prophecy. The prophecy I worked very hard to make sure you lived to hear, I might add."

"See, that's the problem with putting your prophecies in vague poem form. Because I filled it exactly—released all those souls."

His eyes flashed with fury. "You weren't meant to release *them*, you silly child. You were meant to release *me*. Us."

"What's that supposed to mean?"

"It's hardly your business now!"

"Sorry. Guess you should have been clearer. Now, if you don't mind, I'd like to go back to sleep."

He stood. "I am not finished with you yet."

I lifted my hand, palm toward him. "Really? Because lemme tell you, having all those souls inside me, I'd be lying if I said it didn't give me a real taste for them. So unless you want to lose yours, I suggest you stay far, far away from me. Got it?"

His face went ice cold and he smiled at me. "You cannot last on your own, my love. You will need more, and then you'll become what you're meant to be. When that happens, I'll forgive you." He turned and walked through a door in the wall.

I exhaled. I couldn't believe he had been dissuaded that easily, and I was sure he'd be back someday. But his words wouldn't leave me. I loved life. I loved this world, and I especially loved Lend. I didn't want to leave it, but I wouldn't become Vivian, no matter how strong the temptation would be.

I pulled down the neck of my hospital gown and gasped. My heart, which I had expected to be as cold and empty as my wrist, glowed with a faint light. It was subtler than when Reth put soul in me, but there was definitely still something there. It was both puzzling and comforting.

The doorknob turned, startling me. I yanked my gown

back into place as Lend burst in, out of breath and upset. "I'm so sorry! The doctor said you probably wouldn't wake up for a few more hours, and so I thought I'd— Evie, I'm so sorry, I wanted to be here."

I smiled as he rushed across the room and took my hand in his. It was nice to see his real face again. As amazing as his soul was, I'd rather see him. "So what happened?" I asked.

He shook his head. "Man, it was crazy. After Reth took you away, I called my dad. We raced back and saw you and Reth. You were all weird and floated up in the sky, then you went stiff and you dropped. I caught you, but I kinda didn't do a great job." He looked sheepish. "Your head hit the ground pretty hard. So Reth said in his stupid commanding voice, 'I'll be taking her with me,' and I said, 'Over my dead body,' and he shrugged like that was fine by him and started toward me. But then my dad, who had gone back to the car as soon as you started floating, came out with his golf club. I never understood why he keeps custom golf clubs everywhere since he doesn't actually golf. But then he held it up in the air and said, 'I've got a nine iron that says otherwise.'"

"You're kidding me."

Lend shook his head, his eyes shining with excitement. "No, dead serious, it was so freaking awesome. Reth's face went all furious—it looked like he was going to kill both of us. Then he just turned around and walked through a tree and disappeared."

"Wow. Your dad rocks."

"I know. So then we took you inside— What happened to the doorknob, by the way?"

"Umm, oops?"

He laughed. "Anyway, we found Vivian on the floor. I thought she was dead, but my dad found a pulse. When you didn't wake up right away we brought you both here. You'll be fine, just some minor burns and hypothermia, which was kind of hard to explain."

I laughed drily. I had managed to stop Vivian, free the souls, and not kill anyone in the process. Or die myself. I had done okay. "Where is Viv?"

"She was here, but I think she's gone now. My dad says she'll probably never wake up, so he found someone who could take care of her."

I frowned, wondering who on earth could do that until I remembered my first visitor. Raquel would take good care of her. The idea of Vivian, asleep and alone forever, made me sad, but at least she'd be safe from the faeries.

I wondered when the same thing would happen to me, when I would burn out.

"So, I've got a question," Lend said. "What did you mean when you said if you kept the souls you could stay with me?"

I bit my lip. Lend had no idea that he was immortal, his soul brilliant and eternal. I opened my mouth to tell him but couldn't choke out the words. It felt like as soon as I said it, that would be the end for us. "I don't know." I shrugged and tried to smile. "All those souls burning me up inside, I was kind of whacked out."

"What did it feel like?"

I shifted uncomfortably. Remembering it made me feel even colder; I wanted to forget how amazing it was. I couldn't have that again. Ever. "Crowded?"

"Well, I'm just glad you're okay."

"Me, too. So, what was so important that you had to leave?"

"Ah." He plopped a bag on the bed next to me. "I thought you'd want something to do until you got released." He pulled out a box. A boxed set, to be more specific. The first two seasons of *Easton Heights*.

"Shut up!" I shrieked. "You really *were* worried about me, weren't you?"

He smiled but the strain showed through. "I was really scared I'd lost you."

I scooted over, patting the bed next to me. "No such luck. And now you get to watch forty straight hours of *Easton Heights* with me!"

He turned on the first disk, shaking his head, then got onto the bed next to me. "Small price to pay for getting to hold your hand."

I wasn't cold anymore.

ACKNOWLEDGMENTS

I owe so many people for the realization of this lifelong dream. So if you'll indulge me? And if not, well, you can go read the kissing scenes again. That's probably what I'd do, too.

First and foremost thanks go to Noah, the love of my life and the best thing that ever happened to me. Thanks for encouraging me, even when I disappeared into Word documents for weeks on end, and for letting me talk and iron out plot points, even if you did suggest I kill Evie. And to my beautiful children, Elena and Jonah, who, while decidedly unhelpful, are absolutely delightful and fill my life with joy.

Next to my family, most especially my parents, Pat and Cindy, for never doubting I was brilliant even when I felt anything but. Thank you for buying me books and filling my childhood with stories and words. And to my siblings, Erin, Lindsey, Lauren, and Matt, for being readers but mostly for being my utterly ridiculous and hilarious best friends. My grandparents, Dee and Mary, for passing on the storyteller gene, and of course my in-laws, Kit and Jim, for allowing us desperately needed access to their washer and dryer (and for being unfailingly supportive).

I couldn't have come this far without the help of my critique partners and friends. Carrie "Zombie Queen" Harris, Renee Collins, and Kristen Record for their spot-on pacing advice, Ashley Juergens, Megan Holmes, Jane Volker, and Fara Sneddon for their enthusiasm. Fara and Kristen, thanks especially for the treats, babysitting, and listening to endless hours of "This will never happen." A million thanks to Stephanie Perkins, who is the best and gentlest reader I've ever known, who taught me how "good" can *always* be "better," and who laughs and cries with me over how bizarre life is. Finally, Natalie Whipple for being my first reader and ultimate cheerleader. I don't know where my self-esteem would be without you, and will forever owe you for gently steering me back in the right directions. Thank you *all* for being alternately frustrated, devastated, delighted, and elated right along with me.

Thanks to the wonderful online community of writers

and readers who humor the silliness on my blog and twitter—your enthusiasm, intelligence, and support are invaluable. I feel blessed to "know" all of you. Thank you to Pandora and the Hellogoodbye station, and to my dear, beloved Snow Patrol, for providing my lucky album.

Huge thanks to Erica Sussman, my genius editor, who loves Evie as much as I do and brought her to my dream house for publication. Thank you for taking her story and making it the best it could possibly be. You've made the entire process a delight and I'm so fortunate to work with you! Thanks as well to the team at HarperTeen and Harper Children's, including marketing, foreign rights, publicity, editorial, and especially design. Alison Donalty and Torborg Davern, my cover is a work of art and I'm still in awe of it. All in all, I couldn't possibly have been better taken care of.

A whole paragraph to Michelle Wolfson, my agent. Thank you for picking me out of the slush, for sticking with me through the months, and for exceeding my wildest publishing dreams. You truly are Wonder Woman, and I'm so glad to have you on my side for this whole crazy journey.

Last of all to you, dear reader, for picking up my book. I hope you liked it, because I certainly like you. As Evie would say, you're all bleeping fantastic.

Blue Lily Photo

KIERSTEN WHITE

has one tall husband and two small children. She lives near the ocean in San Diego, where her days are perfectly normal. This abundance of normal led her to a fascination with all things paranormal, including but not limited to faeries, vampires, and pop culture. PARANORMALCY is her first novel. Visit her online and read her blog at www.kierstenwhite.com.